SECRET NIGHTS

USA Today Bestselling Author

A.M. HARGROVE

Secret Nights

Copyright © 2019 A.M. Hargrove

Cover Design by Maria @ Steamy Designs

Cover Photo by Wander Aguiar

Cover Model: Kaz Vander Waard

Note From The Author

THIS BOOK WAS ORIGINALLY PUBLISHED UNDER THE TITLE Dirty Nights, at first in three parts, and then in one complete novel. Dirty Nights has since been unpublished and Secret Nights has undergone a complete re-editing.

One

Skylar

"Skylar, I swear to God I will beat your fucking ass if you don't do what I say. Now get out there if you know what's good for you. He's been waiting and doesn't like to be late."

"Mom, please." It's my last ditch attempt at begging. This isn't the first time she's dressed me up like a whore and forced me to meet her pimp. Her threats on the beating are true. I've felt her fist more times than I care to remember, and don't want to feel it again. For a small woman, she could knock the daylights out of me.

Her voice suddenly turns whiny. "Sweetie, you know how much I need my medicine. I get sick if I don't have it. And this is the only way. Do it for me, baby. You will, won't you?"

When I look at her, I realize there is no choice. She's skin and bones, nothing like she was when my dad still lived here. She used to be pretty back then. But these days, she takes no pride in herself. None at all. She rarely bathes unless she gets so hard up

3

that she turns tricks on her own. And now that I *look* legal, she's all but sold me off to her pimp and bullies me to do her dirty work. She has ulterior motives. I bring in more money than she ever would. Oh, if she'd clean herself up, she would be okay, I suppose. But she won't do it. So I'm her personal hooker and drug habit supporter. Lucky me, a sixteen year old. Fun times.

"Yeah, Mom," I say, resigning myself to what lies ahead. A night filled with things I can't stand to think about.

Any other mother would die before they'd put their daughter in danger like this. Not mine. Instead, she stands there and smiles. Then claps her hands, like we're getting ready to go on a picnic or something. Some twisted picnic.

"I knew you'd see it my way. Always knowing how to help your poor old mom."

Turning around I walk out the door. Her pimp, Mikey, stands there waiting.

"Hurry your ass up, girl. I don't have time for your shit!" His fingers tighten around my neck. "You better act right tonight or you know what's coming your way, right?" He presses himself against me and his fetid breath would make me gag, but I don't because his grip on me is so tight it restricts any motion in my throat.

"Yeah," I croak, as I squeeze back tears. What he means is he'll beat the crap out of me. He's done it before and won't hesitate to do it again. The last time, the beating was accompanied by a rape. Bile rises up from my gut again, but I force it back into its proper place. What other choice do I have? We get in his car and he drives me to some guy's place. It's in a seedy part of town, and my shaky legs take me up four long flights of steps to get to apartment 4D. The guy answers the door and the urge to turn and run is overwhelming. But I don't. Instead, I walk inside, where the room is foggy with smoke. An open bottle of whiskey sits on a round table and he asks, "Want some?"

"No, thanks."

The place is a mess, clothes strewn everywhere, and dirty

dishes stacked all over the place. But that's not what bothers me the most. It's what I'm going to have to do next.

The guy is old, like my mom. Maybe in his forties or something. He's pudgy with a belly that droops over his pants.

"Take off your shirt. I wanna look at your tits."

My hands tremble as I undo the buttons. One thing I've learned is not to look at their faces. But I make the mistake of doing that now and see him lick his wet lips. Watching his fat slimy tongue slide over his thick blubbery lips almost makes me lose my lunch. My face must show this because he laughs.

"Not into this, are you?"

"Er, uh, yeah, I am." I can't keep the stammer out of my reply.

"Good." His beady eyes darken as his hands move to his zipper. "Get over here. You know the drill."

My feet don't want to move, but I somehow walk over to him.

"On your knees little girl." He puts his hands on my shoulders and shoves me hard to the floor.

My knees sting from the rough carpet. I reach into his pants, and close my eyes. He tastes like sour milk and this is when my daydreams begin.

My mind takes me away from this horrid place, into my fantasy world, where I can dance away all the dreadful things I'm going to have to do tonight.

By the time I leave, it feels like my insides have been stripped raw. Mikey is outside waiting and I give him the cash the man handed me. He snatches it away and counts it, then tosses me fifty bucks. That's all I get for a night of horror. When I get back home, Mom's waiting with her hand extended. After I hand over the money I climb into the hot shower and scrub the filth off of me until my skin is chafed. Then I brush my teeth and Listerine my mouth raw. But I never get the taste of those nasty men out. They linger with me for a long, long time.

The cheap sheets scratch my skin as I slide into bed. A tear escapes from my eye, though I do my best not to let it. This is the time I dread the most, because I'm alone with my thoughts and reminded of how messed up my life is. My dad doesn't want me. My mom is a drug addict. I'm a high school drop-out. My dream of becoming a professional dancer is moving further and further out of my grasp.

When I quit high school earlier this year, it became apparent that going to any professional school was no longer attainable. Mom made sure of that. Whoring for her made keeping up with my school work impossible. And then there were those rumors flying around. I'd hang my head in shame everyday as the girls whispered about me and treated me like I was diseased. But not the boys. They flocked to me like ants on honey. They even cornered me in the stairwell several times and if someone hadn't come by, I'm sure it would have ended up in something awful. So I decided it was time to bow out gracefully and withdraw from high school.

It would be nice if I had someone to talk to about all of this, but that's never going to happen. Not with my current situation anyway. I burrow down into my hard nest of a bed and do my best to go to sleep. But all I can think of is a set of big beefy paws as they painfully pinch and squeeze me, and the tears finally gush out, while my aching body is wracked with sobs.

Two

Reese

EVEN THOUGH MY FATHER'S FACE HOLDS A SMILE, HIS EYES tell a different story. Disappointment, regret, and even scorn weigh me down as I look into them. It doesn't matter that it's closing night for the six month run of *Shatter*, the Metropolitan Ballet Company's production that has blown New York City away. It makes no difference that the critics have been raving about me as the principal dancer since opening night. All that matters is that my chosen career isn't the one he planned since the day I was born ... I'm not the leading goal scorer at Madison Square Gardens.

But my mom ... well, she turns on the high voltage and says, "Congratulations, darling! You were astounding!" Then she leans into me and whispers, "You were the best out there, dear."

While I'd like to stand here and soak up their praise, my quads, hamstrings and calves scream for my attention. There's not enough ice in all of Manhattan to calm them down.

7

Shatter has been running for six months now and my body is bruised, battered, and worn from the six-day-a-week punishing performances I've been putting in and I am ready for a badly needed break.

Unfortunately, I can't help myself, and I snap under the heavy ache of my limbs. "Really Mother?"

Her eyes admonish me. "Of course, Reese. You know I think you're the best."

Before I can even say anything, my dad pipes in and says, "Son, excellent work. You were great."

It's easy to see by the evasion of his eyes that he's not sincere. I'm no fool, but too bad. This is my love and I'm going to continue to dance for as long as my body will hold up.

"Reese, please," my mom says. "I couldn't be more proud of you than I am now."

"Thanks, Mom. But I wonder if it's only because I'm the principal. Would you have been this proud of me if I had only made it to that guy in the background?"

"Of course I would have. You're my son and I love you."

After locking eyes with her and staring into them for a few moments, I nod and say, "I love you too, Mom." Then I turn to my dad and give him a nod and head to my dressing room to change and scrape the tons of goop off my face.

Tonight the troupe is going to party and party hard! It has been so long since any of us have been out, none of us can even remember the last club we entered.

The party is on and it's as if we've brought the stage here. The only difference is our style is edgier than the classical one we recently performed. What would anyone expect though? The club's crowd is enjoying the spectacle as we do our lifts and spins that aren't usually found on the average dance floor. Some of the other patrons are even joining in with us and creating a sort of controlled mayhem. For the few of us males that aren't gay, like myself, the women are all over us. And admittedly, I'm loving the hell out of it.

Selene, the female principal, glares at me as I dance with another woman. She and I have been sleeping together ever since *Shatter* opened. We're not committed but we're sort of an item, I suppose. Her jealous side peeks out tonight, but I choose to ignore it. I'm all about having a good time, and I don't want to deal with her neediness right now.

Alcohol flows and I know that come tomorrow, I'm going to have one helluva a hangover. But right now, I don't care because I am letting it hang loose and loving every minute of it.

"Selene," I call out. She's standing close to me, but ignores me. "Selene, let's dance." Again, no response. To hell with her. Her constant desire to be the center of attention annoys me. I'm positive my night of hot sweaty sex just went down the drain, but I'm high on alcohol and adrenaline, so I don't give a damn. Grabbing another shot of tequila, I down it and head back out to the dance floor. The night speeds on and soon it's last call.

"We're out of here," a part of the group calls out. We all fist bump and I watch as they pile into a cab. Selene and a couple other girls follow suit. She doesn't say a word as she leaves. Heading to the bar, I settle my tab and I'm out the door too.

Since I live in Soho, where the club is, I only have a few blocks to walk home. It's late September, and still fairly warm out so I figure the walk will do me some good.

The streets have emptied out and my ears still ring a bit from the loud music that played in the club. As I'm walking, I think about how pissed Selene looked ... like she wanted to twist my balls off. So much for that easy piece of ass. Looks like it's gonna be a hand job for me tonight. I pull out my phone thinking I'll leave her a message before I realize she'll probably pick up and have a few choice words for me. Since I'm not in the mood for that, I pocket the phone and dig into my pocket for my keys.

I have a decent buzz going so I never hear them approach until it's too late. They slam me from behind and knock me to the ground. My usually quick reflexes are dulled from all the alcohol I've consumed so I'm slow to push myself up. By the time I make it to my hands and knees, they come at me from both sides and pummel me in the ribs with their fists and kick me. Pain explodes in my torso, with each crushing blow, taking my breath away along with the ability to inhale. I'm incapable of rolling over or moving my arms to block their attack. The option of defending myself has been stripped. I'm incapacitated from what my brain is telling me are broken ribs. But they don't stop there. It happens so hard and fast I can't roll over or even kick to fight back. Fireworks of agony ignite throughout my body. I vaguely see something glint and it registers that one of them has a knife. My mind is so pain-addled by now, I don't feel it when they stab me. But the final blow, the swinging of the baseball bat against my leg, is unmistakable. If I live through this attack, I know I'll never forget that sound ... the cracking and splintering of the bones in my leg.

THE STEADY BEEPING OF MACHINES IS CONSTANT BACKGROUND noise. It goes on and on and on until I want to yell. But I can't because it's impossible to speak. I'm caught in a strange dream. Or maybe it's a nightmare. Like the kind where you're being chased and you try to run but the harder you try, the slower you go. I want to speak but the harder I try, the more difficult it becomes. Sleep is intermittent. It's a succession of dozing on and off. But what is brutally unceasing is the pain that pounds my body everywhere. Occasionally it's dulled somewhat, but it's always there, my enemy. I'm trapped in a vortex of it. It takes me down into its furthest depths and then spins me around so fast I want to beg for it to stop, but I can't. My lungs won't allow it. This must be hell because I can't figure out where else I would be that could be so cruel.

"Reese. Reese, can you hear me?"

I have an argument with my eyelids because they insist on staying closed, but someone is trying to converse with me and it's important for me to look at whoever it is. Finally, I persuade them to open and there is a middle-aged woman standing over me.

"Reese, my name is Helen and I'll be taking care of you today."

There seems to be a film over my eyes because her face is blurry. When I move my hands to rub them, they're stuck. The harder I try, the more agitated I become.

"Stay calm, Reese. Your arms are strapped to the bed. We had to do that because you kept trying to pull the breathing tube out."

Breathing tube? Why the hell would I have a breathing tube?

"You must be confused. I'll explain everything to you. You've been in an induced coma for over a week now. You had an … incident. You were injured and you're in the hospital. We just reduced your medicine so you're slowly coming out of sedation."

What the hell is she talking about?

"Don't try to talk, honey. Your throat will be very sore for a few days from the tube. It's best to go with it. We have you on pain medicine and the most important thing for you to do now is rest."

Why would I need more rest if I've been in a coma for over a week?

She places her hand on my forehead but I want to brush it away. I don't like strangers touching me like this.

"You're safe here, Reese. Everything will be fine."

Shifting my eyes so I can check out the room, I'm shocked to see all the machines surrounding me. Then I hear that damn beeping that's been annoying the hell out of me.

"Try to stay calm, Reese. These are only monitors. No one is going to hurt you. You're safe here."

Why does she keep saying that? I swallow and my throat is on fire. Oh how I'd kill for some water.

"Water?" I croak.

"I'm sorry, honey. Nothing to eat or drink yet. But you're getting adequate hydration through your IV."

Can she squirt that damn thing in my mouth and unglue my tongue because it's stuck somewhere inside? It's impossible to win that fight with my eyelids so I doze off.

WOULD SOMEONE *PLEASE* TURN OFF THE FUCKING ALARM clock? Who set the damn thing anyway? I know it wasn't me. Wait, where am I?

When I raise my head, I see all those monitors again, but I'm alone. My head's a bit clearer so I try to take it all in. There is so much shit in here, I can't make heads or tails out of it. One's for my heart rate and blood pressure. But there are other things too that I'm unfamiliar with. A large unit sits next to my bed with hoses coming out of it. And I see these clear tubes hanging off the bed with pink fluid in them. Nasty shit. Oh hell, there's a tube coming out of my fucking nose too! What. The. Fuck. I've got wires and tubes everywhere! Panic floods me. The beeping on that machine escalates and a nurse runs in the room.

"What's happening to me?" I ask. "Why am I here?"

My mom runs in next, takes one look at me and breaks down in tears.

"Mom, what's going on?" No one says anything.

The nurse finally cracks the silence. "Reese, you were mugged and beaten. Badly. You almost died. You've been in the hospital for almost two weeks. You've had several surgeries, but you're going to be fine. Do you hear me? You're going to survive all of this. You're in the ICU right now. But as soon as we can, we'll move you to a private room."

"Mugged?"

"Yes. Your attackers stabbed you and brutally beat you. Luckily, someone found you and called 911."

My mom finally quits crying and says, "It happened on closing night."

Again, I try to rub my face, but my wrists are strapped. The nurse sees this, she loosens the Velcro and frees my hands. When I move my arms, my torso feels like fire is shooting through it. I groan.

"It's your ribs. Your rib cage was a mess. Your lungs collapsed. That's why you have those chest tubes in you," the nurse explains.

"Oh," I say as I rub my face.

"That's not all."

It's not so much as the words, but the way they're said that makes me wary. My head swings to my mom, and her face is stricken with such sadness and pain, I know that whatever they're about to tell me will ruin me.

"Do I have a spinal cord injury?" I know I can move my arms so maybe it's from the waist down.

My mom shakes her head and says, "No, Reese, you don't."

"Oh, thank God. I thought you were going to tell me I couldn't walk or dance again."

My mom's face pales. "Reese, you won't dance again."

"What? Why?"

Mom glances to the nurse and the nurse says, "Reese, the men who attacked you crushed your right leg. Your knee and femur were so pulverized that the doctors are hoping you'll be able to walk unassisted again."

Your knee and femur were pulverized ... your knee and femur were pulverized ... your knee and femur were pulverized. Hoping you'll walk again ... hoping you'll walk again ... hoping you'll walk again ...

Mom sits next to my bed, holding my hand. Like that's supposed to make me feel better? The doctor made an appearance as the nurse was talking and said he hopes ... yeah, *he hopes* I'll be able to put weight on my right leg again. So much for my fucking career. I refuse to have visitors. Selene came by a few times, but I couldn't stand to see the pity in her eyes. I'm a has-been when I barely got started. My life's been ruined by some fuckfaces who wanted a few measly bucks and my credit cards.

The doctor also told me he's going to begin weaning me off the morphine today. Great. Fantastic. Now I'm going to have to face this without the numbing effects of opiates. Apparently my stab wounds have healed sufficiently, along with the surgeries on my leg, that I can be transferred to a restorative unit. I can't go home until I can demonstrate I'm able to move around on my own. How the hell will I be able to do that? My leg is in some kind of contraption with enough hardware attached to it I look like an Erector Set. Maybe the damn thing has a special button on it and it turns into a Transformer, making me a SuperCar or something. Who the fuck knows?

A snarly bastard is what I am. I don't talk. I yell or growl. If anyone asks me something, I either give a sarcastic reply, or scowl at them. I've gone from Dr. Jekyll to Mr. Hyde. I've made my mom cry so many times now I don't even care anymore. Why should I? I've been fucked. And it keeps getting worse. This hardware on my leg … no, wait. Let me amend that. They've just informed me the fucking hardware *in* my leg, will have to be removed. Well, some of it anyway. Screws, pins, bolts, and who knows what else … probably rebar for all I know. One more surgery added to the list.

And then the doctor in his smart ass way, says to me, that I should be thankful they didn't have to amputate it. Because apparently when they initially saw it, that was a strong possibility. Nice. Just perfect. And I'm supposed to be thankful? That a couple of motherfuckers destroyed my life. *Really?*

Oh, and Selene. Dear sweet Selene. Yeah, she dumped me. Didn't want to hang around with someone who couldn't keep up with her career. Bitch.

Three

Skylar

IT TAKES EVERY OUNCE OF STRENGTH AND WHATEVER ELSE I can pull together not to gag when I breathe. The client that's seated in front of me is so darn smelly that I swear he must've rolled around in a pile of dead skunks. Why do I always end up with the stinky dudes?

And then there's his appearance. I'm not usually one to say bad things about the way people look, but holy ravioli! This guy looks like he got run over by the ugly truck. First off, he's skinny. I mean emaciated. And I should feel sorry for him because maybe he can't afford food. But if that's the case, then why the heck is he here? The entrance fee to *Exotique-A*, the dance club where I currently work, isn't cheap and neither are my services. Then there are his shifty eyes. They're sunken into his long, narrow face, leaving huge dark circles beneath them. Cheekbones protrude creating deep hollows and his thin lips have large sores on them. *Gross*. And, *oh my God*, his freakin' hair. Super greasy, almost to the point of dripping. Has the man ever heard of this invention called shampoo? And, to top it all off, he's going bald and has a comb over. Yep. A comb over that's dripping grease. My guess is he's around forty-five. Large nose and missing half his teeth. But honestly, I could get past all of that if the man had just bathed. Eck. There I go again, forcing back a gag. When I take in the whole picture of him, I have to think that he's either ill or on drugs. Lots of them.

He ogles me. I daresay, he hasn't blinked one time in ten minutes and I have twenty to go. Will I make it without puking? Please, God. Just this once. I swivel my hips and sway to that geeky music he requested. Who the heck listens to this kind of stuff anyway? *Night Fever* by the Bee Gees. Now all I need to do is drop to one knee and do a John Travolta-Saturday Night Fever move. Thank God I have a pole in here. My hands latch onto it and I swing my body around, picking up enough momentum so I leave the floor. Using the muscles of my inner thighs, I squeeze it and flip upside down. Looking at him from this angle isn't so bad.

"Come closer."

Oh crap. I was hoping he wouldn't ask that. Clients can't touch, but they can request the dancers to get right in their faces if they want. Please don't let me hurl on him.

I dance my way closer, shimmying and doing my usual moves. I'm topless and he's locked onto my girls, drooling and licking his ulcer-covered lips. Forcing myself to think about something else, my thoughts move to what I'm going to cook for breakfast. Now that was a mistake because the thought of food, combined with his rank odor, makes me want to retch.

"Put them in front of my mouth."

Oh god. If I puke on this dude, J.D. will kill me for sure. He'll put me back down to the list of skank clients. And I can't afford that. Holding my breath for as long as I can, I inhale again when he says, "Turn around and bend over. Put that ass right in my face."

Oh, good grief. At lease the stink pot isn't breathing on my face now. But when I feel his nasty fingers move the string of my thong aside, I straighten up and take the two long steps that get me to the button on the wall. My palm slams it and seconds later the door swings open.

My head motions toward Mr. Smelly and I say, "He touched my butt. Moved my thong aside."

My bodyguard asks no questions. Those are the rules at *Exotique-A* and they're nonnegotiable. Always. And they always go in favor of the dancer. "Out," Jimmy says with his arm extended, finger pointing.

"But ..."

"I said out. You know the rules."

Mr. Smelly stands and the towel that was on his lap falls. His pathetic hard on is standing there, staring at him, begging to be touched. But there won't be any help for it in here.

"Stick your dick in your pants and get out. Now. Last chance or I throw you out."

Jimmy doesn't mess around. I've seen him do it plenty of times. He's strong and very protective of me. Suddenly, he sniffs and says, "What the fuck died in here?"

I want to giggle, but I don't. I shrug and sidle out of the room. My goal is to be well away from the door so I don't get another whiff of Mr. Smelly. My feet carry me to my tiny dressing room as fast as they can and when I get there, I plunk myself down on the chair. But as soon as I do, I leap back to my feet, grab a handful of sanitary wipes off my dressing table, and proceed to rub my butt cheeks. *That gross dude touched me!* He touched my butt! Of all the men I've been with, he was the most disgusting thing ever! Before I can complete my thorough scrubbing, Jimmy pulls the curtain aside and stands there, laughing.

"What the hell are you doing?"

"That smelly thing touched my butt! I'm getting his germs and God knows what else scrubbed off of me."

He laughs and says, "Need a hand?"

"Oh, shut up! He was nasty."

"Damn right. He was one rotten smelling fucker all right." Then he hands me a roll of cash. "J.D. says it's yours. Just for putting up with the smell."

We both laugh. I know J.D. would never give up any cash so that's coming from Jimmy.

"Thanks, but you don't have to do that."

"Do what?"

"You and I both know that J.D. would never give up a buck."

Jimmy puts his hands on my hips and says, "Just take the money, baby. You know I watch out for you."

"Thanks, Jimmy. You always take care of me." I kiss his cheek. Jimmy and I go back a long way.

"You've got someone in the wings, doll. You want me to send him into the box?"

"Yeah, but can you fumigate it?"

"Oh, shit! Let me get on that."

He tears off down the hall, calling the clean-up crew. They're used to taking care of all kinds of icky things in here.

Cara walks in. Her dressing room is next to mine. "I heard you had a stinky one." She laughs.

"Stinky doesn't come close. Nasty one, he was. And the douche bag touched me."

"Ewww! That's so wrong. What is up with those pervs? Don't they know the rules?"

"Guess they don't care."

"Sky, we need to grab drinks soon. I miss my girl. And it looks like you could use a girl's night out."

"Yeah, I could. And I miss you, too." We hug for a second. Cara's my best friend. We both started here at the same time and have been friends since. "Let's make it soon."

"What about tomorrow?"

"I can't. I have a client," I say.

Cara frowns. "I'm on the next five nights after tomorrow. Next week then. Let's try to make it a date."

"Okay."

Jimmy's back, letting me know a new client is ready for me. "You've got props."

"Perfect, just perfect."

"Don't worry baby. It's only a chair and a water bottle."

"Oh, no. Don't tell me. Another *Flashdance*-er. And let me guess what he wants to hear. *Maniac*."

Jimmy lets out a hearty laugh. "You got him pegged. But he wants *Flashdance* too."

I groan. "What is it with these old dudes and their *Flashdance* crap?"

He's still laughing as he says, "All they know is they wanna see a sexy girl that can dance. And *Flashdance* had it all back then."

"But I'm a blond for Pete's sake."

"Yep, and a damn hot one at that. Go on now and score some big tips."

"Hang on." I reach over for the little vial. "Want some?"

"Nah, I'm good."

I dip in and get enough for a good snort. When I'm all nice and coked up, I head down the hallway.

Here we go again. Music is cued and this time it's an over-cologned hairy dude that sits on the chair waiting for me. As soon as I walk in, I hit the music and *Maniac* starts playing. I spray myself with the water bottle, soaking me until I drip.

The client gives me a toothy grin. Way too toothy, in fact. The dude must've spent millions on those puppies. I swear they're so big and white, if we had a power outage, he could guide us out of this building by grinning alone. It takes all the control I have in this body of mine not to break out in laughter.

"Ah yeah, that's right, sister."

Sister? What the hell? What am I? A nun? Sister Mary Skylar, the Private Dancer. Oh yeah, that has a nice ring to it now, doesn't it? A giggle bubbles out of my lips, but thankfully the music is so loud, Big Teeth doesn't notice.

My hips tweak and Mr. Toothy grabs his crotch. There's a towel on the arm. It's there for a purpose. Clients can jack off under it if they choose, but they cannot touch me or display themselves, at any time. I wonder if anyone explained that to Mr. Toothy. I don't speak to clients. They can tell me what to do, but no conversation takes place between us.

The chair is right in front of him and I straddle it, spreading my legs wide. My hands move all over my body, and then I'm up and moving, gyrating, twisting and doing all sorts of things that Mr. Toothy apparently is enjoying because beads of sweat are springing up on his forehead. My *Maniac* routine is perfection and by the time the song ends, Mr. Toothy is huffing so hard, I wonder if he might have a heart condition. His hand is still grabbing his balls and he looks as though he's in pain. Now I move in for the kill with *Flashdance*.

Spinning, I turn and slam my palms on the chair and bend backwards. Now I'm on the floor in a wide split facing him and I put my chest on the floor too and slide forward then leap up and do all sorts of shimmying. I wiggle my ass in front of his face before I move away for some move splits on the floor. Toothy's hand clamps the arm of the chair so hard, his knuckles go white (but not as white as his glowing teeth) and suddenly he groans. Holy moly! The guy just blew his load in his pants! He lifts up the hand that's been holding his crotch and a nice little stain appears, spreading outward.

"Jesus, holy hell, what did I just do?"

You shot your wad Mister, what do you think you did? I don't answer him out loud though, but Toothy sits there and rubs his crotch.

"Jesus, you're a hot piece of ass. Turn around and bend over so I can have a peek."

I do as he asks.

"Oh, God. Oh, God. You're a prize, I'm telling ya. A

real prize."

I flash him a shy smile. They always love that. He shoves his clean hand in his pocket and pulls out a bundle of cash and hands me the whole thing.

"Your name's Lena, right?"

I nod. That's my stage name.

"I'm coming back Lena. Just for you. You're a fucking prize. And next time, I want that sweet ass right in my face."

I lick my lips, nice and slow and give him another little smile.

"What a fucking prize."

Then I sashay out of there because Toothy's time's up. I hit the hall running and when I'm out of earshot, I die laughing. Jimmy hears me and is there in seconds.

"Oh my God. The guy came in his damn pants."

"You've gotta be kidding me."

"No! And look what he gave me!"

I open my hand and show Jimmy the money. It's two thousand dollars in hundred dollar bills.

Simultaneously, we say, "Jackpot," and high five each other.

"Jimmy, did you get a load of that dude's teeth?"

"Sure, but with tips like that, who gives a shit?" Then he gives me an odd look.

"What?"

"I wish you'd quit this shit."

"Yeah. Like that's ever gonna happen."

"Baby, I want you to go to school. Dance school. And become legit. Not do this. And give up the other stuff."

"Stop Jimmy. I know you care. But I can't. You know that's not possible."

"Yes it is. You should audition."

"Please, let's not have this conversation again. We've had it way too many times."

"I know, but Skylar ..."

"Enough!" Now I'm angry. He's sticking his nose into something he knows I don't want him to.

"You're letting that fucking bitch destroy your life. She's taking it away from you, bit by bit. And the thing that pisses me off the most is you're letting her."

"Jimmy, butt out now! You don't know anything about this stuff." But the truth of it is, his comments hit way too close to home. I shove him away from me.

"Where are you going? You have a john tonight. You can't leave."

My chest is heaving I'm so angry. "Damn it!"

Right now, the last thing I want to do is go and service someone. Jimmy has ruined my night. He means well, but he needs to stay out of my business.

"What time is it?"

"Eleven twenty."

"Damn. I gotta get a move on or I'll be late."

Jimmy touches my arm. "Please think about what I said."

I snatch my arm away. "Let it be, Jimmy." I start to rip my clothes off. He's seen me naked more times than I care to count. I grab handfuls of sanitary wipes and run them all over my body. I don't want to smell for my customer. Then I spray on some perfume. It doesn't take long for me to dress, since I'm used to changing clothes between dances. I tug on a lacy thong, a super short mini-skirt, a tight shirt that exposes half of my stomach and displays my perky nipples. After a quick fluff of my blond tresses, I'm ready to go.

"The car should be waiting for you."

Nodding, I dash down the hall. Being late is never an option for a client. And now that Jimmy has effectively spoiled my mood, I'm not looking forward to this at all. This guy is kooky and loves his blow jobs. He likes to watch me get myself off. I'm great at faking, but I am so not into this tonight. Not that I ever am, but now all I want to do is go away somewhere and hide.

The car pulls up in front of the high rise apartment building. I wait for the driver to open the door. When he does, I tell him to pick me up in an hour. That's what I'm paid for tonight.

The building is all glass. Sleek and contemporary. The doorman smiles as he opens the door. Security asks for my name and when I give it to them, they start to tell me which floor, but I cut them off. "Eighty-first. Thank you."

The elevator doors make a soft swooshing sound when they open and close, and the ride to the penthouse is nearly silent. When the doors open, I enter a dimly lit room.

"Hi, Lena. Come on in. Can I make you a drink?"

It's the usual greeting. He knows I don't drink with clients. We don't waste time with chit chat. My head flicks back and forth as my coat lands on the floor around my ankles. I continue to make my way toward him. He's seated in his favorite chair. It's a barstool, leather and expensive. He always pulls it in the middle of the room. Directly across from it is another chair. But it's a wooden one, regular height.

"How was your day?"

"Perfect. And yours?" I use my husky voice when I'm with him.

"Horrible. I thought about you all day and you distracted me."

"Well, now you don't have to think about me, because I'm right here." I drag out the *right here*.

Walking up to him, I lean in and run my tongue along his neck. "Is your cock nice and hard for me tonight? Are you ready to see my wet pussy come all over my hand for you?"

"Oh, Lena, you know I am."

In a firm voice, I say, "Then take off your fucking pants, George. You know I hate when I get here and you're still wearing them."

He jumps up and takes his pants and tightie whities off. George is in his early fifties and is in great shape for his age. In fact, he's not bad looking either. But he has some weird fetishes.

"Now, bend over, George, because you've been a very bad boy." He complies and I whack him on the ass with my palm about a dozen times. I have to stop because my hand stings like fire. "George, if you're wearing your pants the next time I come here, I'm going to whip you with your belt. Are we clear?" And I have half a mind to do it anyway because this spanking crap kills my hand.

"Yes, Lena," he whines.

"Good. Now, grab your balls and squeeze them until they hurt." Don't ask me why he loves this, but he does. As soon as he squeezes, he gets a huge boner.

"Oh, George. Would you look at that? Now you're making Lena happy. Go sit down in that chair over there because you're going to watch Lena make herself come. But George, if you even lay one tiny finger on yourself, Lena will stop. Do you understand? Lena will stop and go home."

"Yes, George understands."

George sits and I undress, slowly, and watch him as he licks his lips. I tug and squeeze my nipples and lean into him. "Lick these, George." He does. "Now suck them. Hard." Again, he obeys. And why the hell wouldn't he? "Oh, George, that feels too good." I back away and see how hard he's breathing. It really can be a heady feeling, having all this control over someone. Too bad I'm not into it.

"Open your eyes George." When he does, he sees that I've pulled the barstool right in front of his chair and I've taken a seat on it. My thighs are spread wide, exposing myself for his viewing pleasure. "Look at me, George and tell me what you see."

"I see your sweet pink pussy."

"What should I do with it, George?"

His breath is busting out of his lips in little pants now and I wonder if he'll even last the hour tonight.

"Rub your slit, top to bottom and back and forth."

"Like this?"

"Oh yeah, Lena."

Once I get going, I ask him, "Now what?"

"Stick two fingers in and pump."

I follow his direction.

"Harder."

"Like this?" I ask.

"Oh, yeah."

"What else, George?"

"Rub your clit, fast," he says.

Taking my other hand, I use my finger to add the little clit play. Since I am in no way into this at all, my acting skills are going to come in very handy tonight. I moan, just a tiny bit. Then in a breathy voice, I ask, "What else, George?"

"Just keep going till you come."

And I do. Keep going that is. I don't come, but I sure give him a good show. By the time I'm done, he's sweating and gripping his knees, bent forward in the chair, eyeing my pussy, like it's going to take off in a sprint and disappear.

He stares as I pull my fingers out of me and put them in my mouth, sucking my juices off of me.

"Oh God, Lena. That was good. That was so good."

"Get up George and get yourself ready for me. I'm gonna fuck you with my mouth. And bring me your favorite toy. You get to pick tonight."

George hops up and is nearly giddy with excitement. His dick bounces around as he makes a dash for his bedroom. Moments later he returns with a bottle of lube, gloves, a butt plug and a condom. George does like his anal play.

After I get all gloved up, I tell George to bend over. While his ass is in the air, I say, "Okay George, now remember Lena's rules. No sound. If I put this butt plug in and you moan one time, it comes out and Lena goes home. Got it?"

George nods and he reminds me of an eager dog waiting for a treat. I lube up his plug and insert it slowly. George sucks in his breath, but that's it. "Good boy." I pat his butt. If I could, I would burst out laughing right now, but I don't dare. There's a couple hundred bucks tip in this for me tonight.

"Stand up, George." He obeys. I must say, George really is a good boy.

"How does that feel? Does George like his toy?"

He nods enthusiastically.

"Give it a whirl, George. Let me see how much you like it."
He follows orders, and pure pleasure erupts on his face. I better
get to work again, or I'm going to have a limp dick to suck.

After I take a seat in the regular chair, I motion for George to
come closer, and order him to put the condom on.

"Good boy, George. Lena likes how you put your condom
on." Then I put my mouth over his hard cock and start to suck. I
twirl my tongue around the head, licking and sucking, taking
him deep into my throat. Up and down, in and out I suck. Hard
and fast, and then slower. My hand moves to his ass and I turn
his butt plug. Seconds later, he makes a gurgling sound. It
doesn't alarm me. This is how he sounds when he comes. The
first time he did it though, I almost dialed 911. I'm used to
it now.

I lift my eyes and smile. George's mouth is wide open and
now he looks astonished, like he has no idea what's happened
and like this is his first blow job he's ever had.

"George, you're such a good boy. You can go and take your
toy out now."

He nods and staggers to his bedroom. My BJ's sure suck the
life out of him. When he hasn't returned five minutes later, I have
a good idea of where he is. I go check on him and just as I
suspect, he's sound asleep in bed, flat on his belly, butt plug
intact.

Shaking my head, I scribble a note, letting him know how
much he pleased me tonight. Then I sign it with lots of hearts
and take the five, yes five hundred dollar bills he left me on the
nightstand. George was a *very* good boy tonight.

By the time I leave the building, my ride awaits me. I tell the
driver where to drop me. He never is allowed to take me all the
way home. No one, not even Jimmy knows where I live. That
would be a huge mistake.

Four

Reese

"YOU KNOW WHAT? YOU'RE PITIFUL, THE WAY YOU WHINE AND moan about how you've been wronged. Look around you. There are people that would trade places with you any damn day of the week." My physical therapist is, get this, a petite red-headed, woman, who's probably around forty years old. And she's over-the-top sick of my attitude. Her name is Dot. And she's a bitch to work with.

"Yeah, yeah, yeah."

"Yeah. You're the most spoiled little shit I've ever worked with. Now get off your sorry ass and do as I tell you. You should be walking unassisted, maybe with a cane. But look at you. You're still clinging to that walker, like some ninety-year-old nursing home patient. Wait, I've had ninety-year-old nursing home patients that have had hip replacements act better than you. You're a miserable little piece of you-know-what."

"You have no idea ..."

27

"Shut up Reese. I don't want to hear it. Now get to work." Dot walks away, leaving me to my own black mood.

In reality, this is my only outlet. My mom acts like she listens, but she doesn't really. She looks at me with pity, but I don't want to see it in her eyes anymore. And I *am* a whiny ass. When I moved away from my parents into my own place last week, my dad shook his head and told me that I need to get a grip on this. He's right and so is Dot. But I'm stuck like glue in this sick place and I don't really have the gumption to get out.

Gritting my teeth, I begin my program for the day. Six long, grueling hours of this crap. I thought my workouts for dance were tough. They were nothing compared to this. This is brutal. Maybe it's because my bones were so badly crushed and all the muscles supporting them atrophied, but by the time my session is over, I'm dripping and covered in sweat.

"When was the last time you showered?" Dot asks.

I shrug.

"Don't come back here until you do. You stink."

That's another thing. Personal hygiene for me has gone down the tubes. I need to keep better track of that. But the drugs make me forget.

Hey, I got this guy I want you to meet," Dot says to me the following day.

"Who is it?"

"Just a guy."

Here we go. He's probably some therapist or something.

"Look, I don't want some dude trying to get into my head."

"Did I say anything about that?"

I grunt as I push my leg into another set of presses. "No. But I know how you people work. You've probably teamed up with my parents or something."

"Or something. No, really. He's a little older than you and he had the same thing happen to him. Was mugged. Left for dead. Anyway, here's his number. He said to call him anytime."

She shoves a piece of paper into my hand, one of those sticky

notes, and walks away. I look at it and all it says is *Case Jordan —
555-1290.* I cram it into the pocket of my workout pants.

Two days later, Dot asks, "So, did you call him?"

"Huh?"

"Case?"

"Who?"

She shakes her head and cuffs the side of mine. "The dude.
Remember? I gave you his number?"

"Oh. I forgot." I think back and try to remember what I did
with it.

"You don't even know what you did with his number,
do you?"

That bitch is a mind reader. I swear it. She's like my mom on
steroids. "No. But I'll find it."

She gives me a nasty look and walks away. A couple of
minutes later, she's back and jams another one of those sticky
notes into my hand. "Don't lose this one. Now give me fifteen
more or I'm gonna make you jog laps." She turns and leaves.
Fucking taskmaster.

I don't want to call this guy. What am I gonna say? "Hey
man, I was mugged. Like you. Can I come over and cry on your
shoulder? Will you rub my back and make me feel better?" Talk
about feeling like a bigger pussy than I already am.

By the time Dot finishes with me today, I'm a whipped
puppy. All I want to do is go home and crash. She helps me to
the door and hails a cab. As soon as my ass hits the door of my
apartment, I flop on the bed. I'd like to lie here and not move
until tomorrow. But I'm hungry. Living is such a fucking chore.
My phone vibrates with a text and I check it out. It's Dot. The
message says: *Call Case. Now.*

Damn. I wish she'd get off my ass already. I dig in my pocket
and pull out that scrap of paper. After a couple of minutes, I
press the numbers and wait for an answer.

"This is Case."

"Um, yeah. My name is Reese and …"

"Oh. You're the guy Dot knows. She's told me about you."

Great. I'm sure she's said all sorts of shit about me.

"Oh, well, then you probably don't want ..."

"Reese, let's grab some coffee."

"Right now?" He doesn't know me from Adam. I could be a serial killer.

"No time like the present. Where do you live?"

"Lower Manhattan."

"Cool. I'm close. How about we meet at this coffee shop near Wooster and Spring. It's called Joe and Mo's. You game?"

Fuck! This is the last thing I want to do. "Um, I ..."

"Oh, come on. It'll do you good to get out."

"Okay. What time?"

"One hour. See you then."

My hands are shaking when I hit end on my phone. I get up in search of my pipe. I need a hit of some weed ... and fast. After two long draws, I get to the shower. What the hell am I going to say to this dude? This was a fucking set up.

As I reach for the door handle to Joe and Mo's, another hand intercepts mine and says, "I've got it. You must be Reese. Case here." A huge hand is shoved in front of mine so I have no option but to shake it.

"Good to meet you." I don't really mean it and I wonder briefly if he can sense it. "On the way here I thought about how we didn't discuss what we looked like ... you know so we could recognize each other."

He doesn't laugh at my sarcasm. My walker makes a clanking sound as it moves across the floor. As usual, people give me surreptitious glances, like they think I don't notice or something. Every time I go out in public now, I think back about how I reacted to people before I got to be this way and I wonder if I stared. Did I give them funny looks, the way people stare at me now?

We find an empty table and Case asks me what I'd like to have.

"Aren't we in a coffee shop?" I refrain from adding the dumbass at the end.

He grins and only says, "Right. Cream? Sugar?"

"Black."

When he leaves, I study him. Tall, good looking, I suppose, with dark hair, he seems fine to me for someone who nearly died. He's back too soon, holding two cups of steaming coffee.

Without preamble, he says, "So how often are you using?"

I almost spew coffee in his face. The damn shit is so hot, I burn the fuck out of my throat. After I'm done sputtering, I say, "What the fuck, man! You trying to kill me or something?"

"Not at all," he says calmly. "Just wanting to know some truths here."

"Well, that's none of your goddamn business."

"Whatever. Listen, Reese, I want to help. I've been where you are."

"Oh? How's that?"

"I was mugged and left for dead too."

"And did they destroy your life in the process?"

"Not exactly. At least not like they destroyed yours. I did that on my own."

"Say that again."

"Yeah, you heard me. In the aftermath, when I couldn't get over what happened. During all the shit I had to go through to get better, my bitterness destroyed my relationship I had with my family. Lost my wife and kid. She's with someone else now. Someone who gives her what I couldn't at the time. I was a mean son of a bitch to her. Angry. Threw things. Came too damn close to hitting her. That's when I turned to drugs and alcohol." He snorts. "Not that I wasn't taking handfuls of the shit for pain as it was. But noooo. I had to add weed, coke, crack, meth, and you name it to the mix. I even started chasing the white dragon."

Fuck. Even I stay away from heroin.

"What kind of injuries did you have?"

"Gunshots. Stabbed a couple of times. Still have pain and

numbness in my left leg because one of the bullets is lodged close to my spine. They say one day it could move and I could be paralyzed."

"Why don't they take it out?"

"Removing it is too dangerous. It's so close to the spinal cord, one tiny movement could end my walking days permanently."

"You mean there's nothing they can do?"

"Not a damn thing. But hey, I'm fine now. So my motto is: *Every day. Live every day like it's your last.* You and I both know there are no guarantees."

The room closes in on me and I need to get out of here.

"Hey Reese. Listen to me, man. You're young. Life threw you a curve ball. Catch the motherfucker and throw it back."

"Huh?"

"Don't let the ball win. It's only a fucking ball. You know?" He stands and walks out of the place, leaving me alone. Alone with the fucking ball that's slamming into me over and over. I don't finish my coffee. I get the hell out of there and go home. Home to my weed. Home to my crack pipe. And home to my self-pity.

Five

Reese

THE MOVEMENT OF THE BED EDGES ITS WAY INTO MY SLEEP, rousing me from the only place where I find peace these days. Refusing to give in to it, I roll to my side, determined to let sleep reclaim me. But apparently, that's not in the plan. Soon after, a warm hand wraps around my limp cock. This is the opposite of what I'm interested in right now.

Shoving the hand aside, my message rings loud and clear —*hands off*! It seems the bitch isn't that bright. Before long, her hair tickles my back as she rubs her tits against me and reaches between my legs for her target. She finds it all right, and commences to massage my balls. Slowly, my cock springs to life. If she wants to play, who am I to deny her?

I roll on my back, giving her better access, and spread my legs to allow her to shift her body between them. Then she goes to town on me, sucking my cock and licking my balls. Suddenly I push her away.

"Get on your knees. On the floor," I demand. She complies. I move to the edge of the bed and say, "Take it all. Deep throat me." My hand wraps around her neck and I force my dick into her mouth. Her eyes water but she doesn't refuse. I pump into her like a piston, letting her throat work my dick until I'm ready to shoot my load. There's no asking if she wants to swallow because I don't give a shit. She's going to whether she wants to or not. As soon as I come, I feel her throat tighten against the length of my cock as she milks every last drop out of me. She loves this; don't ask me why. When I finish, I pull out and knock her away from me. Before I can get to my feet, she scrambles to her knees and is between my legs again. For the first time, I take a good look at her. Bleached blond hair that's nothing but a mass of snarls and eye makeup smeared everywhere. The sight of her disgusts me.

"You need to get out of here." Pushing her away for the second time, I make it to my feet and hit the bathroom. Fuck, I feel like shit. After I take a long piss, I grab a toothbrush and get rid of the nasty taste in my mouth. I hope she's gone, but I know better. She's still naked, sitting on the bed.

"Can I have a hit?"

If I answer her, I'll have to acknowledge she's there. But I can't ignore her forever. I want her gone. Like ten minutes ago. Why did I even let her stay the night? After I guzzle some water, I say to her, "You gotta go. Now."

"But …"

"But nothing. Get out."

"You're an asshole. I just gave you a fucking blow job and you won't even give me a single hit?"

"I didn't ask you to suck me off. That was your choice."

She dresses and leaves in a huff. The idea of what just took place should make me feel bad, but it doesn't. I lost my conscience when I started doing drugs. I hunt down my vial of white happy dust, dip the tip of my key into it, and raise it to my nose. When I inhale and feel the initial sting, and then the numbness, I sigh. Relief courses through me. And then I'm energized somewhat. I glance at the clock and notice the time. Shit. It's after two. Today's the day I promised my parents we would meet for dinner. This is going to suck, in a big way. Dinners with them have turned unbearable. They were bad before those fuckers ruined my life. But now, well, all we do is argue. Worse than before. At least before I had a vision for my future. Now all I have are getting drunk and high. I try to hide it from them but they're not stupid. They can see how strung out I am. My heads starts to pound just thinking about it.

Jeffrey and Juliette Christianson. Proud parents of moi. Fuck them and everything else. I'm not living up to anyone's expectations anymore. They never wanted me to dance. My mom told me I didn't have what it took. But I worked my ass off to get where I was. And I got there … I made it. And for what? To get my damn leg smashed up by some motherfuckers who wanted nothing but a few measly bucks. So my mom was right after all. I'm nothing but a loser, who can't walk without a fucking cane. Oh, and did I mention a fake knee because the one I had was so badly fucked they couldn't salvage it?

My phone rings, making me jump. I check the screen and groan. And so it begins.

"Yep?"

"Reese, honey." She says it and her voice drips it. Sticky, gooey, syrupy shit. I get this image of her with it running out of her mouth and I give my head a rough shake.

"Mom."

"Five o'clock. At the Fish Grille. Sound okay?"

"Sure thing."

"We can't wait to see you, honey."

"Five then."

That tiny brown vial is in my hand faster than I can hang up the phone. I do another hit of coke and head to the shower. When was the last time I bathed anyway? I can't remember.

As I scrub away the stink, I remind myself to go to the clinic and get tested again. My brain is so numb I can't remember if I used a condom last night. If only for this, I need to pull my shit together. Bringing sleazy women home is normally off the menu for me. I swore to myself I wouldn't do that. Why the fuck was she here this morning? The fact that I had my dick jammed down her throat is bad enough, but I wonder if I had it crammed in her cunt last night. Maybe this dinner will do me some good because I need to straighten my ass up.

When I'm done, I get dressed. All my clothes are dirty. Filthy actually. When's the last time I did laundry? No idea. I put my feet into my cleanest and nicest pair of pants, which aren't very nice after all. They hang on me. As I look in the mirror, I notice how thin I've become. When did this happen? I used to be so muscular. My thighs were so bulky I had trouble getting pants to fit. That was *before*. Even my upper body was thick from all the weights I lifted. I had to be strong to lift the ballerinas. So I was diligent in my workouts. No more. I look like some damn sixteen year old who can't keep up with his growth spurts. Scrawny and skinny. My hair is long now and I *never* had long hair. Most of the time it's greasy and nasty. Now it doesn't look so bad because it's clean. But I barely resemble the guy I used to be. No damn wonder I make my mom cry.

I have to stop thinking about this. When I get to the den, if you want to call it that, I flop on the sofa and pick up my pipe. My weed is somewhere around here and after I find it, I put a pinch in the bowl and light it. Inhaling deeply, I let the effects of it take over. Not long after, that edginess dissipates and I'm much calmer. Weed is so much better than alcohol. Numbs my physical pain too. After another hit, I'm in a much better frame of mind. Leaning my head back, I take a short nap. When I wake up, it's after four. Knowing I have to go uptown, I make my way out the door to the subway. Being late is never a good thing with my parents.

I arrive at the restaurant, to find my parents are already

seated. My dad stands to greet me and his eyes narrow as he inspects my attire.

"Dad."

"Reese," he extends his hand and we shake.

"Hi, Mom." I lean down and kiss her cheek.

"Oh, honey. How are you?"

"I'm good, Mom. You?"

"We're fine. But we don't want to talk about us. We want to know about you. What are you up to? You look so thin, honey. Are you eating?"

"Mom." This is the last thing I want to discuss ... my unhealthy eating habits.

"Honey, look at your pants. They're hanging on you."

About now is when I feel the urge to run, but oh wait! I can't run anymore.

"Mom, can we refrain from discussing my size?"

"Honey." She drags the 'ey' out and makes it last forever.

"Mom, I came to this dinner because you agreed you wouldn't do this. I can leave any time."

"Please don't, son." My dad says. "Your mother and I want to talk to you about something. We think you, ah, well we think it's time you pull yourself together."

Really, Dad? "Oh?"

"Yes. Your mother and I have decided that unless you begin to show some initiative toward your future, we will pull all financial support from you."

Why am I not surprised? I've seen this coming for a while now.

"So, Dad, what do you have in mind?" The snarkiness is all over my question.

"School. Some kind of formal education."

"Reese, darling, you could become a professional choreographer. Or a set designer. Or even an instructor."

My hand flies out, my palm extended. "Stop right there. I will not have *anything* to do with dance. Clear?"

37

They stare at me like a deer in the headlights. Why are they shocked? It's not the first time I've said this.

"Look, let me give this a little thought. I know you mean well, but I don't know …"

"Reese, we're not leaving you any options. No school, no money. Remember, we control your trust fund and we can do with it what we please. Now I know this may sound cruel, but you're wasting your life away. You're lying around doing … well quite frankly we don't know, nor do we want to know. We're sure it involves things that we can't even comprehend. Your appearance is evident of that."

"Okay, so …"

"So nothing. Did you not hear what I said? We're giving you an ultimatum. Take it or leave it. School or nothing. We're happy to support you if you go, but if you refuse, we cut you off. It's May now. You have until August to get enrolled in fall classes somewhere. If you opt not to, then you're on your own financially. You're twenty-five years old as it is. You should be on your own anyway. Functioning in some capacity. Yes, you were dealt a blow …"

"A blow? Is getting beaten nearly to death and having my dancing career destroyed only a blow? I can barely fucking walk now!"

"That's enough, Reese. We're in a public place. Act like an adult, not a petulant child. We're terribly sorry this happened to you. We're every bit as upset as you are," Dad says

"Really? I doubt that. How can you be? You prance around in your high society lives like nothing is real to you."

"Stop it, Reese. I'm tired of seeing you behave this way. You need help. Counseling. Therapy. Look at you. You're a mess. And you won't do it unless we force your hand. So, we're forcing your hand," Dad says.

This dinner is much worse than I had anticipated. They're not going to give up on this. It's the end of the line and I'm going to have to comply.

My legs bounce beneath the table, one more so than the other for obvious reasons. My anger over this ambush is palpable. Mom withers as I glare at her. This was the absolute set up. They knew I would blow a fuse if they did this anywhere besides a public place. I could use a hit of weed to calm me down.

"Excuse me." I stand and head to the restroom. Once there, I take a quick hit off the small pipe I carry with me constantly. Then I wait for the calm to hit before I go back to the table.

When I rejoin them, my father asks with disdain, "Feel better?"

Not bothering to answer, I drink my water instead. The trembling in my hands has eased somewhat, but it's there and they can see it. The thing is, they're right. I know they're right. But I can't seem dig out of this hole I landed in. I'm stuck, and as much as I would like to be what they want, I know I'm not capable of it. The night I was attacked, not only was my career stolen, but so was everything I had. My strength, my pride, my drive, my courage and sometimes the will to keep going. All those times when I was growing up and my mom told me I would never make it, I pushed myself because I knew I could. There was something inside of me that told me so. That something is dead and gone now. There's nothing left but a deep, dark void. An empty abyss where it used to be and I don't think I can ever get it back. I don't know *how* to get it back.

The silence is so loud it's become ridiculous. But I really have nothing to say to them. My throat is thick with things I *want* to say, but the words never seem to make it past my lips.

Swallowing, I croak out, "Look, I'm sorry for putting you two through all of this. You don't deserve it. But I need to think about everything you just said."

As I stand, my mom grabs my hand and says, "Reese, please don't leave. Please."

The pleading in her voice annoys me, though for once I know she's sincere.

I shake my head and say, "Nah, your dinner will be better

without me. I'll call you later." Turning away from them, I limp my way to the door, cane in hand as I go.

MY CANE STARES AT ME, MOCKING ME. SOMETIMES IT EVEN speaks to me, telling me I'm the biggest piece-of-shit known to man. I don't argue because it's right. After that disastrous dinner with my parents, my drug use escalated. I'm now using to wake up, to sleep, to function. My parents need my decision regarding school. If I start classes, I can't go like this because I'll fail. I need help. It's as plain as the nose on my face.

So what do I do? I hit the crack pipe. I need a buzz so I can get out of here. And that's not possible without some assistance. Once I'm riding high, I head out to the clubs. Well, I use the word *clubs* loosely. The places I frequent these days are more like dives. Hell holes. Places I wouldn't have thought of going a year and a half ago. But these are the places where my connections to score drugs are and where I find a piece of ass when I need it. Like now.

The place I'm headed to is, ironically, called the Black Hole. It must've been named for me. It's in a seedy part of town and I don't want to think about what it looks like under the light of day, although, it's probably no worse than my own apartment. Foul is the word that comes to mind. But when I walk inside, a calm seeps into my bones. This is somewhere that offers me comfort. Where no one judges me and I can relax. As I look around the room, I see several people I know and realize that these are my people now. It takes a few minutes, but I finally find the person I'm hunting. His name is Zinc. That's the only name I know him by and that's how I want to keep it. He nods when he sees me, and moments later, takes a seat in my booth.

"My boy, Reese. How ya doin', my man?"

"Good, now that you're here."

"Whassup?"

"I need you to hit me around the block."

"Snow, rock, oxy, and weed? No smack?" Zinc asks.

"Yeah, man, but smack only if you can't lay hands on oxy."

"Here? Tonight?"

"If you got it."

"Yeah, but not on me. You gotta give me a few. You got cash?"

"Yep," I say.

"Sweet. Sit tight, dude, and have some beverages. I'll be back."

And he is. About an hour later. With exactly what I ordered. By this time I'm feeling mighty good, reinforced with several bourbons on the rocks. We make our exchange and I hit the john. I need a rush so I do a hit of coke and know that in a minute I'll be riding high.

A girl that's been checking me out, intercepts me as I make my way back to my seat.

"You alone?"

"Not anymore."

She giggles. Why do girls have to giggle? "I'm Tiffie."

"Hi Tiffie. I'm Reese."

Tiffie sits across from me and I learn all about her, from the time she was three years old and how she ran away from home when she was fifteen. I know I should empathize, but I don't. I stare at her pink and blue fluffy hair and wonder how she is able to make it look like that. It reminds me of cotton candy, and not in a good way. It's a shame too, because Tiffie isn't bad looking. She just needs to wear her lipstick inside of her lips, not smeared outside of them. And her eye shadow is neon blue, giving her a scary look.

She leans across the table and asks, "You like whatcha see, Reeds?"

Tiffie is wasted. She can't even say my name.

"No, not really, but you'll do. Come with me, Tiffie."

She follows me to the men's room.

"Get down on your knees and suck my cock. Now."

Tiffie giggles and does as I tell her. Her mouth works me over but I keep getting glimpses of the tower of cotton candy hair and it disturbs my enjoyment. So I say, "Get up, Tiffie. Pull up your skirt and turn around."

"Oooh, you like it from the back."

"Now put your hands on the wall."

Tiffie is very compliant. I slam my condom-wrapped cock into her pussy and she groans.

"Do you like this, Tiffie?"

"Y-y-yessss."

I grab her waist and pump into her. Her fluffy pink and blue spire of hair tilts precariously and I have this image that I'm fucking Marge Simpson. I close my eyes so I don't lose my erection.

"Tell me how much you love my cock, Tiffie. Tell me how much your cunt loves my cock."

"I loves your crock."

My crock. Fuck. Tiffie can barely talk. "Is that all?"

"Huh?"

Tiffie is so damn drunk, she can't even think dirty, much less talk it. I stretch her out along the wall and slam my hips into her ass. It's hard and rough because with each hit, I grind myself against her. When I feel close to blowing my wad, my tempo increases even more. Her breathing sounds like a damn dog in the August heat now. Maybe mine is too. All I want to do is come so I can get this sport fuck over. And finally I do. When my dick finishes its final spurt, I pull out, and rip off the condom. I drop it in the toilet next to me and flush, then wipe my balls off, just to make sure I clean off any traces of her . I don't want any reminders of Tiffie later when I get home. When I'm confident everything is tidied up, I zip junior back in my pants and tell Tiffie she can pull her skirt down.

"Oh. Okay." She turns around and it's hard not to laugh. Her rainbow tower is seriously listing to the right. I try to correct it, but the damn thing is lacquered to her head. She's so hammered, not only is she unaware of her epic hair fail, but she doesn't even realize the fuck fest is over.

"Come on Tiffie. Did you enjoy your orgasm?"

"Oh yeah. It was great."

"Good. Let me buy you a drink."

And that's when it hits me. Is this where I want to spend the rest of my days? Hanging with and banging girls like Tiffie? Girls that don't even know they didn't come?

With my hand on Tiffie's arm I guide her back to the booth. Then I get her another of whatever it is she's drinking and get the hell out of there.

Once home, I rummage through all my things until I find what I seek. It's a crumpled up piece of paper and I tap the numbers on my screen.

"Case here."

"Case. This is Reese. I really need to talk."

Six

Reese

THE NA MEETING IS CROWDED TONIGHT. WHEN I LEAVE, Case is still talking with a few newcomers. I need to get a move on because of some studying on my agenda. Things are going okay. Not great but better than they were. School sucks. Classes are killing me, especially English, Psych and Criminal Justice. It's not that I don't like them, because I do. But the constant battle I'm waging against my body's need to use makes it so diffi-cult to concentrate that I'm doing a piss poor job in them.

At least my parents know the real me now. Case was good enough to help with that. God, he supported me through every-thing and has stuck with me over the last five months, even when I didn't think I would make it. Withdrawal was a bitch. No, let me rephrase that. It was a nasty piece of nightmare. Thought I was dying. Again. There are some days when I wonder if I'm still going through it. The lure of the drugs. To get my hands on some crack or oxy. The way it made me feel. Even a draw off a bowl of weed. Man, what I would give. But then I stop that train of thought and remember where I was and how far I've come. One day at a time.

My parents begged me to move back in with them, but I refused. I have to do this on my own. Yes, it's more of a challenge, but I need to become my own person again. So I moved to a different place ... a better neighborhood and a nicer apartment. And even now, I don't use a cane anymore. Case has gotten on my ass and I hit the gym every day for at least two hours. Weights and then the bike to strengthen all the supporting muscles in my leg. And to chase away the drug demons. My parents, of course, pay for everything. Well, my trust fund does. Someday I want to give back to them because of what they've done for me. NA has taught me that much.

Yeah, they may not have been the most supportive in my youth, but they've come through like champs when I needed them during my crisis. My selfishness in my younger days has made me realize what a shit I was. Just because they didn't fall all over every fucking thing I wanted or did, I was pissed at them. But they were doing what parents should do. Making their kid think about the decisions he chose. And my mom. I used to think she was self-centered. She is to a point, but who isn't? She got pregnant with me in the height of her career as a principal dancer. Who wouldn't be a little bitter and sad about losing something like that? But she could've had an abortion. Only she didn't. She chose to have me. Maybe I was the shit all these years. Not her. NA has taught me more about myself in the last five months, than I knew in the last twenty-five years.

When I hit step eight—the step where you make amends to all the people you've harmed—I visited my parents, and we all broke down. Even my stoic father, which surprised me. I told them how sorry I was for everything, for abusing their kindness, for abusing their support, but most of all, for abusing their love. What broke me up the most was when they both looked me in the eye and my dad said, "Son, love is unconditional." I cried even harder.

Perhaps being an addict was part of my greater plan. Maybe getting assaulted and nearly dying as a result of it was also part of my plan. Part of my plan to become a better person. To become the real Reese. The Reese I was meant to be. I hope so because I'm busting my ass and it's about killing me all over again.

There's a coffee shop right around the corner from my apartment … the same one where I first met Case. I decide to stop in for an extra-large double shot latte on my way home. It's going to be a long night. My phone beeps as I walk to the counter. I'm looking at the text and not paying attention to where I'm walking when I crash into someone.

"Oh darn," a soft voice says and then I hear a splat. I look down to see a cup hit the floor and the contents spill everywhere.

My head moves up and my eyes land on the cutest thing in the world. She's not beautiful in the sense you would think. But I can't stop the smile from forming on my face. Her long blond hair hangs down her shoulders and it's cut so that it has wispy pieces that frame her face. Her lips are full and upturned at the corners and she has an adorable little pixie nose. Her eyes twinkle with a bit of mirth and they are large, round and smoky gray. When she smiles, she displays a perfect set of teeth and there's something about her that makes me want to act like a school boy.

"Please forgive me. I'm so sorry. I wasn't watching where I was going," I say. I bend down to retrieve her now empty cup and move to toss it in the trash. Then I pick up some napkins to clean up the mess. "Let me buy you a replacement."

"Oh, it's no bother. But you really should be careful. You could get run over by a car or something," she says, her soft voice sounding concerned.

"No, I insist. What did you have?"

"It was only a skinny latte."

"A skinny latte replacement, coming right up."

I hit the order line, place our orders and then hand her the cup of coffee. She takes it from me and when she does, our hands brush. A current of heat passes through mine and as I look at her, I notice her eyes widen. For whatever reason, I don't want this moment to end. I want to ask her to stay here with me. So I can get to know her. So I can hold her hand ... *really* hold it. But I don't.

She drops her head, shyly, then thanks me.

"I'm really sorry about the first one."

"No worries." She raises her cup to me. "Well, I suppose I should be going."

I don't say anything but nod slowly. Then she turns and is gone.

Seven

PRESENT DAY

Skylar

HOLY RAVIOLI! WHAT THE HELL WAS THAT? THE DUDE RUNS into me, makes me drop my coffee, buys me a new one and when he touches me I want to melt all over him. Never. Happened. Before.

I'm a hooker. A prostitute. That crap just doesn't happen to me. That's fairy tale stuff. Make believe. I don't live in that kind of world. And the guy was seriously hot. I'm talking, take my clothes off now and do me, kind of hot. And when he smiled. Well, fuck me running. Forget about the running. Fuck me sitting, laying, standing, you name it. I'd do him for free. I need to get my mind back in the game here. I'm due at the club because my ride will be waiting. I have a client tonight. Hurrying, I hit the stairs to the subway at almost a sprint, pushing thoughts of hot dude out of my mind.

Jimmy's waiting at the back door for me. "Wasn't sure if you were coming."

"Yeah, I'm late, I know." I shove past him to my dressing room so I can change. I find the dress my client loves and pull out the undergarments. Crotchless panties, bustier, garter belt and hose. Then I tug the dress on. It's super tight. Thank God for lycra. The car's waiting for me and I'm whisked away to the hotel the client always reserves.

Tonight I'm meeting Clyde. I'm sure that's not his real name but I couldn't care less. Clyde is early forties and wealthy. Not very tall, but very good looking. In fact, at five seven, I'm taller than he is. But he's not too kinky and I like him.

We arrive at the Harrington Hotel and I head to the front desk to ask if there is a message for me. Of course there is. I'm handed an envelope and in it is Clyde's room number and a key card. I head up to room number 724. When I walk through the door, Clyde has a glass of Scotch.

"Lena." His voice actually sends a tingle up my spine. Clyde does have a sexy-as-hell voice.

"Clyde. I've missed you."

"Take off your coat. Now." Clyde doesn't waste time. And he's demanding.

"Yes, sir." I do as he asks.

"Turn around." I do a little spin. "Nice. Now bend over so I can look at your pussy."

Clyde loves my pussy. I bend over and he sits on the edge of the bed. He just stares at it for a while. I'm getting a little head rush because I've been upside down for so long. Suddenly he grabs my hips and pulls me onto his mouth. His tongue is on me and tunnels into me like he's digging for gold. I don't know, maybe he thinks he's going to find some in there. He's positively terrible at this and needs some oral sex instruction, but far be it from me to teach him.

Oh dear, Clyde's tongue is now changing tactics. He's moved from my vagina and is now attacking my clit. Maybe he wants to do a clit-ectomy. Holy cow. The only way I'm going to get Clyde to stop is to fake an orgasm so here goes. "Ah, ah, ah... Clyde." I wiggle my ass, hips, and everything else I can think of, moaning constantly.

Glory be to all that's holy. Clyde finally releases me and says, "Oh, baby, I adore you when you come. You love it when big Clyde eats you out, don't you?"

If only you knew!

"Oh yes, Clyde. You're the best!" I say in a breathy voice. How did I ever learn to fake this crap?

Then he slaps my ass. He loves to give my ass a good slap. Now he's going to get his lube out and finger me up. He loves that too. I have his method down like crazy. Men are so damn predictable.

"Lena, come here." He undoes my bustier and teases my nipples. I moan and groan appropriately. "On your hands and knees." He lubes up his fingers and inserts them, moving them around. I am so over Clyde's routines I start to think about the new movies that are coming out this Friday.

"Lena, doesn't this please you?" Oh, crap! I forgot about Clyde.

"Oh, yes, Clyde. That feels divine." I make a little purring noise, and then moan.

"I have a surprise for you tonight, Lena."

"A surprise?"

"And you're going to love it."

I always get a little nervous when they tell me they have a surprise. My rules are clear. No intercourse. Ever. They can finger me, use toys to a point and with my permission, vaginally and anally, but never ever can they use their penises in me. No bareback blow jobs. Ever. No kissing. Ever. They cannot ejaculate on me. Ever. BDSM is okay to a point and only on them. For me, they must ask permission and only very mild. And that sums it up.

"Are you ready?"

"Oh, yes, Clyde." I hear a buzzing noise so I know it's a toy and then I feel something being inserted in both my vagina and anus. Oh boy, Clyde has been shopping. Hmm. This might not be bad after all. It's even hitting my clit. I can't imagine what kind of contraption covers all three, but who am I to argue? I never have an orgasm with a client. They're all fake. So maybe tonight I'll finally come.

"Oh, Clyde. What is this? This is sooooo niiiiiice." He loves it when I ooooh and aaaaah.

"Oh, Lena. Wiggle your ass for me." I do as he asks and he slaps me, driving whatever he's inserted deeper inside.

"Ooooh!"

Slap.

"Ahhhhh!"

Slap.

"Oh! Oh! Oh!" And damn if I don't come. I want one of these things! I wonder if I'll have to slap my own ass though. That might take the fun out of it.

Suddenly, my contraption is extracted and Clyde is in front of me with his tiny boner. See, here's the thing about Clyde. His dick is teeny. And I mean super teeny. A teeny weenie Clyde does have. I can put the entire thing in my mouth and I don't think it comes close to the middle of my tongue. And that's when he's fully boned up. One might think blowing a teeny weenied man is easy. But it's quite the contrary. You see, on a large-dicked-man, if you suck hard and get carried away, he loves it. But on a teeny weenied man, you can, in fact, injure him, if you're not too careful. No day dreaming for me when it comes to blowing Clyde. It's pure concentration and focus on his minute appendage. Poor Clyde. I wonder if he's married and if so, does he ever screw his wife? Would she even feel that little appendage? I know they say it's not the size that counts, but Clyde really did get screwed in the penis department, no pun intended. I have to wonder where he buys his condoms because they have to be extra-extra-extra-small. Then a thought hits me. As I'm blowing him, I move my eyeballs to the side, trying to get a glimpse of his hands. I'm suddenly curious to see if there's a correlation there. I can't believe I've never paid attention to this before. The urge to slap my forehead is so strong I can barely stop myself.

"Oh baby, oh baby, oh baby, oh baby, oh baby!" And Clyde is finished. Well, that's it for the blow job part. And it's a good thing too, because my curiosity about his hand size is nearly killing me. I finally take a peek at them and it confirms that the long-standing myth we ladies have all been told about is nothing but a bunch of bull. Clyde's hands are quite large. Hmm, I'll have to file that piece of information away for future reference.

Pulling myself back to the present, I notice Clyde is eyeing me. It's most likely because, he's not done with me yet. Clyde has a lot of money and he pays for four hours. So we've only gotten started.

Three hours later, I leave Clyde's hotel room and my driver is waiting. He drops me off at the usual place. I've given him J.D.'s share of the money. The walk home isn't long, but it's late and I'm tired. It's been a very long day. My feet are killing me as I'm still wearing my four-inch platforms. I wish I could figure out what it is about these kinds of shoes that guys love so much. Even short guys like Clyde. Poor Clyde. Small things aside, he really is a nice guy.

My heels click along the pavement and I turn the corner, but as I do, an arm snakes around my waist and jerks me backwards. The cold steel of a knife is pressed against my neck and a voice says, "Make a sound and this knife meets your artery."

A fist presses into my solar plexus and I can't breathe. He drags me a few feet to a dark alley between buildings. My face slams against the side of a building, the rough brick scraping it. His hands grope inside my coat and yanks open the buttons. My heart pummels inside my chest because I know what's coming.

His knee forces my legs apart and then his hand reaches under my dress, groping me.

"Well, what we got here? You've been expecting me?" He's just found my crotchless panties. Then he crushes my body against the wall with his hips, as his fingers penetrate me. I squeeze my eyes shut. It's been quite a while since sex has been ripped from me and never before like this. The vicious manner in which he's violating me has me trembling in fear. His smell is so horrid as his breath hits the side of my face, his touch so abhorrent but his strength far outmatches mine. I can't so much as budge. He throws his hips into mine again and says, "You're gonna love this."

I feel a space open between us and then I hear the sound of his zipper going down.

Oh God. I can't believe this is happening to me. I try to wiggle but he moves his knife and presses it against my neck again.

"Any more and you won't have a reason to move again."

Then suddenly he's gone and there's nothing but cool air behind me. Open space. My mind doesn't register anything but that. I move my arm, afraid to do anything else, for fear he's still there, and just preparing himself, like pulling out his dick. I know that knife will be plunged into my body somewhere and in moments I'll bleed to death. But then I notice sounds, scuffling sounds that are coming from behind me somewhere. When I turn to look, my body shakes so badly I can't move. So I lean into the wall and hang on to it with both hands. I know I should run, but I can't. I pray this feeling passes soon so I can get the hell out of here.

Eventually, the noise stops. Then a voice asks, "Are you okay?"

My lungs won't fill with air and I fall to my knees and start gasping.

Eight

Reese

THE GIRL FROM THE COFFEE SHOP. CAN'T STOP THINKING about her. I'm even daydreaming about her. What's wrong with me? I'm supposed to be studying, which is why I got the coffee in the first place. I have an exam tomorrow and I'm not anywhere near ready. At around 2 a.m., I get up, stretch, and go for a walk. The streets are deserted. And why wouldn't they be? I wish I had gotten that girl's name and number. I'm such a loser. I need to forget about her and prepare for this exam. As I round the corner, I hear a muffled sound, much like a whimper.

My ears perk up and I follow the sound. What I see boils my blood and turns me into a raging maniac. A man has a woman pressed up against a wall and is sexually assaulting her at knifepoint. All those months in the gym, working out my drug demons have paid off because I grab him by the collar and jerk him backwards and then beat the hell out of him. When he's unconscious, I turn to the girl.

"Are you okay? We need to call the police."

"No. No police." She rasps. She's having a tough time breathing.

That's when I get my first good look at her and notice it's the coffee shop girl.

"You're the girl from the coffee shop."

She lifts her head all the way and the right side of her face is badly scraped and already swelling.

Her eyes ping around and she says, "I-I gotta get outta here."

"I'll take you home."

"No, I can't go home."

I glance around, trying to decide what to do. Without giving her any opportunity to object, I reach around her and pick her up. I only live a block from here so I carry her to my place.

"What are you doing?"

"Taking you to my place. You'll be safe there."

When we get to my apartment, I walk her to the bathroom.

"Did he rape you?"

"N-no. His hand ... he ... you got there right before h-he ..."

I go to my room and grab some sweatpants and a sweatshirt. I hand them to her and say, "Here. Shower. Towels are in the cabinet."

"I-I d-d-don't think I-I-I c-c-can ..."

I take a good look at her and she's shaking from head to toe.

"Do you need a hand?" I ask.

She nods. I take off her coat and I'm shocked at what she's wearing. I'm even more shocked at what's underneath her dress, but I shield my reaction. When she's completely naked, she stands in front of me as though she's fully clothed. It's an odd reaction for someone, especially since she was just nearly raped, but I attribute it to trauma. Then suddenly she breaks down and cries.

"You're safe here," I say as I pull her against me. "Everything's okay now. No one can hurt you here." Damn if I'm not hard, trying not to think about it, and I feel like such shit..

Her sobs subside and she looks up at me, sheepishly and apologizes. "I'm sorry."

"No need to apologize."

Why would she be sorry? She was just brutalized for Christ's sake.

Then she gets into the shower. I back out of the bathroom, thinking about that outfit she had on. Women don't wear that shit for the fun of it. She must've worn it for her boyfriend. But why wouldn't she have called him?

The bathroom door opens and if I thought she was cute before, she blows me away now. Long blond messed up hair and no makeup makes her look perfect. And all I want to do is kiss her. Oh shit, why did I bring her here? Now I have to be a gentleman.

"I've made you some tea." I hand her the cup and watch how her hands shake as she takes it from me.

"Thank you." She takes a sip and asks, "You don't have any liquor, do you?"

" 'Fraid not. Recovering addict here." The slight widening of her eyes gives her away, but she quickly covers it up. "I don't hide this fact about myself from anyone. That's why I made you the herbal tea. It's the best I can do."

She sets her cup down and leans toward me. "Thank you. I ..."

"You don't have to thank me. I'm glad you're okay."

"Can I sleep here?"

Her request startles me, but I don't let it show. "Sure, if you want to. By the way, my name's Reese. Reese Christianson."

She gives me a tremulous smile. "Nice to meet you Reese. I'm Skylar O'Donnell." Then she stands and goes to the bathroom. I hear her brushing her teeth. She must be using my toothbrush. How strange. Maybe she's still in shock. When she walks out of the bathroom, she heads to the bedroom on silent feet and that's it. I brush my teeth and sure enough, my toothbrush is wet. She's an odd duck all right. I turn off all the lights and lay down on the couch. A few minutes pass and I feel her hand on mine.

"You okay?"

"No. I want you to sleep with me. I'm scared of the dark."

She leads me into the bedroom and we both get under the covers. It seems natural for her to be here, though it sounds crazy as all hell. When she curls against my side, I put my arm around her and ask, "Better?"

"I'm good now, Reese. Just don't leave."

"I won't."

The sun is bright when I wake up. And as I expect, Skylar is gone. Her side of the bed is cold, so she must've left a while ago. After I brush my teeth and shower, I put a pot of coffee on. That's when I see the note.

REESE,

Thanks for coming to my rescue.

You saved me last night.

Thanks for a solid night's sleep, too.

Skylar xo

THAT'S IT. NO PHONE NUMBER. NOTHING. I HAD HOPED there would be something but there isn't. Maybe I'll run into her in the coffee shop. I can't help but think she lives around here. Why else would she have been in this area so late at night?

Pushing those thoughts aside, because I don't have time to spare, I begin cramming for my exam today.

Nine

Skylar

IT'S JUST AFTER SUNRISE AS I MAKE MY WAY HOME, WEARING Reese's sweats and my platforms. I hope I can sneak in without rousing my mom. She'll want to know where I've been, what happened and so forth. She'll figure out things went south when she sees my face. Then, instead of being concerned for my welfare, she'll get pissed, because this means I won't be able to work for a few days. And that means she won't get her fix if she needs it.

I really do live a fucked up life. I'm a high paid prostitute, a private dancer, I have a drug-addicted mother who lives with me while I support her sick habit. I also dip into the white stuff myself on occasion. My best friend is my bodyguard and my clients range from wealthy men to an occasional woman, I almost got raped last night, and then spent the night with the guy who saved me, who by the way, I'm wildly attracted to. What. The. Hell!

Try as I might, it's impossible to forget the way Reese smelled as I burrowed next to him. Fresh and clean. Not loaded down with cologne like so many of my clients are or covered with stench like my would-be rapist. Just the thought of having him next to me made me feel nice ... comforting in a way I'd never felt before.

I'm pouring a cup of coffee when Mom stumbles into the kitchen. She reaches in the cabinet and grabs a bottle of vodka. Unscrewing the lid, she holds the bottle to her mouth and takes a good hard swallow. Then she looks at me.

"What the hell happened to you?"

"Nothing. Just ran into a wall."

She grabs my chin and tilts my face toward the light so she can get a better look.

"Don't fucking lie to me. Who hit you?"

"No one."

"Is your pimp not taking good care of you?"

"No, Mom. That's not it. J.D.'s the best. I couldn't ask for anyone better. I was ... okay, someone attacked me on the way home last night."

"What? Where?"

I don't want to tell her because it will be admitting to the fact that my driver doesn't bring me back here.

"I had to take the subway last night and it was on the way home from there."

It happens before I can see it. Her hand flies out and she nails me with her palm.

"You stupid slut. You know not to walk around like that, late at night. What were you thinking? Now you can't work for a week or so. What the hell am I gonna do?" And then she smacks me again and again. As if that's going to work in my favor. "I should knock the shit out of you."

She stands there rubbing her arms. She has no idea the amount of money I make. I never tell her because she's so greedy. This way she thinks she can only use a certain amount of meth, crack, heroin or whatever she can get her hands on. I know. I'm being naive in thinking this will restrict her drug use. It won't. But it also won't give her that free for all she so desperately wants either.

My cheek stings from her slaps. Sometimes, like now, I really hate her. To the point of walking away and never looking back. But I can't do that. Won't do that. If I did, she'd die and then I'd blame myself. Jimmy thinks I should. He says she doesn't give a damn about me, why should I care about her? But I do because she's my mom and she's sick. She needs help but won't get it. And someday I'm going to persuade her to go to rehab.

I make scrambled eggs for breakfast and then I get on my old slow-as-hell computer. Like I do every day, I check out the local dance theaters to see if there are any openings for auditions. They usually require some kind of training but sometimes I find one that doesn't. Those are the ones I seek. When I don't see anything that I could apply for, I go and change into my workout clothes and head for the studio.

I'm lucky. This is one of those friend of a friend of a friend deals. Jimmy has an aunt who is friends with a lady who used to dance and then teach professionally. For years she owned a studio and pulled some favors to get me in here. I come diligently and she has no earthly idea that I'm a stripper. She thinks I'm a wannabe and that I practice diligently. She knows I put my time in here because someone reports to her. Then one day, as I was doing my routine, I noticed an elderly woman eyeing me. She stood off to the side and never once took her eyes off me. When I finished my two and a half hour routine, she was gone. About a month later, she was back, watching me again. Afterwards, she approached me and gave me some solid tips. I didn't see her again for a couple more months. When I was leaving the studio someone handed me an envelope with my name on it. Inside was a brief note.

Skylar,
Come to tea at my home — 121 E. 71ˢᵗ St.
This Wednesday at 3 o'clock.
Marianna

IT WAS THE FORMER DANCER/TEACHER.

MY STOMACH RUMBLED AS I SIPPED THE TEA. MARIANNA SMILED AS she heard it.

"*You should eat more, Skylar. Your workouts use a lot of calories and you need to keep up your strength.*"

"*Yes, ma'am.*"

"*So, tell me. What do you want to do with yourself?*"

"*I want to dance.*" Oh my God! Could I have been any more lame?

She laughed. But not a sarcastic one. "*Oh dear, I know that. The way you work out and how dedicated you are tells me as much. But how are you going to accomplish it? What are your plans?*"

My face fell to my lap. "*I don't know. I can't afford the fancy schools. And now it seems that's the only way to get auditions.*"

"*My dear girl, haven't you ever heard of scholarships?*"

"*Yes, but I would never qualify for one.*"

"*Why ever not?*"

"*Well, I, ah, because there's, ah …*"

"*Spit it out Skylar. For heaven's sake, I may be old but I'm not stupid, nor am I fragile.*"

"*I never graduated from high school.*"

"*So what?*" *Her question took me by surprise.*

"*Huh?*"

"*A young lady never says, 'huh.' But what I meant by that was if you haven't graduated from high school, then do something about it. My goodness, if that's the only thing holding you back, you can take care of that in no time.*"

She must've noticed the furrow in my brow.

"Skylar, that's not the only thing, is it?"

"No, ma'am."

"Well, you're not going to tell me, are you?"

"No, ma'am."

"Are you embarrassed?"

"Yes, ma'am."

"Very well. Maybe one day you'll come to trust me. In the meantime, I think there are a few things you can do to make your dancing much improved. And I want to help you. You may not be formally educated but you can still audition for certain shows. Off-broadway productions often take raw dancers because they like to shape them into stars. And if that doesn't work, try off-off-broadway. Someone is bound to discover your talent. So, what I'm telling you, Skylar, is to never give up on your hopes and dreams." And then she patted me on the knee and smiled.

There's something about this woman that I was instantly drawn to. I felt so relaxed around her. And that's quite unusual for me. Smiling from ear to ear, I said, "Thank you, ma'am."

"And you can stop calling me ma'am. I have a name and it's Marianna." Then she winked at me. I was in love with this woman.

AND THAT'S HOW MARIANNA AND I BECAME FRIENDS.

Ten

Reese

IT'S AFTER ELEVEN AND I'M WALKING HOME. I'M TIRED. THE
NA meeting went on longer than I would have liked. New
members like to talk about their issues. Sometimes it's hard to
put myself in the moment. But I can't skip a meeting ... I'm too
new to sobriety. Too new to being drug free to trust myself.

Thoughts of Skylar keep clouding my mind. What's her deal?
My curiosity is taking over everything. A week's gone by since
her attack. Everywhere I look, I hunt for signs of her, but nothing. I'm about four blocks from home when I hear shouts and
sounds of fighting. When I see what's happening, I pull out my
phone and hit 911 to report it. Then I rush the attackers. There
are two versus one. The guy being attacked is giving it back
pretty good, but still. I surprise one of them by grabbing him
from behind and when he turns, I pop him so hard in the old pie
hole, he buckles. The other one starts to make a break and I grab
him before has a chance.

"Oh, no you don't. I think you're gonna wait it out until the blues get here and haul your ass to jail."

By then the victim gets up, wiping his bloodied face, starts thanking me and the cops pull up. I give them all my information and statement and I head for home again. Damn thugs. If someone had intervened for me, maybe I'd still be dancing. But then again, I'd still be that selfish fucker I used to be. *Quit thinking about this shit, Reese.* I can't change the past and can only focus on the present and future.

By now it's close to one a.m. as I unlock my door. I scrub my hands and wash my face, making sure there isn't any blood remaining. After I brush my teeth, I decide I need a hot shower to relax me. When I'm done, I turn on the TV and a little while later, I hear the buzzer on my door. Who would be visiting me at this hour?

"Yeah?"

"Um, hi, it's Skylar. Can I come up?"

What the hell!?

"Yeah, of course." I buzz her in.

A minute later she walks through the door and I gape. She's wearing a trench coat but drops it when she walks through the door. Her dress is skin tight, short and has a plunging neckline that goes to her navel. Her hair is done up in some kind of fancy style, twisted around her head, wispy pieces falling around her face. She has black fishnet stockings on and black stilettos.

"Hi Reese." She flicks off her shoes and heads to my bathroom. She doesn't bother to close the door. I can hear her turn the shower on. Not long afterwards, she brushes her teeth and comes out, stark naked. "Come to bed with me."

"You wanna tell me what's going on?"

"You have to ask?"

I've never had an invitation quite like this before. She's not coy about it at all. It's a blatant come-fuck-me.

Standing, I move toward her. When I'm right in front of her, she reaches for my pants, but I brush her hands away.

"What are you?"

"A girl who wants to sleep with you."

"Skylar, when I fuck, I like it dirty. Are you willing to take it like that?"

"Why don't you find out?"

So I give her what she wants. First my shirt goes, then I rip my pants off and tell her, "Suck me. Hard."

She kneels and wraps her lips around my cock. At first she hesitates, but as I grab her head and push it down, she gets my meaning. She swirls her hot wet tongue around me, and slides that perfect mouth up and down sucking as she goes. I moan. Damn, but this girl knows how to blow cock. She pulls me in deep and releases her throat, but then makes a swallowing movement that massages my entire length. Fuck is this hot. Her mouth slides up and down and then she moves to my balls and starts licking them. Pulling them into her mouth, she lightly sucks, and then moves back to my stiff cock and resumes her lapping. Her tongue is like hot velvet on my skin. Then her lips tighten around me and start to suck me off again. As she sucks, her hands slip down to my balls, massaging me and I'm so close. So damn close. But I don't want to come in her mouth so I grab a fistful of her hair and pull it … hard. She lifts her eyes and it destroys my resolve. I want her to continue until I shoot off down her throat. As she eyes me, she flicks her tongue across my slit. Not once, not twice, but a dozen times until I'm helpless as she watches. Then her hand moves between my legs from my balls and slides up to my ass cheeks, fingers sinking in. My hands pull her head, hard, forcing my cock deep into her throat and I thrust back and forth.

"Suck me off, hard."

She does, as I push as deep as I can. Her eyes water but she doesn't refuse me.

"Don't fight it."

Her throat tightens against me and relaxes slightly and then she starts to move on my cock again. She sucks and pulls on me.

I groan as my cum spurts down her throat. "Fuck. Skylar." She looks up at me, my cock deep in her mouth, cum dripping out of the edge of her lip. I pull out and she licks that remaining bit off. That tiny motion makes me want to fuck her in the worst way.

She slides up along my body until she's standing and then takes her tongue, the same tongue that's still laced with my cum, and runs it all over my lips. She sucks first my upper, then lower lip and I can't take anymore as my tongue pushes into her mouth, tangling with her own, until she moans. This woman drives me crazy. She grabs my index and middle fingers and plunges them into her, fast and deep, then pulls them out and slowly licks her dewiness off. My mouth waters as she sucks on them … hard. Then she takes her own fingers and repeats the motion. But instead of sucking on them herself, she runs them across my lips and says, "This is what I taste like, Reese."

Before she can even finish saying my name, I pick her up and toss her on the bed, spread her legs, and my tongue laves her pussy. I run it along her slit in one long swipe and then plunge in deep, tunneling it as far as I can, then pull it out and lick and suck her clit. She's so fucking wet, her juices coat her. I rub them all over, back and forth until she writhes, sliding two fingers inside her, making sure to pay attention to her g-spot. But I don't let her come. I'm going to save that for when I fuck her. Every time she starts to clench her fingers and thighs, I stop until she's moaning and whining.

"Are you on the pill?"
"Yeah."
"Are you clean?"
"Yeah."
"So am I."

I flip her over and stuff pillows under her hips. My cock is so hard again it's about to blow. I quickly roll on a condom, and sliding my cock up and down along her slit, I circle it against her clit until she moans. Then I slam it into her.

"Ahhh!"

I pull out. She whimpers. And I repeat the whole process over and over. I wrap my arm around her waist and pull her back onto my lap and she cries out.

"Oh my god!"

"Go with it, babe."

"Ah…ah…ah!"

I move her to my rhythm, my hand on her core, her arms thrown back and around my neck. I look down at her as we fuck and her nipples are like rocks. Damn she's hot and sexy. But she's never been fucked like this before. Swiveling my hips, I rock back and forth, rubbing her clit with my hand. She rolls her head from side to side as it rests on my chest.

"Oh God, oh God, oh God!"

"Come for me Skylar." I whisper in her ear. I can feel all of her muscles tighten and there is that telltale series of spasms against my cock that I love so much. "Ah yeah, your cunt is perfect, baby. Just perfect."

"Ahhh, ahhh." Her nails sink into the flesh on my shoulders.

I wait for her to come down from her orgasmic high and say, "On your knees. Bend over." Now I fuck her hard. Really hard. This is where I get off the most. Sometimes, they come again. Sometimes not. I don't care either way because she just had a damn awesome climax. My hands hold her hips steady and it's a constant pounding. But she's absolutely getting back in the game.

"Ahhhhhhhhh!"

"That's it baby. You have an amazing pussy. It was made to be fucked. Hard." And then I can feel it building in me again. Right as it hits me, she milks me dry. As she kneels there I know she's on the edge so I rub myself over her clit and slip my fingers back inside her. "You have a gorgeous ass. Now roll over. I'm going to suck you off."

She flips on her back and I push her legs in the air, spreading her wide. She's so fucking wet. I rub her juices all over and slip two fingers inside her, pressing my thumb against her ass. When she moans, I know she's into it. I start to suck on her clit, hard, and when my thumb penetrates that sweet tight backdoor of hers, it pushes her over the edge and she comes all over the place.

Crawling up her body, I make it to my destination, and lick her lips. "This is what you taste like." Then I kiss her. She's a hungry animal on me, kissing me, licking and sucking my mouth.

"Reese."

"Yeah."

She maneuvers on top of me and says, "I've never climaxed during sex before."

"I know."

She sucks in her breath. "How did you know?"

"By your reaction."

"Who knew?"

"I did, but you never asked."

"Right."

"Go to sleep, Skylar."

She snuggles against me and closes her eyes. She's an odd one and the way she showed up here tonight, dressed in that outfit, makes me wonder what her deal is. But right now I'm too damned tired to dwell on it. I'll figure it out in the morning.

Just as I'd imagined, when I wake up and feel the bed next to me, she's gone. I get up and check the kitchen, but once again, nothing. She'll be back though. After last night, that smile she had on her face, I have no doubt she'll be back. And I'll be here waiting. Because that body of hers is made for mine and I can't get enough of it. But one thing's for certain … she has a secret and I'm going to find out what it is.

Eleven

Skylar

THE SUN IS ABOUT TO RISE WHEN I SNEAK OUT OF REESE'S place. I don't want to be here when he wakes up because if I see his face, I'm afraid I'll never leave. The man undoes me. And the sex. What is that all about? I've never in all of my life imagined sex could be like this. He takes me to a place I never knew existed. A place that isn't real.

As I walk home, my mind races with images of the things he did to me with his hands, mouth and his cock. I thought I was having an out of body experience. And the funny thing is, I went in there acting like I was the one in control. Like I was the one that was going to bring *him* to *his* knees. I'm pretty sure that happened when I sucked him off. He totally got into that. But who am I kidding? He was in control the whole time and those eyes of his as he watched me toward the end. How they got all deep blue and hazy. And his mouth. I've totally messed up here. He's going to be impossible to stay away from. And that's dangerous for me. I *need* to stay away from him. But the real question is, *can* I?

When I run up the steps to my place, I pray Mom's still passed out. She has her fixes and her vodka. But she suspects something is up with me. I open the door as quietly as I can and the place is silent. So I head straight to my bedroom.

"Where've you been all night, girl?" She rounds the corner and her arm nails me in the throat. Damn, she knows exactly how to hit. And what the heck is she doing up this early? She's never up before eleven.

"Um, I stayed with a client."

"Like hell you did. You don't stay with clients dressed like that."

Double damn!

"You're right. I stayed with a friend."

It amazes me how fast she can move for someone who is always under the influence of something. Her palm finds my cheek this time and it stings like all hell.

"Mom!"

"Don't you 'Mom' me. And don't you lie to me girl. I know you've been out whoring around."

Oh my God!

"Mom, I'm a prostitute, remember? You're the one who forced me into this life."

Smack. Her hand connects with my face again.

"Don't you sass me, girl. You know what I mean. You stay away from those boys. And I mean it. If I catch you whoring around, I'll whip your ass, Skylar."

"Mom, I'm twenty-three years old. You can't whip my ass anymore. I'm an adult. Besides, I can walk away from this. From you. And where would that leave you? Huh? Who would support you? Where would you get your drugs from?"

"Why you conniving little cunt! After everything I've done for you all these years. I've given up my life for you."

"Don't you think you have that backwards? You forced me

into a life of prostitution so I could feed your stupid drug habit. If it weren't for you, I'd be out of school, dancing somewhere. But no, I'm a damn hooker, whoring around because of your nasty drug addiction!"

I've never spoken to my mother like this before. She stares at me, mouth agape. I'm positive she's in denial. It's amazing to me how she's built this false world around herself and is under the misconception that she's done all of these wonderful things for me. All of the drug abuse over the years must have destroyed her brain.

"You little liar."

Her arm flies out, only this time I intercept it, my hand clamping down around her wrist.

"That's it, Mom. You strike me one more time, and I'm gone. I'll leave here and never come back. You'll be out on the streets, going through withdrawal with no drugs to pump into your body. You hear what I'm telling you? Do you hear me, Mom?" I scream.

She stares at me, her face ashen. Maybe I've finally gotten to her. Who knows? I turn and walk to my tiny room, slamming the door behind me.

I need a shower. I don't really want to take one though. Washing Reese's luscious scent off of me isn't something I ever want to do. Grabbing a fistful of the sweatshirt I'm wearing, I raise it to my face and inhale. His scent floods me and wetness pools between my thighs. Images flash through my mind again of how he pulled me on him, how his cock was so deep inside me that I have to clamp my hand over my mouth to stop a moan from escaping. This is an unprecedented level of arousal for me. My belly tightens and my breasts even ache with the mere thought of him. My hand slips between my legs and I rub myself to a quick orgasm. But it doesn't bring the relief I expect. Only one thing can do that, and he's still asleep in the bed where I left him. I quickly change clothes and head to the studio. Expending energy will be the only way to get my mind off of him.

THAT NIGHT AT *EXOTIQUE-A*, JIMMY WALKS INTO MY DRESSING room. "What's going on with you?" he asks.

"What do you mean?"

"You seem different."

Jimmy knows me better than anyone.

"I had a huge fight with my mom. I told her if she hit me again, I would leave and she'd be on the streets. I may have gotten through to her."

He nods slowly. He's not buying it. "You still working out at the studio?"

"Uh huh. Why?"

"Curious."

"Is that all?"

Jimmy's got something to say, but keeps his mouth clamped shut. His eyes get twitchy, just like they are now, when he doesn't know how to approach a touchy subject.

"Just say it Jimmy."

He sighs. "My aunt said that Marianna told her you hadn't gone to any of the auditions she set up."

Damn.

"Yeah, well ..."

His hand comes up, palm facing me. "Here's the thing, Skylar. Marianna is influential. She knows a lot of people. I mean *a lot.* She's taken an interest in you and thinks you've got potential. She's going out of her way to help you. And now you're lying about this shit. This isn't good. If you're not serious about dancing, that's one thing. And it's okay. But don't lie to her. You're hurting my aunt. And you're hurting Marianna. She's only trying to help you and you're slapping her in the face."

"Oh, God, Jimmy. I'm so sorry. It's just that when I got to the first audition, all those dancers looked so professional. Like they had all been through the routine before and knew what to do. And there I stood like a damn outsider. A nobody. Which is what I am. And I started thinking — who am I trying to fool? I'm never going to make it there. I'm a fucking stripper for God's sake. So I ran. I was embarrassed. And now, every time I think about going to one of those again, it totally freaks the heck out of me."

"Damn, Skylar. Why didn't you say something? I'll go with you, if you want. I'll put those uppity assholes in their places. You're the best and I'd put you up against all of them any day of the week."

He's such a great friend and he honestly means what he says. But he doesn't know the professionalism of the dancers and how they walk and talk. I don't even have the proper attire to wear to those auditions.

"Thanks Jimmy. But it's so much more than that. I don't think I'm cut out for it. I don't feel like it's my place."

"You won't ever know unless you try. In any case, you need to talk to Marianna about it."

He's right. I do. And I've wronged her by not telling her the truth.

"I will. And I'm so sorry I hurt your aunt after all she's done."

"Enough. You need to get ready. You have someone in the box, waiting."

"Shit."

The night speeds by, but there's only one thing on my mind and it's one tall muscular guy that I plan on paying another visit to later.

My belly's in knots when I press the buzzer.

"Come on up Skylar."

The door buzzes letting me know I can push it open. I walk up the flight of stairs and his door stares me in the face. This time, it's cracked, waiting for me to walk through.

"Hi." His voice is low and if I thought Clyde's voice could

send a tingle down my spine, Reese's sends mega volts of electricity racing through my body. I want to know everything there is to know about this man. Except not right now. The only thing I want is to shower and then have him do what he did to me last night. Because I've thought of nothing else all damn day.

I walk up to him, stand on my tiptoes, take his lower lip between my teeth and nip it. Then I suck it hard. When he pulls me to him, I back out of his hold and walk toward the bathroom, stripping as I go. By the time I get to the doorway, I'm down to my thong. His eyes burn a hole in me and I want so badly to turn around, but I don't. I turn on the water, but I stop to brush my teeth while it's getting hot. Then I strip off my thong and get in. My body is all soapy when I hear the shower curtain slide open.

No words are spoken as he pulls me against him. I'm already wet with anticipation. His mouth hits the place where my neck meets my shoulder and he slides his tongue up and down, then moves south to my nipples. They're like diamonds reaching for him, and I'm positive they could cut glass. He takes one in his mouth and puts his teeth around it, clamps down hard and flicks his tongue back and forth, until I squirm. But he doesn't release me. His fingers tweak my other nipple and my head falls back as I moan. I may come just with this going on. He continues the mouth action on my nipple but his other hand moves to my mound. His fingers slide in and out spreading my wetness around. My hands grip his head to my breast. Something needs to happen soon, because the ache between my legs threatens to turn me into a rabid animal. The fierce sensations are so powerful and intense they're approaching pain. Suddenly he stops everything. What the hell? My breath is locked somewhere between my lungs and throat. I open my eyes to see him stroking his cock. He stares at me with lustful eyes.

"You're not allowed to come yet."

Oh hell. I can't think straight. His hands move to my hair and he shampoos it. When everything's rinsed, he pushes me to my knees and says, "Suck my dick." His cock stares me in the face, stiff and glistening. I can already taste it as my mouth salivates. My tongue flicks his crown and he says, "No. Suck. Hard. Deep."

I take him in all the way and he groans. That sound spurs me on. I love that sound. My hands reach behind him and pull him closer. But he takes one hand away and puts it on his balls. He likes his balls held. I massage and squeeze them as I suck his cock but his hand pulls my hair, jerking my mouth away from him. When I look at his face, his eyes are half closed and his nostrils flare. He pulls me up and spins me around, slamming my arms against the tile. Then he takes my hands in one of his and he spreads me with the other. I feel the head of his cock rubbing me right before he plunges in.

"Ah!" I can't help the sound that's forced from my mouth. He pushes against me, hard and rough. His cock reaches a place I've never felt before.

His hips crash into mine over and over, punishing me, pushing me to the point where pleasure meets pain. And it's so good. Everything builds inside of me and then his fingers find my swollen clit and rub it between them. When my orgasm hits me, I call out his name. Loud. And then, just like last night, he really starts to fuck me hard. He pulls me back and says, "Bend over, feet together and hands on your knees."

After that last orgasm, I thought I was done, but in minutes, he has me coming all over the place again. His cock pressures my clit in this position like I've never felt and he hits me so deep, once more, I cry out his name when I come. Afterwards, I feel his hot fluid spurting into me as he grinds out his own climax. Before I can even gather my wits, he turns me so fast that I'm dizzy and kisses me. My arms hang onto him so I don't fall, but in truth I never want to let this man go. He does things to my body I didn't know it was capable of feeling.

He breaks off the kiss and says, "Skylar. You were made to fuck." Then he reaches around me and turns off the water. "Dry off. I want to lick off your pussy now."

Whoa. That's so not what I expected. He hands me a towel and I dry off. Then he pushes me into his bedroom and onto his bed. When I spread my legs, he says, "Uh uh. Sit on my face."

He lies on his back and I do as he asks. "I want you to play with your nipples while I lick you." So I do. It doesn't feel nearly as good as when he did. And I tell him. He laughs.

Then his tongue flicks over my clit and I jerk. "Hold still."

He starts again and I wiggle.

"Skylar. Don't move." His voice is really stern. Jeez. "Do you want me to tie you up?"

"No."

"Okay. Do. Not. Move." He starts again and I try not to squirm but I can't help it. In a flash I'm on my back and he's up. He goes to his closet and comes back with some rope. Holy crap. He wasn't joking.

"On your knees and sit back like you're on my face." I do as he asks. Then he proceeds to tie me up in a fashion where my wrists and ankles are bound to each other, so I can't move. One bit.

"I can't move."

"That's the idea."

"But ..."

"Be quiet, Skylar. Now I'm going to eat you out. And you're going to love it."

He lies back down and lifts me so I'm on his face. And I. Can't. Move. He eyes me as he starts to lick my pussy. He half smiles because he knows I'm pissed. His tongue is liquid fire and my body burns for it.

"Ah ... ah Reese."

He stops. "Tell me you love it when I tongue you."

"I love it when you tongue me." I practically moan the words out.

His tongue dives back into me. Then out again to flick my clit.

"I'm not going to let you come yet, Skylar."

The frustration has built in me. He brings me to the edge and backs off.

"Do you know why?"

"No!"

"Because you disobeyed me."

"Please."

"Please what?"

"Let me come!"

"Like this or do you want me to fuck you again?"

"Both!"

"Greedy girl."

"Yes!"

He licks me and then centers on my clit, sucking it hard and I come. I want to buck off of him, but I can't. He doesn't let up and I'm so sensitive now that I beg loudly for him to stop, but he doesn't listen. He licks, nibbles and sucks my clit until I think I'll go insane and then another orgasm rolls over me like a tidal wave, annihilating me and leaving me whimpering. Finally, he ceases his torture and chuckles, lifting me off of him. I'm lying on my chest and knees now, still tied, completely weak and helpless.

I hear him moving about, but I'm not sure what he's doing because I'm barely conscious.

"Skylar, are you still with me, baby?"

"Uh huh."

"Good. Are you an anal virgin?"

"Huh?"

"Are you an anal virgin?"

"I don't know."

Now his voice is firm. "Skylar, it's either a yes, or a no."

"I've done anal toys but no sex."

"I see."

I feel his fingers enter me again. I'm so wet I need him inside of me.

"You're ready for me, aren't you?"

"Yeah. Please, Reese."

"Not yet. I need to get you ready for me."

Then he slides a finger in my other entrance. Very slowly. It's strange at first, but I'm not opposed to this. I have a lot of clients who love this so there must be something to it.

"So tight and ready for me." His finger is gone and then something much larger is there. "Push out against me, baby." I do as he asks and he slowly inches in. At first, it hurts, with a burning sensation. I suck in my breath. "Relax for me, babe." It's not easy, but I try. He moves in a little deeper, inching in past the pain to where it feels full. So different. Not exactly great, but not bad either. Eventually, it begins to feel good to where I'm highly aroused. When he's finally all the way in and moving slowly, he asks, "Are you okay?"

I breathe, "Yes."

He picks up a little speed, but not as fast as when he's in my pussy.

"Ahhh!" It feels really good.

His hand slides down and he puts his fingers on my clit. I'm not going to last long like this. There something so strange yet primal about this.

"Reese, I'm gonna come."

"I know. I can tell." He gives a little laugh.

He rocks into me very gently, not at all rough like he does when he fucks me the other way, and it's somehow softer like this. His arm tightens around my waist as he still slides his other fingers around my clit. The multitude of sensations come crashing together.

"Skylar, I need for you to come now." He focuses on moving in and out faster but shorter strokes and I cry out as I come. He follows closely behind and we both stay still in this position for a few seconds. Then he pulls out and unties me. He disappears into the bathroom. When he returns, I'm still in the same position as I was when he left. He uses a warm cloth on my behind to cleans me.

"Just so you know, I always wear a condom for anal."

"Hmm. Do you do this a lot?"

"Do you show up at men's apartments late at night a lot?"

"Touché."

I roll to my side and look at him. He's perfect. Dirty blond hair, gorgeous blue eyes, and the most perfect body on a man I've ever seen. And I've seen more than my share of naked men. He has multiple tattoos and one day I'm going to find out what they all mean. They're mostly script. Some are tic marks and numbers. They cover his torso, arms and legs. But tonight is the first time I've noticed his scars. He has a lot of them. One of his legs is covered in them, like he's had a multitude of surgeries. But he's tried to mask them with tattoos.

"Like what you see?" His beautiful eyes are narrowed.

He doesn't ask as though he's pleased I was staring at him. He makes me feel as though I've been caught doing something wrong.

"No. Actually I *love* what I see."

His mouth slams shut. He leaves the room and I think I've offended him. After he doesn't return, I get up in search of him, to find him standing in the den, staring out the window. As I look at his naked back, it's then I notice more scars. Something terrible happened to him. But nothing can take away his beauty. He could be scarred on every inch of his skin and he would still be perfect in my eyes. Something within Reese speaks to my soul. I don't know what it is nor do I wish to analyze it right now. Whatever it is, it's there, it's solid, and it's strong.

I pad across the floor and when I reach him, my arms slide around his waist, and I press myself against his back. His skin feels like heaven against mine and I can't stop from rubbing my cheek against his shoulder blade.

"Come back to bed, please. It's lonely in there without you."

"Skylar, what are we doing here?"

"I'm hugging you."

"Always elusive."

He grabs my arms and turns to face me. His eyes search mine

but eventually give up. Then his hands move to frame my face and he kisses me. Wet, deep and passionately. Instantly, I melt. He has such control over me, it's ridiculous. No man has control over me, yet Reese breaks me apart with one kiss.

He sweeps me into his arms and carries me to bed. After we're under the covers, he asks, "Can I expect for you to be gone when I wake up?"

"Hmm," I mumble as I snuggle in next to him. I can't answer him.

A myriad of thoughts rush my brain, like I just tapped the coke vial. Major boundaries have been crossed ... boundaries I *never* under *any* circumstances cross. Hard limits have been broken. He trussed me up like a Thanksgiving turkey and I allowed it. Worse yet, I *loved* every second of it. Then there's my checklist: bareback BJ—check; bareback intercourse—check; anal sex—check; bondage—check. What the hell am I doing here? This is all sorts of wrong and I don't even feel bad about it. In fact, I'm obsessing right now over when I can do it all again. And then there's his nagging question ... the one I can't answer. Because I don't *want* to be gone. I want to stay in his arms forever. But I know that's not possible. Once he finds out who or rather what I am, he'll shoot me out of his life faster than a damn bottle rocket on the Fourth of July.

Twelve

Reese

WHEN I WAKE UP TO AN EMPTY BED AGAIN, I KNOW EXACTLY what I have to do. My phone is in my hand before I know it. Case promises to meet me at Joe and Mo's in an hour.

"Case. I need a favor. I want you to put one of your guys on someone for me."

Case laughs. "You mean you're hiring me?"

He never expected me to be one of his clients. "That's right. You are a private investigator, aren't you?"

"Yeah. The best. Give me the details."

So I do.

"Reese. You involved with this girl?"

"That's none of your business."

"Wrong, buddy. As your NA sponsor, it is."

My mind chews on his response and he's right. It is his business. He's my best friend, too, and I know he has my best interests at heart.

"Yeah. She shows up at my house. We fuck. She leaves."

Case laughs. "Sounds like a damn good arrangement to me. Why the hell do you want to follow her?"

"Here's the thing. I met her while saving her ass from a rapist."

"Did you call it in?"

"No. She wouldn't let me."

"Did she say why?"

"No. And she wouldn't go home either. Said she couldn't. And now she shows up at my house every night."

Case is silent for a bit. "You got a name?"

I give him everything else he asks for and he says he'll have something for me ASAP. Case used to be a cop. That was before. He has a before, just like I do. He was beaten and left for dead. His aftermath, like mine, included drugs. A lot of them. He got kicked off the force. Then he went to rehab and ended up at NA. While he was in rehab, he met my physical therapist Dot. Meth was her vice. Small world we live in. When Case couldn't be a cop anymore, he decided to use his connections and open up his own PI firm. He does well now and has several guys working for him full time. Cops work for him part time when they need extra money. He pays well and it works out great for both sides.

"Reese, what if we find out something you don't really want to know?"

"I'll deal. Just find it. Follow her, Case, and let me know what you come up with."

"I love you Trust-Funders."

I laugh. "I know. We like to give you guys business, right?"

MY PARENTS ASKED ME TO MEET THEM FOR DINNER. I TAKE A cab uptown and they already have a table. We meet at their favorite Italian restaurant on the upper East side. Nowadays, my mom is almost giddy when she sees me.

"Reese," she says as I bend down to kiss her. She grabs my shoulders and laughs. "You're huge!"

"I'm working out a couple of hours a day," I tell her. "Hey Dad." I shake his hand and he pats me on the back.

"You look better every time we see you, son. I don't think I could be any more proud of you." His eyes glisten.

Looking him straight in the eye, I say, "Thanks Dad. For everything. But mostly for believing in me. And for giving me that ultimatum. I hated you and Mom for it at the time. But you did the right thing."

He nods and I know he can't speak right now.

"So tell us what's going on with you," Mom says.

"Oh, the usual. Classes, working out, and Narcotics Anonymous of course." I laugh.

"How's school?" Mom wants to know.

"Kicking my butt."

They laugh.

"I'm glad we're together. I wanted to tell you this. I've decided on a major. Criminal Justice."

Their faces both register shock. Mom's looks like it's turned to stone and Dad's is a cross between 'Holy-Shit-I-Can't-Believe-It' and 'Thank-God-He's-Doing-Something-He-Can-Actually-Get-A-Job-In.'

I break out into laughter. "Let me explain. I want to get my undergrad degree in Criminal Justice and then I want to go to Law School. I want to prosecute people like the ones who attacked me."

When it finally sinks in, they beam. Really beam. If they could reflect light, they would. Tears dribble past my mom's lids and my dad clears his throat a few times before he says anything.

"Son, you make a father proud."

"Thanks, Dad."

"Oh, Reese. You'll make a fine attorney. Yes, you will." She digs in her purse for a tissue, then dabs at her eyes. "Now look, my mascara is running I'm sure."

"Mom, you're beautiful, even with the black raccoon circles under your eyes," I tease.

"What? Oh dear." She stands up and tears off to the restroom.

"Son. You know you can't ever joke about things like that with her."

"I know. But I wanted time alone with you. To thank you, Dad. These last months weren't easy. Kicking the drugs was ... well, there were times I didn't want to live. I know you and I had our rough spots and that things weren't always the greatest between us, but the only reason I'm alive today is because of your ultimatum. That and the fact that you and Mom believed in me. So thanks for kicking my ass and making me man up on all of this. It's made me a better man."

"Jesus, Reese. I'm more proud of you now than I've ever been." He pats me on the back and I notice his eyes are glistening.

"Thanks but save that for when I graduate. I have a long haul ahead of me."

"You do, but you're young. It'll fly by. You'll see."

Out of the corner of my eye, I see Mom coming back. Dad laughs at her expression.

"Reese, one of these days," she says.

"Yeah, Mom?"

We all laugh. The rest of the dinner is light hearted filled with easy conversation and trivial things. As we're leaving, my mom mentions something to me.

"Oh Reese, give your Aunt Emmy a call. She says she hasn't spoken to you in a while."

"She's right. I feel awful about that." Aunt Emmy, who's really my mom's aunt, is one of my favorite people. She was my huge supporter when I was a little kid starting out. She always believed in me when I wanted to dance and was the one who talked my parents into allowing me to pursue that path. She's my Mom's father's sister, but she was with me throughout my recovery, even when I hit rock bottom. She always believed in me and never stopped loving me.

"I'll call her tomorrow. I'm sorry, Mom. Time seems to slip away from me."

"Please don't forget. You know how much you mean to her."

"I promise. I love her too."

We hug and my parents head off toward their place a couple of blocks away. I decide to walk to the corner to grab a cab and I happen to glance across the street. Getting out of a dark sedan is a beautiful blond, dressed in a tight white skirt with a gold sequined top showing two inches of skin, and gold platform pumps. Her hips sway as she walks into a high-rise apartment building. I'd know that woman anywhere. I've memorized those legs and hips, that hair and the rest of that body. Now where in the world could she be going at this hour, dressed like that?

That night I wait for Skylar, but she doesn't show. My night is sleepless, and my cock is hard. All I can think of is her mouth on me, the sounds that come out of it when I fuck her, and the feel of her lips on my mouth and tongue. When the sun comes up, I head for the library because there'll be no studying in my own home for me. Everywhere I look reminds me of hot, hard sex and Skylar.

A few days later, just about the time I think she's gone forever, the buzzer rings and my gut clenches. Funny how one little sound can make my dick get hard.

When she walks in the door, I don't look at her, nor do I say a word. I know she will take a shower and brush her teeth, but I want to punish her for abandoning me. I'm pissed at her. My cock has missed her and it's been hard for several days. Jacking off isn't fun, knowing the relief will be short lived.

She walks out of the bathroom and looks at me.

"Come here, Skylar."

She hesitates, but then walks to where I'm seated. When she stands before me, I ask, "Where have you been?"

"Around."

"That's not good enough. Answer me, please."

"I was busy and couldn't come over."

"What was more important than us?"

She looks down, unable to meet my gaze.

"Skylar, look at me when I speak to you." She won't meet my eyes, so I reach out and pull her into my lap. Her naked body is almost more than I can endure, but I ask her again. "What's more important than this?" And my mouth crushes hers. I take everything she gives back, until she's breathless and pushes me away. My hand moves between her thighs and seeks out that place I know will make her come. "You're wet for me, Skylar." I turn her in my lap, so her head rests on my knees and I spread her legs, exposing her smooth pussy awaiting my mouth. Sliding my hands under her ass, I lift her and say, "Put your legs on my shoulders." My head dips and I swipe my tongue from her opening to her clit. She sucks in her breath. "Did you miss this?"

"God, yes. I couldn't stop thinking about it. I tried to stay away, but I couldn't."

"Why did you try to stay away?"

"Because I'm … just because."

Giving her ass a firm squeeze, I say, "Tell me, Skylar. Why did you try to stay away?"

"Because I'm not good enough for you, Reese. I'm nothing," she cries out. Her hands cover her face, as if she wants to hide from me.

Grabbing her hands in one of mine, I pull them down and say, "That's not true. You're beautiful. Don't ever say that again." Then my mouth finds what she needs, what she wants, and she cries out for something altogether different now. After she climaxes, I pull her into a sitting position and tell her to unzip my pants. She does and then manages to maneuver my stiff cock out of its prison. Her hand wraps around it and she does a slow pump. Damn, it feels good.

"Turn around and ride me."

One thing I love about Skylar, she always does what I tell

her. She turns and slides my dick into her wet pussy. Such nirvana. She feels so sweet when she comes all over me.

"Lean forward." I'm close to shooting off, but I want her to come, because I fucking love to feel her spasms rock my cock. She's so wet, she's getting my jeans damp too. I take my thumb and get it lubed up using her own juice and slide it into her ass.

"Aaaaahhhhh!" she cries out. Her fingers dig into my thighs and she pants so loud it turns me on even more.

Once I get past her tight opening, I move my thumb in and out a tiny bit and that makes her come. Fast. Always makes me wonder why women are so opposed to anal. Not Skylar. She's coming all over the place.

"Ahh. Oh God!"

When I feel her inner muscles tighten and clench my cock, that's all I need to let loose. I thrust into her, hard and fast. And then I get mine. I grab her and pull her down on me, grinding into her as I shoot off. She whimpers as she leans back against my chest. My hand moves to her nipple and I tug on it until she moans. I want her to turn her head so I can kiss her. She does and our lips meet in a feverish exchange of tongues.

"Go get in bed. I'll be right there." I watch her ass as she walks to the bedroom. She really does have a beautiful ass.

I grab a piece of paper and an extra key. Then I scribble down my security code for the building and lay the note and key on her coat. Afterwards, I join her in the bed for some more fucking. The night is still young.

TWO DAYS LATER, I'M HEADED TO CLASS WHEN MY PHONE rings.

"Hey Case."

"I got some info on your girl."

"Shoot."

"Nope. I don't work like that, especially not with this kind of information. When are you free?"

The hairs on the back of my neck rise. "I'm on my way to class. I'll be done in about three hours."

"Fine. Meet me at Joe and Mo's then."

"Cool. See you there." I wonder how I could even concentrate during class now, distracted by what was waiting for me at Joe and Mo's.

Thirteen

Reese

I'M RIGHT ABOUT CLASS. THE CRIMINAL JUSTICE PROFESSOR
drones on and on about due process and I can't keep my mind
focused on his words. Class can't end soon enough. My mind is
not where it needs to be because I'm absorbed with what I'll
learn when I meet up with Case. The buzzer goes off and I all
but sprint to Joe and Mo's. When I spy him already seated, I can
tell by the set of his mouth, he's not happy. This isn't good.

"Hey," I say, nudging his shoulder. "Coffee? Refill?"

"Nah, I'm good."

"Be right back." I pick up a coffee and join him.

He has a file in his hand and slides it across the table to me.
The file is labeled, "Skylar Mara O'Donnell."

Hmm. Didn't know her middle name. I open the file and see
her date of birth as October 14. Born New York, NY. Lenox Hill
Hospital. Parents: Michael Brian O'Donnell and Mary Elizabeth
O'Donnell. Blah, Blah, Blah.

I look up to see Case's eyes trained on me.

"What?"

"Go on. Keep reading."

"Why don't you just tell me? I get the feeling I'm not going to be pleased about any of this."

"If you want it that way. Skylar is an only child. Her dad was a stockbroker, mom a pharmacist. Everything was great. Until."

"There's always an 'until' isn't there?"

"Usually. Anyway, the mom started stealing drugs from the hospital she worked for and got caught. Went to prison. The marriage ended. Skylar lived with the dad for a while but when the mom was released, he sent her back. Apparently, he got remarried and the new wife was young. It says she didn't want a daughter around. Who knows? So Skylar goes home to a drug-addicted mom who can't find a job because she's an ex-con who lost her license to practice pharmacy. She's now doing street drugs because we all know the prison system feeds those addictions. She's also a hooker, feeding her drug habit. We're not a hundred percent on this part, but we think mommy dearest pushed daughter into hooking for her. There's a bit of a disconnect here. But jumping ahead a few years, when she's eighteen, she goes to work for *Exotique-A.* Ever hear of it?"

"Nope." By now I'm getting antsy as hell.

"It's a strip club. Owned by a guy named J.D. Rowe. J.D. also has an escort service, a.k.a. a prostitution business, on the side. Skylar is a hooker for him. But she's one of his 'special' girls." He curls his fingers when he says special. "Meaning she only gets the richest most elite clients. She has a list of restrictions, or hard limits, that her clients have to abide by."

"Restrictions?"

"Yeah. No intercourse. No blow jobs without the use of condoms. No kissing. Things like that. Oh, and Skylar, or Lena as she's known professionally, is closed for new clients. In other words, she's got her list of regulars and doesn't take anyone new."

"A fucking prostitute? She's a fucking hooker?" I'm incredulous and sick at the same time.

"Pretty much in a nutshell. Yep."

"Fuck! I knew there was something, but this? Goddammit!"

"Look man, I'm sorry. Looks like you were feeling something for her."

"Uh, yeah. That and she has a key to my place. Why the hell did I jump the gun on that? I should've waited to give her the damn thing until you came back with your information on her. Damn it!" I slam my hand on the table in frustration.

"Reese. In all of this, we really couldn't find anything bad about her."

I laugh. Derisively. "Oh, and being a prostitute is good?"

"No, but being a drug addict isn't either. People have all sorts of reasons for doing things. Don't discount hers. Sounds like that mother of hers is a piece of work. And her father. Sent her back there because the new young wife didn't want a kid? Really? Wouldn't that fuck any kid up?"

Ignoring his analysis, I ask, "So where's this *Exotique-A*?"

"Not too far from here." He gives me the address. I know exactly what I'm going to do. Lena is going to have a visitor.

Fourteen

Skylar

MOM'S BEEN ACTING LIKE AN ANGRY HORNET. EVERY CHANCE she gets, she slaps me (or tries to anyway) or makes some low blow comment about how I'll never amount to anything. Really Mom? You pretty much sealed that deal when you forced me into hooking at the ripe old age of sixteen. It never fails though. As many times as I've heard her say those ugly things to me, the words always sting. She's cracked my heart so many times I'm surprised it's still intact. There should be little pieces of it scattered all over by now.

My nerves are all jangled up by the time my hand presses the bell. When the buzzer makes that loud sound, my anxiety claws through me even more. This is going to be awful. My hand is fisted and getting ready to knock when the door opens and there stands Marianna.

"Skylar. It's so wonderful to see you, dear." Her thin arms enfold me and for a small woman, her strength is astounding.

She squeezes me and I suddenly find myself teary eyed. My mom used to hug me, all those years ago. Things were different then. The only times anyone's hugged me since has been for sex. Other than Marianna. And it feels so good I have to rein my emotions in. *Pull yourself together Sky, or she's gonna think you're cuckoo.* I duck my head so my hair curtains my face, and quickly swipe my tears away.

"It's wonderful to see you too, Marianna. And I owe you a gigantic apology."

"Come and sit." We move into her living area and I can see she has tea prepared. She always serves hot tea when I come to visit.

After I take a seat, I jump right in because I have to get this off my chest. "I'm so sorry for lying to you. But the honest truth is after I went to the first audition, I lost all the confidence and faith I had in myself. I saw those other dancers and how they looked and knew I was just a girl from the other side of the tracks and could never be like that. So I never went back. But I want you to know how much it meant to me for you to help me. No one's ever done anything like that for me before and I appreciate it so much. But I'm sorry I didn't live up to your expectations.

"Are you finished?"

"What?"

"Talking. Are you finished?"

"I suppose."

"Good. Now listen up young lady. If you don't want to dance, fine. But if you do, then you need to buck up and quit feeling sorry for yourself. Most, yes most, of those dancers you saw aren't worth a hoot." My mouth drops open. "You heard me. The only reason you *think* they can dance is because they give the impression they can. But they stink. Unlike you, they don't work hard yet think they deserve to be given a part just because. Listen to what I'm telling you, Skylar. Start auditioning. You will bomb on your first several. Only because your nerves will rattle you to the point that they will affect your performance. But that's why you must keep doing it. Each time you audition, you will improve. And tell all those tight ass dancers to get screwed if they bother you."

Now my eyes pop open as wide as my mouth.

"I see I've gotten your attention. Jimmy said he'd go with you. Let him. It will bolster your confidence, and if that's what it takes, then do it. You understand?"

"Yes ma'am."

"And stop calling me ma'am, damn it."

"Okay, Marianna."

"Good. I'm glad that's settled. As soon as I find another audition, you're going, even if I have to drag you myself. Do I make myself clear? I'm not getting any younger and I want to see you on stage before I die."

"Marianna! Don't say that."

"Why? It's true! You don't seem to understand something. You are an extremely talented dancer, and I'm going to do my damnedest, even if I have to harass you, to get you out there. So stop being a such a coward and do it already!"

"You're shocking me!"

"Good. Now tell me the latest gossip. How's the strip club coming along? I love your stories!"

So I tell her about my latest crazy clients and she laughs and laughs. When it's time for me to get back I look at her and say, "You make me feel good and no one's done that in a long time."

She grabs my hand and squeezes it.

"Good. Then return the favor and dance for me, darling."

When I get to work that night, Jimmy is waiting for me as usual.

"I visited Marianna today. I love that woman."

"I know. My aunt called. She was happy you came."

"I wish she could've been my mom."

"I wish so too, Sky."

Tonight's busy for midweek. I haven't had a break all night

and I get back to my dressing room to guzzle some water. Dancing is hard work, though most people don't think of it as such. I totally throw myself into it because even though it is a strip club, I still love it.

Jimmy sticks his head in. "You've got someone waiting. Lights are super dim. He only wanted you lit on the pole. And you get to choose your music.

"Oh, that's great." I'll choose Kesha's *Your Love Is My Drug*. I love dancing to this song.

When I walk in, the client is seated and it's so dark I can't really see him. He's wearing a hoodie, the hood shielding his face. I can only see shadows created by the light. His legs are extended and crossed at the ankles. He wears jeans and running shoes and keeps his hands in the pockets of his hoodie.

His instructions were the pole and that's fine by me. This way I don't have to get near him. I love the pole anyway. I spin, grip it with my thighs, hang upside down, maneuver my way around, all to the beat of Kesha. The next song plays and I waste no time picking up the beat. Soon my time's up, and I move away from the pole. Usually the client says something. Not this one. He just sits there, staring, I presume, because I can't really see him. He offers no tip, nothing. After a couple of uncomfortable moments of silence, I leave.

Back in my dressing room, I think about him. Jimmy sticks his head in and I tell him about it.

"Maybe he was mute."

"Maybe. Whatever. It's over now."

"And you got yourself a thirty minute break, doll."

I check the clock and see it's close to closing. "How many more after this?"

"I need to check to see what's going on with the other girls. You don't have any clients tonight, do you?"

"Nope. Free night."

"Let me see if I can cut you loose early."

"Okay."

I'm daydreaming about Reese when Jimmy interrupts me. "Sorry babe, but your last client wants you till closing." "What? That's weird. Now I won't make any tips." Jimmy pats my arms. "Sorry, doll." "Same deal?" "Yep. Two more pole sessions." "Ugh, I'll be exhausted." "Right? Your thighs will be rubber." "Dang!"

After my break, I go back to my little box and there is mystery man. I cue up the music and begin. He never moves a hair. Sits there like a statue. After two full sessions, I can barely stand anymore. When I get ready to head out, he clears his throat. I turn to look at him and his arm is extended, money sticking out between his index and middle finger. Smiling, I take it and leave. When I get to my dressing room I look at it and find he handed me two five hundred dollar bills. What. The. Hell. My exhaustion was well worth a thousand bucks.

Using Reese's security code and key, I let myself into his apartment, but come up short when I find it empty. He's not here. Neither are any of his belongings. His bed and couch are still here, but all of his clothes and personal items are gone. He's moved out. I find a note on the bathroom mirror.

S,

The place is yours, rent-free.
Keep it.
R

WHAT THE HELL IS GOING ON? HE JUST MOVES OUT AND GIVES me his apartment? Like that? This is so weird, I don't know what to think. All the sheets are new. The towels are new. His dresser is empty. He left nothing behind that would remind me of him, other than the bed, couch and building itself. Where did he go and why would he leave? It all crashes down on me that I know absolutely nothing about Reese Christianson. Not a blasted thing. I don't know what he does, where he works, nothing. And the worst thing about it is, all I want right now is him. I want him inside of me; I want his mouth on me, everywhere. Because thoughts of him are so consuming, they're all I can think of. My stomach clenches in response and even the mere idea of being in his apartment has me wanting him. My hand automatically slips between my legs and before I can contemplate what I'm doing, my fingers massage myself to a quick climax in search of some relief. But there is none. I'm every bit as frustrated afterward. Because I want his hot breath on me, his tongue inside of me, but most of all, I want all of him. My clothes land in a pile around my feet and I crawl between the sheets. Sleep is fitful and I'm cranky as hell the next day when I go home.

Over time, I move things to the apartment. My mom is curious about it, but I refuse to give her concrete answers. Every now and again, her hand still tries to connect with my face, so I know this idea of taking Reese's apartment over is even better than I'd imagined. But it's still a shell without him. My body aches for his touch. Whenever I think of him, my breasts swell and my nipples harden into painful peaks. Sometimes I have to run home to ease my discomfort. This is damn crazy! What the hell has he done to me?

The other night, when I was with George, I made him bite my nipple. He was shocked and then became so excited over the prospect of doing it to the other nipple, he started barking and howling like a dog. I almost had to pepper spray him. I have to pull myself together. Next thing I know George will be slapping *my* ass. Holy hell. Maybe I need a vacation or something. I know one thing. Reese has ruined me for all my clients. It's getting harder and harder to act around them. I daydream and can't separate myself anymore. If I don't pull my shit together and fast, J.D. is going to start getting complaints from my men. That would be the kiss of death for certain.

I need to talk to someone about this and the only one I trust enough is Cara. I send her a text and we arrange to meet for lunch the next day.

I'm sitting at the table, waiting on Cara, when she waltzes in. Every head turns and stares. Long, straight black hair, Cara is Asian and stunning. You can't look at her and let it go. She has the kind of beauty that traps your eyes and then lures the rest of you in. She must be a siren because sometimes even I can't stop staring at her. Too bad I don't swing both ways.

"What are you thinking? You have that crazy-ass look on your face."

Laughing, I say, "I'm upset that I don't go both ways. You're damn hot, girl."

She laughs and says, "You're nuts. And if I went both ways, I'd go for you too, Sky."

"Gah, we're a mess, aren't we?"

"Nah, just two nutty girls. So what's up?"

"Well, I *am* a mess." I explain the whole situation with Reese.

"Well, hot damn. I'm aroused just listening to you. But Sky, you don't know a single thing about this guy. Do you trust him?"

"Yeah, I do. That first night he saved me from getting raped, he could've done something terrible to me then, but he didn't. And then all those other nights I've been with him, I've felt safer than I've ever felt before."

"You are legit hooked on this guy. You have to find him somehow."

"I know, but how?"

"You know he was at that coffee shop, right?"

Smiling, I nod. I never gave that a thought. "Yeah. Joe and Mo's. He's a recovering addict so he doesn't drink. But he does teas and coffees. I *do* know that much. He offered me that herbal tea after I was attacked."

"So he's a recovering addict. Like does he go to meetings?"

"Uggghhh! I never asked. It just seemed like the wrong thing to dig into at the time. Honestly we mostly had sex. A lot."

"My bet is that he's thinking about it as much as you are. Come on. If he gave you his apartment and paid for it, he has to know something about you."

My heart slams to the floor. I suddenly feel like throwing up. "Oh God. Do you think he knows? I mean I'd go straight there in my clothes after a client. But I'd always shower before we'd do anything."

"I don't know, but how could he know? Do you think he followed you?" Cara asks.

I rub my thighs, trying to dry off my now sweaty palms. "But how? My driver always picks me up at the club. And he never drops me off at home. Usually a couple of blocks away."

"Does he know you work at *Exotique-A*?"

"No!"

We both sit in silence, puzzling this thing out.

Cara finally breaks the quiet and says, "I don't know sweetie. But if I were you, I'd start paying frequent visits to that coffee shop. And I mean real frequent."

Fifteen

Skylar

JOE AND MO'S HAS A NEW BEST CUSTOMER. I DIDN'T KNOW A person could consume this much coffee. The people here are becoming my besties too. I had no idea they made these many kinds of coffee drinks. And after all these visits, I haven't had one single sighting. But I'm not giving up. If anything, I'm persistent.

Joe and Mo's is on my way to work, so I stop and grab an extra-large coffee for the walk in. I've really given up seeing him again. It was too good to be true. A girl like me would never find someone like him … on a permanent basis anyway. So it was probably a good thing that he left when he did. My thoughts are still jumbled as I walk to work. The big thing on my mind is how long before I'll be evicted from his apartment. It's been such a pleasant change, not having Mom on my back every day. The absence of putting up with her bitterness and anger has been a breath of spring air. Thinking of going back to the way it was sickens me to no end.

When I walk into the back door of the club, Jimmy meets me and is all excited. He tells me that Marianna has signed me up for an audition the next afternoon.

"Seriously?"

"Yeah. She says she tried to call several times but your phone acted weird."

I dig through my purse and find my phone. There are zero missed calls. "That's strange."

"Maybe it's time for a new one. You know how those things are."

"Yeah, maybe. I'll check into it."

"Oh, and one other thing. Your client from the other night? The one that never said a word? He's coming in at ten. He wants you for the rest of the night."

"Oh, hell yeah! I'll take that kind of tip any day!" The mystery dude just made my night.

"He's requested you wear only a black G-string. Nothing else."

"Got it. I'll wear one with his name on it if he wants," I laugh.

Jimmy shakes his head and walks away.

At ten, I walk into the box and there he sits, exactly like before. I dance for him until closing time. I'm not sure how long it is. Again, he never speaks. No requests, nothing. I do my own moves and when his time is up, he hands me my tip, between his two fingers again. This time he gives me three grand. Holy. Moly. I skip, yes, skip back to my dressing room. Jimmy and Cara come in and we all laugh and I'm as giddy as can be.

"Hey, let's go out for drinks. Tonight."

Neither of them can make it. I cover up my disappointment by saying, "Hey, no worries. I'm tired anyway. And I have that audition tomorrow. It's best not to go with a hangover."

Jimmy pipes in and asks, "You want me to come with you?"

"You're the best Jimmy, but I've got this." I kiss his cheek.

After I get changed into my jeans and a T-shirt, I head out the door. Knowing it's not the smartest idea, I decide anyway to walk home anyway. I need to clear my head and get my shit straight. On the way, I get the sense I'm being followed. When I look over my shoulder, I don't see anyone. But still, I pick up my pace, until I'm in front of my—Reese's apartment. It's not possible to think of this place without thinking of him. I'll always think of this place as his.

When I unlock the door, I head to the bathroom to brush my teeth and take a shower. The hot water soothes and calms me after a long night of dancing. I wrap the towel around me and walk to the bedroom, in search of a T-shirt.

"You shouldn't dance like that for strangers."

"Eeeek!" I scream. The hooded stranger is sitting on my bed, feet stretched out and crossed at the ankles.

"Drop that towel, Skylar." I'd know that voice anywhere.

"Not until you take that hood off." He reaches up and tugs it off. "When did you find out?"

"Your dirty secret? The same time I found out you're also a fucking paid whore. That you sell yourself to other men." He spits out the ugly words like they're acid on his tongue.

Those words bite much deeper and hurt far worse than anything has ever wounded me before. Worse than when my dad walked out of my life and abandoned me. Worse than when he believed my evil stepmom over me. Worse than when my mom sold me to Mikey. And greater than any physical blow anyone ever landed on me.

My fists clutch the towel against me as I hang my head in shame. Tears instantly blur my vision and the urge to get out of here overwhelms me. But my clothes are in the dresser and he's standing next to it.

"Are you deaf? I told you to drop the towel." His voice is vinegar to my wounds.

I back out of the room, away from him. My brain tumbles with thoughts of what to do, where to go. My coat … it's in the living room, but my shoes are in the bathroom. I can make do with them and figure something out later.

"Skylar," he calls out, "I'm paying you. Is my money not good enough?"

Paying me? What is he talking about? I don't care to find out because every one of his words is a razor slicing up my heart and soul and I can't bear for them to be sliced any more. I stumble into the bathroom, attempt to push my feet into my shoes, but they aren't cooperating. When I try to run to the living room, I trip and fall, letting go of the towel as my hands smack the floor. My palms sting like fire and as I lie there, I see a pair of feet in my line of vision.

"You're a kept woman, Skylar. Where do you think you're going?" I cringe at his scathing tone.

I must escape ... get away from here because his words make me feel dirty ... so much filthier than I already am. Scrambling to my hands and knees, I crawl to my coat. Shoving my hands through the sleeves, I somehow manage to get it on. But I can't button it because my hands are trembling so much. With one shoe on and one off, coat unbuttoned, I run out the door. Tripping down the steps, I twist my ankle and fall the last three, slamming onto the floor and bruising my knees. My vision is so blurred from my tears, I can't see.

Bands of steel wrap around my torso and lift me. He carries me back to that horrible place I want to part of. When he gets inside, he slams the door behind us and drops me on the couch. He returns with some tissues and removes the one shoe I'm wearing. Then he examines my ankle, which is already swelling. I realize then, that I've ruined my chance for the audition the next day and I burst into sobs.

His hands start tugging off my coat and then I start to fight. My fists fly out at him and I punch him and want to hurt him for saying those cruel things to me.

"Don't touch me! Haven't you humiliated me enough? Now you want me naked as well?" My chest heaves from the exertion of each breath and my hands are fisted as though I'm ready to strike again.

"I only want to help you change into these." He holds up a pair of sweats in his hands.

When I see what he has, it brings on another round of sobs.

"Come on, Skylar, let me help."

I give no resistance as he takes off my coat and puts the sweats on me. Then he pulls me onto his lap where I bawl my heart out. When they eventually give way to hiccups, he asks how my ankle is.

"It's ruined everything."

"Ruined everything? How so?"

"I was supposed to audition for a dance production tomorrow." Hiccup … hiccup. "My friend went through a whole lot of trouble to help me and now I won't be able to dance."

"Hmm. Maybe you will. I can wrap it for you. I know a lot about ankle injuries."

I rub my face with my sleeve, drying the tears. I move to get up but his arms tighten around me.

"I'm not letting you up, Skylar."

I lift my eyes to his and try to figure him out. I see nothing in them to give him away.

"What do you want from me, Reese?" I sniff.

"The truth."

Gritting my teeth, I say, "You already know the truth. You said it yourself. I'm a fucking paid whore and I sell myself to other men. Oh, and while we're on the subject, I'm a sleazy private dancer, too. I'm a slut, Reese. A nasty slut. My mom's a drug addict who sold me to her pimp when I was sixteen. I've been used, abused, raped, you name it. When I turned eighteen, I found someone who thought I was worth something." A bitter laugh rushes out of me. "A better pimp, who treated me with a bit of decency." No one knows this. No one. Why am I telling him this? I guess it's because none of it matters anymore. I always had a small element of pride in myself. Maybe it was because I was forced to do what I do. But he's reduced me to nothing … stripped me bare so I don't even have that tiny bit any more. "I've taken care of my mom since then. What else do you want to know? Do I like what I do? No. I despise myself for it. Every fucking day. And you just drove that point home, like a damn arrow straight into to my heart. Why don't I quit? What else can I do to keep my mom off the street and her drug habit paid for? I can't go to school. I can't wait tables. It doesn't pay enough. So now you know. Can I get up and leave now?" I've finally run out of steam. My voice sounds dull and lifeless even to my ears.

I'm not aware tears are flowing again until he takes my face in his hands and wipes them away. He stands, still holding me and puts me in bed. Then he lies down behind me and pulls me close to him. I don't want to like being next to him. I don't want to like the way he smells when he curls behind me and tucks my head under his chin. I want to hate him and everything about him. But I don't. God help me, I don't.

"Shhh, it's going to be all right Skylar."

"It won't ever be all right, Reese. Ever. You can't possibly understand any of this."

I must've cried myself to sleep because something awakens me in the middle of the night. When I realize what it is, I come fully awake.

"Go back to sleep Skylar. I'm only icing your ankle."

I glance down to see he's wrapping a bag of ice around the sprained joint. I watch his hands adeptly handling the Ace bandage, like he's done this a million times. When he's finished, he places my ankle on a towel and gets back in bed with me. He wakes me up a few more times in the night doing the ice thing.

When the morning comes, I hear the shower running. My head pounds from all the tears I shed. I test my ankle by rotating it and it hurts, but not nearly as bad as I thought it would. When I look at it, I see it's swollen and slightly purple. My audition is at one so I still have a few hours where I can ice it.

Since I'm in dire need of some coffee, I hop to the kitchen and start a pot brewing. The bathroom door opens and Reese walks out, wearing a towel wrapped around his waist. My heart drops to my stomach and my mouth suddenly goes dry. I don't want to face him today. He knows every single one of my terrible secrets and the thought of seeing disdain or contempt in his eyes will be too much for me to bear.

"Hey," he says. "I didn't expect you to be out of bed. You need to keep your ankle elevated and iced for as long as possible. What time is your audition?"

"Um, one." I squeak the words out through my constricted throat.

"Good. That gives us some time." He busies himself with his towel.

He can't mean to stay here. I don't think I can hold myself together if he does. Can't he see I'm unraveling at the seams?

"Reese. You have to leave. Or I do."

His head snaps up. "Not happening."

"But ..."

"I'm staying until you leave for your audition. And then you won't ever have to see me again if you don't want."

If he thinks that makes me feel better, he's crazy. I wish I could go back in time ... to yesterday morning. When I thought I was just a girl who stripped and hooked for a living. And I wasn't that girl who had some guy she barely knew destroy every fairy tale she had ever dreamed about.

Sixteen

Reese

WHEN I CALLED HER A FUCKING PAID WHORE, SHE WILTED AND then crumpled before my eyes, like I took my fist and punched her in the gut. The pain that washed over her face was so visceral I fucking *felt* it. When she told me her deal, I wanted to kill her fuck of a mother. Who the hell sells their sixteen-year-old daughter to their pimp? A pimp that abused and raped her? And then when she told me why she does it— all for the woman that sold her in the first place— I wanted to ram my fist through the wall. But when she told me that I—Reese Christianson—humiliated her and drove the point through like an arrow no less, of why she hates herself, I wanted to die. Right there and then. I've never hated myself more than at that particular moment. Not when I was so fucking high that I used women left and right or even used my parents. But the way I hurt Skylar slammed me to my knees. And the way she fucking sobbed. Off and on all night long, waking me up with her pitiful cries while she slept. There won't be a day I live for the rest of my life that I won't think about it.

But today she needs to go to some audition. She said a friend pulled some strings to get her there. And now her ankle is totally fucked up because of me. I have lots, and I mean lots, of experience dancing on sprained ankles. Had to do it all the time. Ballet requires dancers to do all sorts of leaps and jumps from the grand jete to the rivoltade. Ankle injuries were common. This is an area where I can help her. I need athletic and kinetic tape and I can teach her how to wrap it.

"Skylar, I was an ass to you last night. I'm sorry. It wasn't my business to barge into your life and assume you have no worries or problems to contend with. And that this was a path you've chosen for the hell of it. That was selfish and foolish of me. I'm not asking you to forgive me, though I would like that. What I am asking is for you to let me help you. I can help you with your ankle for your audition. All I need is some tape. While I run out to get it, why don't you shower? I'll also pick up some breakfast. Then when I get back, you can eat and we'll do some heat and ice treatments. An hour before you leave here, I'll tape you up and I promise you, you'll be able to dance. I won't guarantee you'll be your best, but you'll be able to dance. Do we have a deal?"

Her eyes narrow as she studies me and then she eventually nods.

I dress quickly and head out for supplies. It only takes me about forty-five minutes to get everything I need because I know exactly where to go. On my way back, I pick up some bagels and coffee.

When I walk in, she's sitting on the couch with her leg elevated.

I grab two buckets. In one, I put some of the ice I bought and fill it with water. Then I plunge her foot into it.

"Yow! That hurts!"

"I didn't say this would feel good."

In the other bucket, I put warm water. After one minute in the ice, I take it out and put it in the warm water.

"Ouch! Are you sure this is supposed to help? It's killing me!"

"Yep. Contrast treatments. It constricts and dilates your blood vessels. It allows your body to get rid of all the swelling and accumulated fluid around the injury." I hope my explanation suffices and she doesn't think I'm hurting her on purpose.

After four minutes in the warm, I put it back in the ice. I keep this up for thirty minutes.

"Now for breakfast and some ibuprofen." I make her a toasted bagel with peanut butter and give her the pills. I also hand her some more coffee.

"I still think you're trying to kill me."

"No, please trust me on this, Skylar."

After several rounds, we stop and elevate. Then when things have calmed down for her, I tape her up and show her exactly where to put the tape for the best support.

"How do you know all this?"

I shrug. This will not be part of our discussion today. "Lots of sprained ankles when I played tennis," I murmur.

When I'm finished, I ask her to test it out. She stands and hesitantly puts weight on it. Then she does a few moves, light steps and smiles a little.

"Pretty good," she says.

"Do you wear shoes?"

"Yeah."

"Go put them on and then I want you to try some of your more difficult moves. We can alter the tape if need be. To add extra support, you know."

"Right." She disappears and comes back with dance sneakers on. Suddenly she starts moving to an unknown beat and spins on one leg. I glance down and notice it's her bad ankle she's been spinning on. Then she takes off and does a series of spread eagle jumps and ends up with a flip. She's good. Really good. She could be in a music video. I knew from her pole dancing she was talented, but this takes it beyond great.

"This feels pretty good. I can tell it's not right, like something's off, but still it's better than I'd hoped."

"How long have you been dancing?"

"Forever, it seems. Started when I was a little kid. I wanted to go to Juillia ..." she stops and shakes her head. "Never mind. It was just a dream." Her blue eyes have dimmed considerably. It was her future ... the dream she harbored for years. I know. I shared that same dream. To dance my heart out. The only difference is I got the chance, I had the opportunity. I had the special training. She never did. She ended up with a drugged up bitch who sold her life away.

"Skylar, go to this audition and dance your heart out. Dance as if your life depends on it. You're good. Really good. You have great potential."

"Thanks Reese, but you don't have to say that."

"I mean it. Just go and give it your all. What's your phone number?" I ask as I grab my cell. She tells me and I immediately text her my number and save hers to my contact list. "Text me when you're done. Now good luck. I have to go. Peace out." I pick up my stuff and leave, not really wanting to, but knowing I need to give her some space.

Emotions whirl through my body, things I've never felt before. But I shove them down and keep walking. I'm late for class as it is. I've already missed English. I'll need to suck up to my professor and see what I can do to make up for it.

My Criminal Justice class has just been dismissed when my phone vibrates. I snatch it and see it's a text from Skylar.

S: *IT'S OVER. NOT SURE HOW IT WENT. DON'T KNOW HOW TO gauge it*
Me: *Congrats on finishing! Proud of you*
S: *Thanks I think*

Me: *Coffee?*
S: *When?*
Me: *Now? Or whenever you can get there*
S: *Where?*
Me: *Guess*
S: *Joe &Mo's?*
Me: *Yep*
S: *See ya there*

I'M ONLY A FEW BLOCKS FROM JOE AND MO'S SO I GO straight on over. Since I don't know where she's coming from, I figure I can get a bit of studying in. My English professor is going to make me pay. I have to write an extra paper. Fun times.

I grab a coffee and pull out my laptop. I've decided my paper is going to be a story about Skylar. So I start typing away. I'm astounded at how easy the words seem to flow from my mind onto the screen. But what shocks me even more is reading what I've written.

"Hey," a voice startles me. I nearly spill my coffee.

She stands before me, looking radiant. She's holding a cup of coffee so she must have slipped in and I didn't even notice.

"Hey."

'What're you working on over there that has you so engrossed?"

"Oh nothing."

"Um, wrong. I've been standing here for at least three minutes and you haven't noticed me. At all. Give it up, Reese."

There's not a chance in hell I'll let her read this. I exit out of the doc and close the lid. "Really, it was just some stuff for school."

Skylar is not good at hiding things. Her face shows surprise at my statement. "You're in school?"

"Yep. NYU. Criminal Justice."

"Really?"

I laugh. "Yeah. Is that so hard to believe?"

"I don't know. I had all kinds of ideas about you, but school never entered my mind."

"So what you're saying is I don't look very scholarly?"

"No, that's not it at all." Her face immediately explodes into a bright shade of fuchsia.

Before I can help myself, my hand reaches out to feel her cheek with the back of my fingers. "A little hot there, are you?"

She smiles shyly, and ducks her head. "I'm sorry, that came out wrong."

"So, tell me. I want to know what you had me pegged for."

She snorts. "A fighter."

My smile disappears and I lean forward and whisper, "Oh, Skylar. You, of all people should know that I'm not a fighter. I'm a lover. Especially when it comes to you."

She does a quick inhale and then licks her lips. When she does that tiny little thing with her tongue, my my pants suddenly feel too small. Our eyes latch on to each other's and my hand reaches for hers. "Please forgive me for the way I treated you last night. I've no right to judge. Ever."

A slight nod from her lets me breathe easier. Lacing my fingers with hers, I say, "So tell me about your audition."

"Oh, Reese, I was so nervous. I don't think I did very well because of that."

"The first ones are always the worst. Was this your first, by the way?"

"Yes. And I'm sure I messed it up badly."

"I see. Since this was your first, you were bound to be nervous as hell. You need to do a lot of them."

"Yes. That's exactly what my friend says. She said that even if I'm not interested in the production, I should try out anyway because I need the experience."

"You should listen to your friend. She sounds very knowledgeable."

"So do you." Her eyes drill mine.

"Well," I hedge, "it's really only common sense. Like a job interview. The more you do it, the more desensitized you become."

"I suppose. Anyway, the tape totally helped. Thanks for doing that."

"I'm glad and you're welcome."

"So, Reese, what are we doing here?"

She rips those very thoughts right out of my head.

"Having coffee?" I dodge because this may be uncomfortable.

"You know that's not what I meant."

"What do you want to do here, Skylar?"

"What I want isn't possible."

"Why do you say that?"

She looks around the coffee shop and then back at me. She now wears a defeated expression. "You know my story. All the ugly details. Well, most of them anyway. I'm stuck and things aren't going to change. My mom ... well, she is who she is and that's that. I can't walk away from her. I've tried, but I just can't do it. So I'll always be that dirty paid whore who earns her living to buy drugs for her mom's habit. That's why."

"Skylar, I'm sorry your mom is the way she is. But that's not your only option. There are other ways."

She sneers, "Oh yeah. That's right. You've been there. You know."

"Yes, I have! And there are places that can help."

"That's all fine and good Reese, but the person has to *want* to go to those places. My mom doesn't want to go. You ought to know that. Sometimes I think she's gotten to the point now where she doesn't even know she has a problem anymore."

"Let me at least talk to her or meet her."

Skylar is quiet for a second and then says, "No. That would go over like a damn bomb at the Macy's parade. Can't do it."

"So, we're at an impasse."

She picks up her phone and checks the time. "I've gotta go. I promised my friend I'd stop by and I have a, er, work tonight."

My gut roils with the thought of her being with another man. "I don't want you to be with any other guys."

"Your wants don't count here, Reese. Neither do mine. I do what I have to do. Not because I want to do it."

"Tell me again that you hate it."

"Every minute of it." She stares me straight on when she says it. And I nod in return. I watch her as she leaves and I decide there and then I know what I'm going to do.

Seventeen

Skylar

MARIANNA WAS EVERY BIT AS EXCITED AS I WAS WHEN I TOLD her how the audition went, even though I wasn't lucky enough to be chosen. "The fact that you auditioned with an injured ankle tells me how serious you are. You need to keep auditioning to get to understand the process and lose your nervousness." As I was leaving her home, she pressed an envelope into my hand. Giving her a puzzled look, she only shrugged and then winked.

I'm on the subway, headed back downtown. I want to open the envelope, but I want to wait until I have some privacy. As I sit and think, my phone vibrates. When I check it, I see it's from J.D. with instructions for tonight's client. Oh for Pete's sake. I'm meeting George and he wants to do his doggie act. Dear God. Not tonight. I'm so not in the mood to walk him around his apartment in that damn harness and leash he loves so much. Good lord, where does he come up with this crap?

Running up the steps to my old place to check on my mom, I walk inside and call out her name. No answer. "Mom!"

I open the door to her bedroom and walk into something I wish I hadn't. She's in bed with some dude and it's not pretty.

"Get the fuck out of here you slut!" she screams.

I back out of the room, shutting the door behind me. Oh, God. It never dawned on me that she still did that. She always seems so drugged out that ... eww. I have to stop thinking about it.

When I get back to my/Reese's place, I plop on the couch. The whole idea of what I just saw makes me want to puke. But then I remember the letter Marianna gave me. Digging through my backpack, it's in my hands and I'm tearing it open. It's a note card and when I unfold it, a necklace falls out.

My Dear Skylar,

I'm so proud of you for taking the plunge and going to the audition. It takes courage to wade through a crowd and force yourself to do something you find uncomfortable. But I promise the more you do it, the easier it will become. Just know, I think you're a true winner. Please take this necklace. It was given to me a long time ago when I was just beginning my career in ballet. A dear friend gave it to me as a good luck charm. And now I'm passing it to you. It worked wonders for me and I'm hoping it will do the same for you.

Much love,

Marianna

I PICK UP THE NECKLACE AND INSPECT IT. IT'S A DELICATE gold chain that has a pair of ballet slippers hanging from it. It's beautiful in its simplicity. I'll treasure it for two reasons. One, because it's from Marianna and perhaps it will bring me some badly needed luck. And two, because no one has ever cared enough for me to give me something so perfect. Well, not since I was a child, before my parents divorced. Forcing myself to stop thinking about that, I head to the shower. It'll be time to meet quirky George soon so I need to get ready for tonight.

The car meets me at *Exotique-A* and takes me to George's. My stomach churns with acid. It feels like my first time. This is becoming more and more distasteful to me. We pull up in front of the building and I walk in. Security stops me, as usual, then allows me to pass. The elevator doors open, and the ride to George's penthouse is silent and smooth. When the doors open into his penthouse, there he sits, on his favorite leather stool. His harness and leash are already on, awaiting me.

"Hello George. I've been told you've been a very bad dog. Is that right?"

"Woof woof."

Crap, this is going to be a long night.

"Come!" I snap my fingers. George hops off his chair and crawls to me. He stays on all fours as his harness and leash are attached. His eyes follow me as I reach for the riding crop that awaits me. "Now George, are you going to obey your master tonight?" I flick the crop against my palm several times.

"Woof woof."

"Good. Let's see how obedient you are. Turn and face away from me." He does and I start to whip him. I don't know why George likes to act like a dog. As I whip, he howls like a wolf.

"Ah woo! Ah woo!"

"Roll over George." He does and his boner pokes straight up in the air. "Ah, George has been a naughty dog. Look what he's done. He wasn't supposed to do that." Clicking my tongue on the roof of my mouth, I lightly whip his boner with the crop. Then I smack his balls. George starts howling like a wolf again. This means he likes it. If he growls, I'm supposed to stop. The weird thing about when George acts like a dog, I don't really have to do much but spank, whip and smack. Oh, and he likes his ass fucked, but he jacks off while I fuck him with a dildo. How hard is that? Heck, he could do that by himself, but he pays good money for this crap.

"Come on George, it's time for a walk." He gets on all fours and I walk him around the apartment, smacking his ass or balls every now and then, just as he likes. When his butt is red, it's time for his big games.

"I think it's time for George to have his obedience lesson. What does George think?"

George howls. I scratch his head.

"Does George want to sniff my pussy?"

"Ah woo!"

"Sit." My voice is firm. George sits. I undress as he watches. When I'm naked, I sit on the floor. "Come," I say, tugging on his leash. He gets on his belly and inches forward until his face is right in front of my crotch. "Lick me, George." And he does. I fake my orgasm and George howls.

"George was bad. Very bad. It took waaaaay too long for Lena to come. Now George must pay."

"Ah woo!"

George has his toy set out along with his lube. I prepare things and tell him, "George cannot touch himself until Lena tells him to. Or George gets punished."

Out comes the crop again and I slap him repeatedly until he squirms. His ass is red and must be stinging, but he's moaning like crazy. When I slap his balls, his groans get even deeper. Then in goes the dildo. George has ceased his howling and is groaning and gurgling so loudly, it's a damn good thing we're in a penthouse.

"Do not touch yourself George or Lena stops." He can come either way. But I like to prolong this. It means an extra hundred bucks for me.

"Roll over George." He flips on his back. I twirl the dildo and tell him, "Jack off George." His hand grabs his boner and in two seconds, he shoots his wad. In another two minutes he'll be asleep.

"Get up George. Now."

He stands.

"You can go to bed now." He staggers to his room.

Five minutes pass. I get dressed and walk into his room. Sure enough, there he lies, face down, sound asleep, dildo still intact. I take the money from the nightstand. He's left me another five hundred in tips. But I always wonder if George will ever make it to bed *after* he takes the dildo out of his ass. How the hell can he sleep with that thing in there? It doesn't seem to bother him though. He's out like a light.

Closing the door behind me I head down to the car that waits for me. Handing J.D.'s share of the money to the driver, I hop out at *Exotique-A* and decide to walk home. It's a nice night and it's not too far.

When I walk in the door, I gasp when arms come around me and pull me close. As soon as I smell him, I know it's Reese.

"You scared the crap out of me."

"Mmm," he says as he nudges me with his nose. "Get cleaned up." We haven't been together in this sense in a while and immediately, my core tightens and my belly flutters. He knows where I've been. It's written on his face. Yet he's here.

"Now, Skylar."

Wasting no time, I go straight to the shower, undressing on the way. My routine is the same—turn on the shower, brush my teeth while the water heats, then get in and scrub, scrub, scrub. When I'm done, I open the curtain, and there he stands. He reaches for me and puts his hands on my waist, lifting me out of the tub. I'm dripping water, but no mind. He wraps me in his arms and grabs my bottom lip with his teeth. He bites me. Then rubs his nose on my face. He backs me against the wall, drops to his knees and puts his mouth on my sex. His hand picks up my leg and puts it onto his shoulder, and he tongues me hard and fast to an intense orgasm. My fingers are tucked into the thickness of his hair as I pull him closer to me.

"You taste so fucking good." He stands, cups the cheeks of

my butt and says, "Wrap your legs around me." I obey. I briefly think how my role has reversed from my time with George. His hand moves between us, unzipping his jeans. Then I feel the crown of his cock spreading our wetness around. He stops for a second and our eyes lock. Then he bucks into me and, oh God, every other thought except for Reese flies out of my mind.

"You feel so good," I tell him. He slams me into the wall over and over as he thrusts into me.

"You like my cock then, huh?"

"Ah, ah." I can't answer him because I'm about to come. But he pulls out. Right at that crucial moment. He unwraps my legs and sets me down.

"What the hell, Reese?"

"You didn't answer me."

"I couldn't. I was about to come."

"Always answer me, Skylar."

My mouth hangs open. "Yes. I love your cock! I've never felt like this. Ever."

"None of your clients …"

"No! They don't get to do this with me."

Then he spins me around so fast, I don't see it coming. His cock presses into me and he's back to where he left off.

"Now tell me how much you love my cock when I'm fucking you, Skylar."

"I love your cock, Reese."

"You love it like this?" And he pumps me hard and then grinds himself against me. His arm comes round me and pulls me into him, and he's so deep he's hitting me just right.

"Yes. Yes. Ahhhh. Yes."

Over and over, he thrusts until I come. And then, and I don't know why he always does this, but right afterwards, he really picks it up. Faster and harder than before. Until I don't think I can possibly take anymore. His hand slips between my folds and finds my clit. When he rubs it just right, I orgasm again and so does he. He leans into me and stays there, his warm breath fanning my neck.

"You were made to be fucked, Skylar, but only by me."

His words startle me. Why does he say things like that? Then his mouth begins a series of light kisses along the back of my neck, down to my shoulder and then my cheek. He pulls his dick out of me and I feel our fluids running down my leg. But his mouth is on mine and I soon forget it. He carries me to the bed and I can't take my eyes off of him as he strips. He's perfect.

He stands at the end of the bed and his eyes rake over my body. His hands take my ankles and spread my legs apart. He sees the trail of liquid and he licks his lips.

"Does this repel you or turn you on, Skylar? The thought of me licking this off of you?"

"It turns me on." It never did before Reese. I always wanted that stuff off of me. But not with him.

"Good. Because I'd lick it off either way." His tongue follows the line and he drags it to the apex of my thighs. Then drills straight into my vagina. If his hands weren't holding me down, I would've flown off the bed.

"Skylar, hold still."

I squirm. He stops and I know exactly what he's going to do. He gets off the bed and returns with that piece of rope.

"Raise your knees." I comply. He binds me again, my wrists tied to my ankles. Then he blindfolds me. I'm exposed, yet so turned on. All I want right now is for him to touch me. But he gets up and leaves. At least I think he does because I don't hear a thing in the apartment.

"Reese?" No answer.

I'm not sure how much time goes by but suddenly I feel something ice cold enter my opening. Then a warm tongue is on me, licking me, sucking me. I writhe. Then he's gone again. Soon he's back, repeating this torture, until I quiver at the tiniest touch.

He runs something soft along my arm and I moan. Then I feel it on my foot. Then he whispers, "Suck my cock, Skylar."

I'm so greedy for anything right now, I eagerly open my mouth and take him all the way into my throat. He moves in and out, and then his mouth on my sex, tonguing and sucking, and I groan. Soon he pulls out and I whimper at the loss of him. Fingers enter me. Massaging me, pressing me in every way that's right. Every nerve ending is on fire for him.

He turns me over. My ass is in the air. I'm at the point where I don't care what he does. I need release of any kind. But he still only plays with me. Something cold travels the length of my spine and then I cry out as it enters me. He rubs my ass and then smacks it. It hurts so good. I never thought I'd feel like this. Each stinging slap elicits a louder moan until I finally cry out.

"Please. I need you. I need you inside of me."

"Where do you want it, Skylar?"

"I don't care!" I cry. And it's the truth. I don't. He can do whatever he wants right now because I'm so damned aroused I can only think of how good it will feel when he enters me and is inside of me.

"One day, Skylar, I'm going to fuck you in both places at the same time. But not tonight."

"Yes! Tonight. Do it. I need it. Please." I beg him to.

Right as I finish begging he pounds his cock into me so hard, I scream.

"Ahhhhh!" I cry out. He's never fucked me this hard, at least my mind is so numb with want right now I can't remember if he has.

He's kneels behind me and presses himself close against me as I climax. I tremble all over, it's so violent. But he keeps on going, not slowing a bit. It's as if I never came. I'm about to cry out when another one rips into me and keeps coming.

"Ah, ah, ah, ah." I'm caught in a cycle of short bursts and they finally quit, leaving me a boneless heap.

"Damn, babe. You just multipled on me." He's breathing like he ran a marathon. "Always knew you were made for fucking."

Right now, I'm so exhausted I can't think straight. He's pushed me to my limits. Correction. He took me beyond any limits I had previously been up against. My body is limp and my eyes close. I don't even feel it when he unties me.

My nose twitches. Is that coffee I smell? What is this? A dang Folger's commercial or something? That thought makes me giggle because if it were, it would be an X-rated one. When I open my eyes, I'm butt-assed naked and sprawled across the bed. Yep. An X-rated one for sure.

The next thing I see is Reese, standing next to the bed, wearing nothing but his jeans. The top button is undone and they ride low on his hips, exposing much of his toned six-pack, including his V. My tongue licks my lips.

"Coffee?"

"Mmm." I reach for the cup, but I'd rather have him. When he doesn't move, I decide to be bold. "Here." I hand him the cup back and sit up. My hand hooks into the waist of his jeans and I pull him towards me as I sit up. I slowly unzip him, watching his eyes take in the scene. My mouth takes him in and I give him a super duper morning special. When I raise my eyes, I let out a tiny giggle. He's watching me with a smile on his face, but he still has the coffee cup in his hand.

"You wanna do something with that?" I ask.

"With this?" he points to the cup, "or with this," he points to his semi-stiff cock.

"Hmm, tough choice. Though I may have sucked the life out of him."

"We'll see about that," he says as he sets the cup down. Then he jerks my butt to the edge of the bed. "Let's see if you still think so after this."

My thighs are spread wide and his fingers start to tease me. "Damn, Skylar. Are you always ready?"

"Only when you're around."

He raises my ankles and starts to tease me with his dick as he circles my clit with the tip. Then he drives it home. Gah, this man knows how to please me. He holds my hands and uses them to find the right rhythm as he thrusts into me until I climax. And like he always does, right afterward he picks up speed and takes it to the next level. He knows my body better than me. He must have some kind of cock radar, or maybe it's pussy radar, because he knows exactly at which threshold the pleasure-pain begins and that's where he always hovers. And it's where I crumble into one giant orgasmic mess.

After he comes, he lowers my legs and falls onto the bed next to me. He nuzzles my neck and then laughs. "Fucking you is like going to the carnival, Skylar."

"What?" I'm not sure if this is a compliment or an insult.

"Oh, babe. It's like being inundated with a million different sensory experiences. All for the first time. Every time we have sex, I'm blown away. Like the first time I went to the carnival. You know, tasting cotton candy for the first time. Or riding the Ferris wheel and seeing everything from up high in the sky. Or biting into a funnel cake. That's what you do to me."

"The carnival, huh?"

"Yeah. The carnival. Simply amazing."

"I've never been."

He raises up on his elbow. "What?"

"I've never been to the carnival."

"Never?"

"No. Never."

"But ..."

"Reese, my parents split when I was seven. They had issues before then. My dad left and my mom went sort of nuts. She was a pharmacist at the hospital and that's when all the drug use started. I don't know if she'd been using before, but it escalated when he moved out. Then she got caught. The hospital fired her and she was charged with stealing with the intent to sell and trafficking. She went to prison. I moved in with my dad and his new wife. The new wife hated me because I wasn't part of her plan. She made up lies about me. Said I slapped her and …" I take a deep breath and rub my eyes because they've become blurred with tears. "She accused me of stealing money. It was rough. My dad believed her, of course. Why would he ever believe his twelve-year-old daughter? She told him the apple didn't fall far from the tree." Sarcasm oozes out of me and though I try to pretend it doesn't hurt me anymore, it always gouges into my heart. Guess I'm not very good at covering it up. "Anyway, my mom got out on good behavior when I was fourteen. So that's when they sent me back to her. There were no carnivals. No picnics. No holidays. We had Christmas for a few years, that I can remember. But I never got to dress up for Halloween. Never went on Easter egg hunts. So yeah, no carnivals for me."

He holds my hand and raises it to his lips. Kissing it tenderly, he asks, "Do you have to work tonight?"

"Yeah. I work almost every night. It's a money thing, you see."

"Any chance you can get a night off soon?"

"Yeah. I just have to let my boss know."

"Skylar, tell your boss you can't work on Friday."

"But Friday is busy at *Exotique-A*."

"Tell him to find someone to take your place and that you need the night off. If you won't tell him, I will."

His face is all kinds of serious so I agree.

"Good. Glad that's settled. Be ready for me around two."

"You gonna tell me what this is about?"

"Not a chance. Just be ready. Wear jeans and comfortable shoes. You'll be walking a lot."

"Walking a lot?"

"Yep. And don't eat. I want you hungry as a bear. Oh and one other thing. I don't want you walking home alone any more from the club."

How the hell did he know?

He gives me that look. The look that tells me he knows what I'm about.

"Reese, I'm fi ..."

"No. If you feel the need to walk home from work, call me and I'll come and walk you home. Have you forgotten you almost got raped? Because I haven't."

He's trying to tell me what to do and I don't like it. I'm independent and have always been.

"You can't tell me what to do."

"Look. You have a job that I despise. You have to know how I feel about it. Other men get to see you naked. They get to fucking *touch* you. They do things with you that only *I* should be able to do. But this is your life and you have to do what you have to do in order to get by. I'll deal with it. Doesn't mean I like it, just means I'll deal. But this walking home alone. That's a totally different thing. It's plain stupid and dangerous and you know it. So don't do it. And if you insist, I'll hire people. I'm not gonna take a chance where your safety is concerned. I'm begging you, Skylar."

He's right so I agree with his terms. "I'll call if I want to walk. Otherwise, I'll have the driver bring me here."

"Good. Now, getting back to that coffee." He smiles. I melt. Totally, completely melt.

Eighteen

Reese

At two o'clock on Friday, I walk into the apartment to find Skylar dressed and waiting for me. And she looks cute as hell. Dressed in worn jeans and a sweatshirt, she looks like a high school kid.

Tossing my backpack on the couch, I rifle through it and find my wallet. Then I grin at her and say, "You ready?"

"I guess so. Where we headed?"

"It's a surprise." I hold out my hand and she takes it. Her hand feels right, like it belongs in mine. We head for the subway, but when it's time to get off the train, I won't let her look.

"Close your eyes and keep them closed. And Skylar," putting my mouth right next to her ear, I whisper, "if you open them, or so much as peek, I'm going to punish you later on tonight." When she sucks in her breath, I want to find a secluded spot so we can have a quickie.

"Reese, stop." Her hand squeezes mine and I lean down to kiss her.

When we get on the next train, I tell her she can open her eyes again, but I put my arm around her and hug her close to me. After a couple of train changes, we exit the subway and walk the couple of blocks to Luna Park. My eyes are focused on her face the entire time and it's like watching a kid get their first bike. Or maybe seeing them blow out the candles on their birthday cake. She looks like I just handed her the world. And it's a only an amusement park.

"You ready to experience your first carnival?"

"Oh my God!" Then she turns to me with the most amazing expression on her face, like the sun is shining right out of her. She's glowing. She throws her arms around me and buries her face in my neck. "I can't believe you brought me to Coney Island!" Her voice is muffled against me, but her excitement is contagious.

"Only wanted you to experience what I was talking about the other night. Let's go."

We ride the rides first. And then dive into the food. I spare nothing. She has to taste it all from the cotton candy that makes her fingers sticky to the funnel cakes I knew she'd be addicted to. My phone stays in my hand because I constantly snap pictures of her.

"These are amazing!" she says as she licks her fingers.

Suddenly, and I don't know why, a thought strikes me. "Skylar, I've noticed something about you. Why don't you curse very much?"

Her face turns to stone and she stops chewing. She sets her funnel cake down and finishes swallowing the bite she's working on. Then she wipes her mouth and takes a drink of her Icee. Her eyes have looked everywhere but at me, and when they do, the pain that clouds them makes me flinch.

She inhales and says, "My parents fought. Nasty fighting. Mom would hit my dad. Then he would hit her back. They yelled and screamed at each other constantly. Said terrible things. Cursed all the time, while I stood there and watched. I heard everything because they never tried to hide it from me. Then when I lived with my dad, his wife called me all sorts of awful things. 'Little Shit' was one of her favorites. Or the 'Spawn of the fucking crack whore.' And she did it in front of my dad. She never called me by my name. Not once. And then there's my mom. Fuck is her favorite word. 'Skylar, where the fuck is my stash?' Or 'Get your fucking ass in here you goddamn slut.' Anyway, I hated it so much I made up my mind that I would do my best not to ever speak like that. So that's why. I despise it and everything it represents."

Skylar's been traumatized her whole life. The abuse she's lived through is beyond tragic. It's a wonder she's functional.

Now it's my turn to wipe my hands and mouth with my napkin. Then I get up and move to sit next to her. We're seated at a picnic table. So I pull her onto my lap.

"You amaze me. You had a shit childhood, and yet here you are, a strong and beautiful young woman." Then I hold her because I'm not sure what else I can do. "I'm sorry I asked you that. I didn't mean to pry or to spoil this for you."

"Reese, it's me. This is the way I've lived forever. I don't know anything different so don't be sorry. I don't usually talk about my life with anyone. You're the first. No one knows everything about my past."

"Then I'm honored that you chose me to tell your secrets to."

"What about you, Reese? What kind of secrets do you have?"

Well, fuck me. There are too many painful secrets that I can't delve into right now. Maybe someday. "You know the worst. I'm a recovering addict. That's not exactly something to write home about."

"Yeah, but there's more you're not telling me."

"Skylar, you know more about me than most people."

"Oh? How so?"

"You know what I like best in the bedroom. No one can say that."

Her throat works around as she swallows. And it's true. No one knows as much as she does because I haven't been with any one woman as many times as I've been with her. A change in subject is needed so I add, "My Aunt Emmy used to bring me here all the time. We would call it our Coney Time."

"Your Aunt Emmy?"

"Yeah. She's my favorite aunt. My grandfather's sister. She was my hero growing up. My parents hated this place. My mom wouldn't be caught dead here. But not Aunt Emmy. We'd come here once a month. And when she'd take me home, I'd have the worst stomachache in the world. And my mom would be so pissed at Aunt Emmy. But the following month, she'd show up for Coney Time again."

Skylar laughs. "What would you do in the winter?"

"Oh, Aunt Emmy would come up with something. The circus, the zoo. You name it. She'd hunt down places to take me that had Coney Time food. She's hilarious. You'd love her. She used to tell my mom that she needed to loosen up a bit or that her ass would bite off a lead pipe if she ever got near one!"

"That's too funny!"

"That's my Aunt Emmy. My mom's gotten used to her over the years, but it would drive her crazy. Back then, she would say I couldn't go anywhere with her. But Aunt Emmy would come over when my mom was gone and steal me away. My nanny would laugh."

"You had a nanny?" Her eyes look comical.

Damn! I didn't mean to let that one slip.

"Uh, yeah. Her name was Martha and she was great. I still talk to her."

"Whoa. You must've had a great life growing up with all those people who loved you."

God, I sure did, but at the time I was too self-absorbed to

realize it. And now I look at Skylar and see what she's faced and …

"Yeah, I did. I was too spoiled for my own good, though. I should shut up now. You don't need to hear me go on about how I grew up."

"No, please. I love hearing about it. How it was for other people who had it good, you know? I used to dream about how it would be to live in a home where I could feel safe and surrounded by warm fuzzies. My dream was that I would run away from home and some family would find me and take me in. There would be dinner time every night and someone would be there to help with my homework if I needed it. And I'd have a warm bed with clean sheets to sleep in. And then in the morning, the mom would wake me up and fix me breakfast and have a lunch made for me to take to school."

"Skylar, who taught you to dance?"

She ducks her head. I find it so odd that she can strip in front of strangers but gets shy when I ask her a simple question.

"The neighborhood kids. We used to play music and it started with hip hop. Then I sort of created my own style by blending it with other stuff."

"And your gymnastic moves?"

"Oh, I started doing cartwheels and walkovers and stuff when I was a little kid. I always dreamed of dancing or doing gymnastics. Then, like I said, I blended the hip hop stuff with flips and other moves and I took it a little further."

"I'd like to watch you do an entire routine."

"Oh, I don't know. I'm okay I guess. Maybe someday."

"Well, remember, I've seen you at *Exotique-A*."

Her face flushes scarlet.

"Um, yeah."

"You're excellent. On the pole. You're really strong."

"Reese, that was a strip tease dance." She huffs.

"Doesn't matter. I watched the way you moved. You're really great."

135

"Oh? And how would you know. Are you some kind of dance expert?"

Okay, I need to change the direction of this conversation again.

"Well, no, but I think you need to give this dance thing a go. Now, are you done eating?"

"Oh, yeah. I'm stuffed."

My hand moves under her sweatshirt so I can rub her belly. "Oh, seems to me you have a little more room in here."

Her hands move to my face, she grabs me and kisses me. She's taken me by surprise. Her tongue pushes past my lips and tangles with mine but when I move mine into her mouth, she starts to suck on it, playing with it the same way she does my cock when she blows me. My cock strains against my tight jeans and I moan into her mouth. Not even thinking, I slip my hand down the back of her jeans so I can caress the cheek of her ass and damn it feels so good. That's when I feel a tap on my shoulder.

"Sir, this is a public park. If you wanna do that, you need to take it elsewhere."

Oh, hell!

"Right. Sorry, man."

When he leaves, Skylar and I look at each other and laugh. Hard.

"Let's move away from here. I'm afraid if I sit here any longer, I'll might have a little issue in my jeans."

"You would not."

"Babe, I have a stiffie that could rival granite. Come on."

She laughs again. We spend the rest of the evening at Luna Park and I even win a giant stuffed panda bear for her. It's a bitch lugging home, but she loves it, so I'm happy.

When we get there I take the panda and put him in the bed. Then I turn to Skylar and say, "He can keep you company when I'm not here."

"Are you not staying tonight?"

"Not tonight."

"Why?"

I take her in my arms and kiss her. Like she means something to me. Like she's the most important thing in the world to me.

"Sleep well, Skylar." Grabbing my backpack, I head out the door.

I know she's puzzled, but the fact is I can't stay tonight ... or any other night. She's exposed a piece of herself that I really didn't want to see. She's opened up to me and now I want all of her to myself. I don't want to share her with any of her johns. Or the scumbags that watch her dance. I want her to dance only for me, and me alone. Now that she's shared that part of herself, I feel wounded too. And possessive. I don't want her to hurt anymore. To feel the pain of abandonment. Each night when I've waited for her to come home, I could take out my anger on her with hard, dirty sex. But now I want to fuck her, softly and sweetly. I want to show her that side of me too. But I can't. Not until she leaves that ugly part of her life behind. So I'm the one that will have to leave her behind. Even though it hurts. Like recovering from the beating that nearly took my life. And I know staying away from Skylar will be like going through withdrawal all over again. But it's not an option for me to sit by and watch her prostitute herself any longer. This is the only way I know to say goodbye without destroying her.

Nineteen

Skylar

AFTER SPENDING THE MOST WONDERFUL NIGHT OF MY LIFE with Reese, he walks away and leaves me alone with a giant stuffed panda. For hours I stare at the door, thinking he'll walk through it again. But when the sun begins to turn the room a golden hue, I admit to myself that he's really gone. Every day I come home from work, thinking he'll be there, but he's not and the disappointment crashes into me time and time again.

Cara meets me for lunch one afternoon at our favorite sushi restaurant.

"You look awful, girl."

Nodding, I try to speak, but my tears choke me up and a sob escapes instead. She grabs my hand and says, "Oh honey, I didn't know it was this bad." She motions for the waiter to come over and orders us some sake. Then she stuffs some tissue into my hand.

At last, the gripping burn leaves my throat and I launch into my pathetic Reese saga.

Cara is quiet and looks pensive for a moment. "You've obviously called him, right?"

"Yeah."

"Can you go to his apartment?"

Groaning, I say, "I am *at* his apartment. I'm living in it. And that's the other thing. I can't keep doing that. Here's the weird thing too. He must show up there sometimes because the refrigerator is always stocked with food and stuff. Like he still takes care of me or something."

"Now that's a little creepy."

"Why?"

"I don't know. It's like he's spying on you or something."

I think about it and then say, "I don't look at it like that. I think of it as he wants to make sure I have everything I need."

"Okay, whatever. But are you gonna keep on living there?"

My hands sink into my hair as I say, "Ugh! I don't know. I want to because it's a great place and I don't have to listen to my mom rant and rave. But then I feel so guilty not paying him rent. But I can't afford my mom's rent and this place. I'm so confused."

Cara grins. "Hell with it. Stay until he asks you to leave."

"You think I should?"

"Hell yeah! I mean, he allowed you to move in, right?"

"Yeah."

"Then if he wants you gone, make him ask you to leave."

Cara's strong. Much more so than I am. Staying at Reese's would be nice, but how humiliating would that be if he shows up one day and asks me to leave? It would be better if I just go on my own.

"I'll figure it out."

"You're gonna move back with your mom, aren't you?"

"Probably."

"You can stay at my place when I don't have a client."

"Thanks, Cara."

Unlike me, Cara entertains at her place. She likes it that way and sometimes they spend the night. She makes huge bucks when they do.

"Listen Sky, I know you don't want to hear this, but one day you're going to have to set your mom loose. Jimmy thinks so too. She's a noose around your neck and she's slowly squeezing the life out of you, honey. I know you feel obligated to her, but one day, something's going to happen and it scares me to think about it."

Cara and Jimmy are right. But if something happens to my mom, and I'm not there to check on her or to help her, I'm not sure if I could live with that.

"I know but ..."

"She's a grown woman and she's chosen her path, Sky."

"Yeah, but she's sick."

"Sky, you're making excuses for her. She is sick but she also can get help and refuses to do so. By giving her the money to support her drug habit, you're enabling her, honey. You're helping her kill herself."

"Cara, stop. I don't want to discuss this anymore."

"I know, but it needs to be said. You can be pissed off at me all you want, but the bottom line is she's ruined your life and you've let her. Answer me this. Would you be dancing and a working girl if it weren't for her?"

"You know the answer to that."

"See, that's the difference between you and me. I do it because it gives me a high. I love the fact that men thrive on looking at *me*. I love that men *want me*. You, you're different. You hate doing this. It disgusts you. Go to your mom. Give her an ultimatum. Tell her to get help or you won't support her anymore. Tell her no more drugs. Do it for her, but more importantly, do it for you, Sky. You deserve a chance at a better life for yourself—one that involves dancing, and not the exotic kind."

She's right, but I don't think I have the guts to do it. On the way home, thoughts of my mom, dad, and Reese race through my mind. Something's gotta give because I can't go on like this. Tonight's my free night. But since it's been a few days since Reese has been by, my hunch is that he'll stop by to do his grocery thing. So I dress up and head out, like I do when I have to work. Only this time, I circle around the block and keep an eye on the apartment.

My suspicions are correct. At around nine thirty, here he comes, his arms laden with groceries. After about five minutes, I head inside. No question about it, he's startled when I walk through the door.

"Hello Reese."

"Skylar. What are you doing here?"

"I might ask you the same thing."

"You might."

"But you won't answer, will you?"

He's silent as he stares at me. As I look back at him, I'm shocked at his appearance. He was built like a brick wall before, but now he's ...

"Reese, what have you been doing?" Before he can back away, I lift the tight T-shirt he's wearing. He's nothing but pure hard muscle.

"Um, yeah, I've been hitting the gym a lot."

"A lot. Looks like eight hours a day. Are you taking steroids?"

A bitter laugh rips out of him. "Skylar, really. I'm a recovering addict. Do you honestly think I would dope?"

"No, but from the looks of you, I ..."

"I'm pumping a lot of iron and hitting the bag pretty hard. That's it."

"Frustrated much?"

"As a matter of fact, I am. Extremely. You see, there's this girl and she ... never mind." He rubs his neck. "I need to go."

"No, don't," I say in a rush. "Please stay." I put my hand on his arm. *Please, Reese don't go. I want you to stay so badly because you mean so much more to me than my lame words.* That's what I want to say to him, but I refrain.

His chest expands with a breath and his hand reaches back to rub his neck again. But then he says, "I can't. I have to go."

Without another word, he leaves. And my heart aches again like he just walked away with a piece of it and left the rest of it broken and scattered across the floor.

Twenty

Reese

"Case, it's me. I need your help."

"Wassup?"

"Can you get me Skylar's dad's addy?"

Dead silence.

"Case? You there?"

He groans into the phone. "Buddy, what'cha doing? Why do you need that?"

My grip tightens on the phone. "Case, I just need to do something."

"Where are you?"

"Leaving the gym. Why?"

"Meet me at Joe and Mo's."

"Yeah. Okay." I know better than to put up a fight on this. He'll win. He's waiting when I walk in the place, seated with a cup in his hands, and an extra one for me.

"Decaf?" I ask.

"Yeah. You've been too jacked for regular. Spill."

"I just wanna go and talk to the guy."

"What're you gonna say that will change the outcome of things?"

"Nothing. But Skylar deserves it."

"Does she know?"

"Nope. Haven't talked to her in a couple of weeks."

Case leans back in his chair and crosses his arms. His eyes don't leave mine. Hell, he doesn't even blink.

"You look like the strings on a tennis racket you're wound up so damn tight. Don't think I haven't noticed."

"I know. I'm taking care of it in the gym. Don't worry about it."

"The gym only does so much. Look at you. You look like the fucking Hulk. And it ain't working, my man. You need to talk to someone."

"I'm not doing that psychobabble bullshit. I already know I'm fucked up. I don't need some shrink to verify that."

"Reese, please …"

"Case, all I need is his address. If you won't do it, I'll find someone who will."

He sighs. "Right. Okay, but I go with you. And we come right back."

"Fine. But you don't say a word when I'm in front of the man."

"Deal."

"Book the tickets. And make 'em first class. I don't do coach."

"Goddamn. Who are you? The Prince of England?"

"Right, Case. I'm sure the Monarchy has its own private jet. Book the fucking tickets."

SKYLAR'S DAD LIVES RIGHT OUTSIDE OF L.A. WE FLY FIRST class and Case is happy we did. It was a long flight and we leave for New York again in five hours. We pick up our car and head straight to Mr. O'Donnell's. When we pull into his driveway, my fury hits an all time high. He lives in a McMansion, equipped with two Mercedes and in the meantime, his daughter is prostituting herself out to support herself and her drug addict of a mother.

"You good with this?" Case asks.

"Yep," I say through my clenched teeth I'm seething but I'll get through it.

I push the button for the doorbell and leave my finger on it. It buzzes continually.

"Is this really necessary?" Case asks.

"Probably not, but it does give me some degree of satisfaction, however small."

The door opens and a man in maybe his late forties to early fifties looks at us and says, "That dang buzzer must be sticking."

"No, wasn't the buzzer. It was the buzzer pusher. Are you Michael O'Donnell? Born in Brooklyn, New York. Formerly married to Mary Elizabeth O'Donnell and father of Skylar O'Donnell?"

"Yeah. What's going on?"

"Mr. O'Donnell, you are one piece of crap. That's what's going on. Do you know that your daughter, that beautiful amazing human being that you somehow miraculously fathered, was forced into prostitution by her mother when she was sixteen years old so she could buy drugs for her? Do you know that bitch of a female, that piece of shit you're married to, lied to you about Skylar? Told you things about her that weren't true? Skylar would never steal anything from anyone. You have to practically beg her to take something from you. But steal? Never in a million years would she do that. Look at her!" I have a five by seven picture from our day at Luna Park where Skylar is tasting cotton candy for the first time. I pull it out of the envelope and shove it in his face. "She's twenty-three years old and this is the first time she'd ever tasted cotton candy for Christ's sake.

And here you sit, in LA, with your fancy house and cars, while your daughter strips and fucks men, so she can keep her mother off the streets. Now how does that make you feel? Look at that beautiful face, Mr. O'Donnell. LOOK AT IT! Because I hope to hell that piece of shit you're married to is worth the way you fucked up your daughter's life, your own flesh and blood, you worthless prick! You belong together. Have a good rest of your fucked-up life." My palm smashes the picture against his face right before I spin around and stomp to the car. Case is on my heels and we get in and drive away as Michael O'Donnell watches us, mouth hanging open, from his fancy front porch.

When we get a few blocks away, Case says, "Well, that went well."

I turn to look at him and he has a smirk on his face. A second later I burst out laughing. "Indeed it did. I didn't punch him, like I wanted to, but I did grind that picture on his face a bit."

"Hmm. I almost punched him for you. Nice work, buddy."

We fist bump. But in reality, I want to punch my hand through the windshield for the pain Skylar has experienced because of that bastard.

After we land, we grab a cab. Case wants to know where I'm headed.

"The gym."

"Please talk to someone. I'm serious."

"Yeah. Sure." He knows I won't do it.

We're silent for the remainder of the ride. When I get to the gym, I wrap my hands and go to it on the bag, pretending it's Mr. O'Donnell's face I'm tearing into. An hour and a half later, sweat pours off of me like water and I break for some rehydration. Then I go at it again. There's an undercurrent of energy in me … a raging inferno that needs to be extinguished and I hope that another round with the bag will do it.

It's late and the gym is closing up when I finally leave. My stomach rumbles with hunger and it reminds me that it's been hours since I've eaten. There's a pizza joint between here and where I'm hanging my hat these days, so I duck inside for a quick bite. A large sausage and pepperoni pie later, I head back to Case's place. Well, it's not really his place. It's a place he maintains for NA. Some of the recovering addicts need temporary housing and this place is set up for that. He's reminded me several times that this place is supposed to be temporary. Guess I've sort of passed that since I've been holed up here for three months now.

As I round the corner, I see two guys taking it out on some poor kid. Great. This is exactly what I need. Blowing off some more steam may ease the fire within me. My fists connect with bone and I hear crunching and their screams. But I don't stop until I'm satisfied they're down for the count. Then the kid who they were beating up looks at me and I ask, "You okay?"

"Yeah. Thanks."

"Call 911. Get the cops here."

"Okay."

"They'll be out for a while so you're safe till the police get here."

"Hey, thanks."

I don't really know why I don't stay. Maybe it's because I'm not in the mood for questions. Whatever the case, the walk to my temporary home is short and fast. Since I'm bloody from the fight, I hop in the shower and get cleaned up. By the time I'm done, my eyes barely stay open.

The next morning, Case is beating my door down. Now what? When I roll over to get out of bed, my body feels like it had it out with an armored tank and the damn tank won. Turning the door knob is even an effort.

The door swings open and Case stands there holding my bloody clothes in his hands.

"Wanna tell me what this is all about?"

Ah fuck. I must've left my clothes on the bathroom floor. "Morning to you too," I huff.

"Jesus, what the hell did you do last night?"

"Went a thousand rounds with the bag. Then on my way home, some kid was getting his lights punched out by two punks so I punked them instead."

"You call the cops?"

"Nope. I told the kid to when I was leaving. Didn't want to hang around for questions."

He eyes me something fierce. "Any particular reason?"

"Yeah! Look at me Case. If they start to dig, what will they find? A drug abuser. I don't need that shit."

"Okay, calm down."

My ass drops back on my bed and I rest my elbows on my knees. "Jesus, I'm sore."

"I can tell. Let me look at your hands." I hold them out for his inspection. "You ice these?"

"Nah. Too tired last night. That's why I left my shit in the bathroom. My eyes were slamming shut."

"Be right back."

Case is the best. Don't know where I'd be today if Dot hadn't sent me his way. In the morgue, most likely. He charges back in with two large bags filled with ice and holds the tops of them open.

"In you go."

"Man, I hate this part."

"Yeah, well, if you'd go talk to someone like I keep telling you, this ice wouldn't be part of your day."

"Damn, I don't know what hurts worse. This or leaving them alone."

"I know what you mean. By the way, Happy Birthday," Case says.

I shoot him a look that lets him know I think he's off his rocker. "Not my birthday."

"Oh, hell yeah it is. Today is the anniversary of your first year of sobriety. It's your birthday, man. Your first birthday of your second chance at life."

How the hell did I forget this? I've been carrying around this chip for twelve months now, rubbing it between my two fingers like it's a fucking piece of gold. And today, when the one year mark is reached, my mind totally blanks it out. What. The. Fuck. My hands that are stuck in two big bags of ice, cover my face and I cry. Like a fucking baby. When my pussy-ass finally shuts up, my eyes connect with Case's.

"Yeah, man. I cried like a baby too. It's cool. One year is a landmark. But that doesn't mean you're out of the woods. My toughest time was at eighteen months. Hang tight. You're gonna make it."

"Case, this thing with Skylar ..."

"Yeah, it's eating a hole in you. I can see it. Talk to her, man. You've gotta tell her how you feel."

"I don't know if I can. She's ... she's trapped and I don't want to make her feel any more trapped."

"But you have to tell her how you feel about her."

"Maybe."

"When do classes start?"

"Summer session starts next week."

"Talk to her. You can't live here forever. I gotta go. See you at the meeting tonight."

"Right. Thanks Case."

When I'm finished icing my hands I decide to pay a visit to Skylar. It's been over a month since I've seen her ... since I've taken her groceries or anything. A bagel would be a nice surprise. And maybe a latte.

Hurrying up the steps, I unlock the door and find an empty apartment. All her belongings are gone. The place is nice and tidy but she's left nothing behind. Even the giant stuffed panda is gone. On the kitchen counter sits a note and her key to the apartment.

R,

Thanks so much for allowing me to crash here.

But I know I've been an intrusion so it was time I moved on.
I waited and waited for you to drop by, to tell you in person,
but it's obvious you don't want to see me anymore.
I understand and don't blame you a bit.
But I did want you to know that you made me
feel safer than I've ever felt before, so thanks for that.
And thanks for taking me to Luna Park.
It was the best time of my life and
I'll cherish that memory forever.
See you around.
S

AN ICY HAND GRIPS MY HEART. WHAT DID I EXPECT? THAT she would stay here forever? She's not someone that willingly takes a thing, so I should've known she'd leave. I pull out my phone and go through the pictures of her from Luna Park over and over and over. And each time I look at her, my heart cracks a little more. What did I do? Why did I leave? Why wasn't I willing to accept her the way she was? Now I'm paying the price and it hurts. No, it doesn't simply hurt. It burns. It kills. It destroys.

This is the night it begins. The night when people start to pay. I purposely hunt down those who are hurting others and I make it my mission to destroy them. Muggers and rapists don't stand a chance around me. I hunt, and when I find them, I bring them down to a bloody mess. It's the only way to assuage my pain … to make me forget her and to take my mind off of drugs.

Twenty-One

Skylar

As soon as I hit the back entrance of *Exotique-A*, Jimmy tells me that J.D. wants to see me in his office. He says he doesn't know what he wants, but I have a good idea. I head upstairs. The bodyguards let me pass. They recognize me and he's told them to expect me.

When I knock on the door, J.D. tells me to come in.

"Hey J.D. What's up?"

"Sit." He motions for me to take a seat on one of his leather sofas. He shuts down his computer and walks around to take a seat next to me.

"Baby doll, we have issues. I've mentioned this to you before, but you brushed it off. Now, you wanna tell me what's going on?"

"Nothing. I'm fine."

"No, you're not. You're my number two girl. Cara's my number one and the reason she's number one is she's willing to do things with her clients that you're not. And that's cool. I'm cool with that, baby doll. I've got you matched up with my highest paying johns that are willing to play by your rules. But baby, I'm getting complaints from them now. You're not into their games. Clyde's called me twice telling me you've changed and aren't into his technique. He says you don't come anymore. Georgie boy told me you didn't want to play the dog and pony show like he wanted last time. Now Big Daddy's taken care of you since you were eighteen. I've done all I can to keep things the way you want baby doll, but things have gotta change with you. I need my old Lena back and fast, or I'm gonna have to pull you off my client list."

"No, J.D., please. I promise to get my head back in the game."

"You gotta, Lena. I mean come on. How hard is it to fake an orgasm? And George? Seriously? Slap his ass and tell the man to howl like a fucking wolf. I don't care what stupid crazy ass shit the guy likes. Put a fuzzy dog tail up his ass for all I care. But keep the guy happy. He pays and tips like a mutha. Okay baby doll? And the next time Clyde goes down on you, act like it's the best thing you've ever had. Got it?"

"Yeah, I got it."

"Okay. Now who loves you best?"

"Big Daddy loves me best."

"Now give me some sugar right here." He taps his cheek and I kiss it.

"Good. Now get your ass to work, baby."

I've really got to get my head in the game. Reese has screwed with it so badly. I can't stand being with someone else, when I want to be with him. When I'm with any of my clients, it makes me sick thinking about what I'm doing. The only one I want to do those things with is Reese. He's completely ruined me.

Jimmy's waiting for me, as usual, right outside my dressing room. "Everything cool?"

"Yeah. I just got chastised. I haven't been a very good hooker, apparently."

"Sky, you need to get out of this."

"You know that's not going to happen."

"She needs to get help, just like Cara said."

"Did Cara tell you?"

Jimmy's face turns bright red. So bright that I can even see it in the dim lighting of the hall.

"Damn it. Are you guys talking about me behind my back?"

"Only because we love you and are worried about you."

"Listen to me, Jimmy Ratcliff, I've been taking care of myself since I was eight years old. I'm fine. I'll be fine. Got that?"

"Yeah. But I'll still worry."

I punch him in the arm as I pass to go to the box.

The night flies and I'm finally down to my last dance. He's rude, obnoxious and drunk. Normally, these guys don't make it back here so Jimmy must've missed him somehow.

"Get over here, bitch."

I bite my tongue, but do as he asks. He can't touch me, but I can get very close to him, if he wants.

"Shake those tits in my face." Again, I comply. His arms snake around me so fast, I don't have time to react. He pulls me on his lap and squeezes my breasts so hard I yelp. "Shut up, whore," he says as I feel the hard cold steel of a knife blade press against my chest.

Oh God. This has never happened. This guy's going to assault me in the box. I do a quick calculation of how much time he has left and it's probably close to fifteen minutes. I'm way too far from the panic button on the wall for help. If I move, he can slice me in seconds.

"What do you want?" My heart pounds, practically beating out of my chest.

He laughs. "What do you think?"

"Think about this first. You won't get away with it. You're

the last customer. If I don't open that door in fifteen, my body-guard comes in. You'll be toast either way."

"Wrong. You and I will walk out of here together, just like two love birds."

"They won't buy it. I never associate with the customer."

"Oh, they'll buy it or that knife at your back will slide right on through."

"Tell me what you want."

"Everything comes off." This is stupid because the only thing I have on is a G-string. I slip it off.

He stands up and I back away from him. He's drunk and I'm hoping my reflexes will save me. That panic button is my only hope, but if Jimmy charges in here, either one of us could get stabbed. *Think, Skylar.*

As he stalks me, he holds the knife in one hand and unzips his pants with the other. His massive cock springs out and I gasp. "Like that don'tcha? Wait till I push this baby up your cunt and make you squeal."

Backing into the wall, I slam my head against the button. Deciding I'd rather be stabbed than let that monster rape me, I go for it. Jimmy opens the door and everything happens at once. The guy feels my knee hit his groin and he doubles over. I feel a slight stinging in my side, but pay it no attention. Then the guy lunges at Jimmy. I scream at the top of my lungs. At this point I'm not sure where the knife is but the drunk guy is strong. Using my head, I keep pounding the panic button. The room erupts with all kinds of muscle as they take the guy down. Suddenly I feel really cold so I wrap my arms around myself and that's when I feel my side is warm and sticky. I look at my hand and it's covered in blood. I never did care for the sight of blood. Always made me cringe. This time, it makes me pass out cold.

NEXT THING I KNOW, I WAKE UP IN A HOSPITAL BED AND CARA is sitting next to me, reading a *People* magazine.

"Well, look who's awake. How do you feel?"

"What's going on?" My throat is scratchy.

"Sky, you got stabbed, remember?"

The drunk guy in the box. Groaning, I say, "Now I do. Is Jimmy okay?"

"He's fine. Not a scratch."

"Everyone else?"

"Just fine. Except that guy with the knife has a set of bruised balls on him. Your knee did a real job on him."

"Good to know."

She pats my hand.

"What's my damage here?"

"Nothing serious. It nicked your ribs but mostly surface stuff. You'll be out in another day."

"Cool."

"Yeah. Um, well ..." she stammers.

"What?"

"Jimmy and I called Reese."

"You did what?" I attempt to sit up but she pushes me back down.

"Yeah. At the time, we didn't know how serious it was. He's kind of outside."

"Kind of outside?" My body goes into a full-blown panic. Heart in throat. No. Maybe in stomach. All of a sudden I'm pouring sweat. "I have to get out of here."

I roll out of bed and Cara says, "Sky, calm down. Please."

The floor is cold on my feet and now I shiver. My sweat has made me cold. There's an IV attached to my arm so I push the pole around in the tiny room.

"Sky, what are you doing?"

"I don't know. I have to go." The door swings open and there he stands. One look at him and I lose it. Totally. One hundred percent. Strong arms encircle me and my head falls on his chest.

I breathe in his scent and it makes me cry even harder. Why is this happening to me?

"Shhh. You're safe. I've got you." My fists curl into his shirt and I cry uncontrollably, feeling like a fool. Somehow he lifts me up and puts me back in bed, never letting me go. Tissues find their way into my hand and I sniff and wipe my nose. His hands brush the hair off my face and he looks me over, making sure I'm not hurt anywhere else. Then he lifts my gown and sees the large bandage. His lips thin and his cobalt eyes turn dark and stormy. He's not happy about this. At all.

"I'm so sorry. I should've been more careful. I ... this has never happened before and I didn't know what to do. I should've been more prepared or more cautious ..." His hand gently grabs my shoulder and gives it a little shake. My eyes meet his and they soften.

"Babe, this is not your fault. Do you hear me? You have nothing to be sorry for. I'm sorry you got hurt and I'd like to kill the motherfucker that did this to you."

"He's not worth your time. Besides, my knee gave him bruised balls with."

He chuckles. "Does this mean you'll come stay with me again?"

Does he want me to? Can I go through this again? Can I be what he wants me to be? Probably not. I won't ever be that girl until my mom straightens up and goes to rehab. But as long as I have to support her and her habit, I'm trapped in this rotten life of mine.

"As much as I want to say yes, you know I can't. You hate what I am and I hate what it does to you. I'm so sorry for everything, Reese. You don't deserve this. You're too good for someone like me."

"That's fucking bullshit and you know it. I'm a recovering drug addict. Do you have any idea of some of the things I've done? The lows I've stooped to just to get high. No, you can't know. So don't pull this shit about me being too good for you. If anything, *I* don't *deserve* you. That's right, Skylar. Maybe you're too good for me. But let's be real here. Bottom line, you won't leave your mom. You won't force her to make the decision to give up using. To go to rehab. You enable her. You *allow* her to buy. Hell, you give her the money to do it. And *that's* the real issue. Yeah, I hate the fact that other men see what only *I* want to see. And I hate the fact that I want to be the *only* one you dance for. But what I hate even more than that is you're not willing to make your mom give it up … or even try. She's done her best to fuck up your life and you keep letting her to do it. You lie down and let her walk all over you. So now you know. And before you start in with the—oh you don't know how it is. Just remember one thing. I *do* know how it is because I've been there myself."

He leaves me with nothing to say because he's right. I know it, he knows it, and he knows I know it.

"Life's tough, Skylar. It's not a cakewalk. It's a road paved with pieces of broken glass and half the time you're not wearing shoes while you walk through it. But eventually your feet toughen up and it gets easier and easier. Call me when you're ready to do something about your mom. I can help. That's the one thing I *do* know something about. That and my feelings for you."

He kisses my forehead and walks out of the room, leaving me with my turbulent thoughts and my body twisted with emotion. The sound of the squeaking door makes my head jerk up. Has he changed his mind? My heart crashes to the floor when I see it's Cara walking back in.

"I heard everything. He's right, you know."

"Yes, damn it! I know he's right! All of you are right! What more do you want from me?"

"It's not what we want, Sky. It's what you want. Do you really want to go through life, carrying on like this? Look at yourself. You're so in love with that guy it's ridiculous. How long is it going to take before you admit it? And then the question is how long can you keep up the pretense with your clients? J.D.'s already busted on you. He's not going to keep letting you get away with it. It's going to crash down around you sooner or later."

"What can I do?"

"Well, for one, get pissed off at the woman who birthed you. She should've taken care of you, instead of the other way around. Let her know you're through. Then get a legit job. Go to school. And dance. Dance your big heart out. That's what you want to do anyway. It's what you've always wanted to do. You've got the talent. Go for it."

The next morning, after a sleepless night, the doctor comes and examines me. He proclaims I'm free to go home. The stitches will need to be removed in a week to ten days but other than that, I'm good as gold. It takes forever for them to complete my paperwork, but a nurse shows up in my room with a wheelchair.

"What's that for?"

"Hospital policy."

"But I can walk."

She shrugs so I get in and she wheels me to the entrance. Talk about feeling goofy. She deposits me outside the hospital doors, where I stand and start walking home. What a load of crap rule is that?

My apartment is only ten blocks from the hospital so I decide to hoof it all the way. I only make it a couple of blocks when I hear a sexy voice that sends chills down my spine.

"You sure you're okay to be walking this far? I was just on my way to see you."

He strides right next to me. "I'm fine, Reese. Really. And yeah, they released me."

He must think I'm weak because he picks up my arm and tucks it into the crook of his own. "Are you in any pain?"

"Not really. Just a little sore."

He doesn't say anything for a little bit but then, "I'm sorry for the way I spoke to you yesterday."

"Don't be. You're right. We both know it."

"Still ... I'm sorry. I shouldn't have been so hard on you. Especially right after you were attacked. That was wrong of me."

"'S'okay. You made me think. Fact is, I haven't slept a wink all night. Part of me is afraid to talk to her for fear of what she'll do to herself. But the other part of the issue is that she's mean, Reese."

"What're you saying? Does she hit you?"

"She tries, but it's nothing I can't control. But that's not what I meant. She's mean and won't listen. She shuts down."

"Don't I know that well. She doesn't want to hear the truth of it all. That's why she's doing it. I can help."

"Thanks. But I need to try this by myself first. If she won't come around on her own, I may take you up on it."

"Okay. You know where to find me, Skylar. Anytime, day or night."

He leaves me at the entrance to the run down building that I call home. My dread of being back here increases with each step I take. But this has to be done. I can't go on like this. I've finally come to realize that my life is every bit as important as hers and if I don't do this, neither one of us will have a life left to live.

Twenty-Two

Reese

SHE WALKS UP THE STEPS AS I STAND THERE AND WATCH. FISTS clenched by my side, I can't bring myself to walk away. My phone buzzes and pulls me out of my trance. It's Case.

"Hey, man. Where are you?"

"Just walked Skylar home."

"They released her attacker. On some technicality."

"You've got to be kidding me? There were several witnesses. He tried to rape her. He fucking stabbed her."

"Calm down, man. I know what he did. Don't shoot the messenger. I just wanted you to know."

"Find out where he lives."

"Oh man. Don't go there, Reese. You could end up in prison."

"Case. I know what I'm doing. Find his address. If you don't, I'll get someone else to."

"Shit, man. You're always backing me up against a wall."

"That fuck will do this again. You *know* he will. I'm gonna make sure he doesn't. That's all."

"Goddammit."

Stupid court system. Always protecting the criminals. That's why I'm going to law school. I'm going to make things change ... in favor of the victims. I don't care what I have to do, or how long it takes. It shouldn't take a year for these violent offenders to go to trial. Or for a rapist to be set free. This is bullshit.

I hurry to class because I have a full schedule today. My goals have changed since last year. When I started classes, I waffled through the process, not having any idea of what I wanted to do. Everything's different now. There's a burning desire in my gut to do something. To make a difference. And I'm going to make that happen.

Case texts me later that afternoon with an address on my buddy. After I hit the library and complete my studies for the night, I check out his place. He lives in a not-so-nice part of Brooklyn. He's easy to track and not very subtle about how he dresses. Flashy. White flat brimmed ball cap. White T-shirt with black lettering. Baggy jeans. Gold chains. White tennis shoes. Swaggers. Thinks he's hot shit. That's about to come to an end.

He walks for a couple of blocks and I tail him. When he turns the corner is when I strike. He's on a deserted street, dark with no one around. I shove him into an empty doorway, face first, and handcuff him. Then I put a burlap sack over his head and commence to beat the crap out of him. My fist connects with his cheek, feeling the resistance of bone. That's not going to stop me. This man becomes my punching bag. I'm on automatic: jab, cross, hook, uppercut. Bones crunch beneath my gloved fists. His breath rasps, and I stop right before he loses consciousness.

"Don't ever attempt to rape another woman, or the next time, I'll cut your balls off and shove 'em down your throat."

He slumps against the wall as I remove the handcuffs and walk away. As soon as I'm home, I ice my hands, but the gloves will help with the prevention of swelling and bruising. My friend will be hurting for days after this. Hopefully, the next time he thinks about hurting a woman, he'll think about this beating first.

NA MEETS EVERY NIGHT. WHEN I FIRST STARTED, I USED TO go every day. I don't anymore. Now I go whenever I need it. Lately, my attendance has increased. Case mentioned that his most crucial time was at the eighteenth month. Mine seems to be at the thirteenth. Thoughts of Skylar have me messed up. Some days I want to use so bad I can even taste the bitterness of the coke on the back of my tongue. I can feel the tang of the crack when I inhale and I imagine the smell of weed in my nostrils. Just to have that numbing effect fill my body makes me go out of my head with need. I live on the edge all the time. Spending three or four hours in the gym isn't helping any more. My legs are constantly in motion. Thump, thump, thump.

When I walk in, Dot heads me off and shoves me in the corner. "You look like shit."

She never was one for beating around the bush. Always went straight for the kill.

"Oh, hi Dot. Nice to see you, too."

"What are you doing? Getting ready for Mr. America? You look like an animal."

"Fuck off. I remember a time when you gave me shit for not working hard enough."

"Yeah, well, that's when you were acting like a pussy. Seriously, what's going on with you? You're not using, are you?"

My breath whistles as I blow it out between my tightened lips. "No. And if I ever get to that point, I promise I'll call you and Case first."

"You know I really do care about you, right?"

"Yeah."

"You need to talk to someone. Here."

She crams a sticky note in my hand. I look at her and shake my head.

"Not this again?"

"Look what happened last time."

"Did Case put you up to this?"

"Maybe. But what if he did? He only has your best interests at heart."

"I'm not interested in that psychobabble bullshit."

"Reese, she's good. Really good. I wouldn't tell you to call her otherwise."

"She? So *she's* gonna dig around in my head and all that shit? I don't know about that."

"Why do you have to be such a dick? It's not like that. Just go talk to her. Once. Then if you don't like her, call it a day. Please. I'm asking you to do this for Case and me."

"Okay. One time."

Dot smiles. What the hell did I just agree to? Now I'm going to have some shrink rooting around in my head, making me feel all sorts of shit I don't want to feel. Damn Dot and her meddling.

"Don't look at me like that," she says.

How does she do that? *She* should've been the damn shrink. I head to the coffee pot. Her voice hits me from right over my shoulder.

"And stay away from caffeine. You look like you just hit the meth pipe."

My head swivels and I shoot her the nastiest look I can muster.

She shrugs. "Sorry, but it's the truth." And she walks away.

My hand automatically reaches for a bottled water instead.

That night, as I lay in bed, insomnia suffocates me. Thoughts of Skylar and how she lives tear into me. It's so disturbing, I end up pacing most of the night. When eight a.m. hits, I tap in the numbers for Dr. Gabriella Martinelli.

A soft voice answers and I ask to make an appointment. She must hear the desperation in my tone, so she sets it for that afternoon. It surprises me I'm able to get in that quickly, but I'm thankful. After I shower, I head to class.

At three, I'm sitting in Dr. Martinelli's office. When her door opens and she calls me in, I'm surprised at how young she appears. She laughs and says, "I can tell by that look, you're surprised, Mr. Christianson. I suppose you expected some bespectacled old woman?"

That's exactly what I expected. "Uh, yeah."

"Come on in and have a seat."

She leads me into a small but cheery office. No desk, but two comfortable chairs that face each other.

"And you don't get to lie down and fall asleep either."

I laugh. She puts me at ease.

"So, just a bit about myself. I'm fairly fresh out of my residency. I trained at Bellevue and worked a ton with substance abusers. That's probably how you got my name."

"And how did you know I was a substance abuser?"

"Look at you. You're jittery and rubbing your arms. You look like you're withdrawing. Are you?"

"No. I did that thirteen months ago. I'm dealing with something altogether different now, which makes me want to use again."

She takes my personal history and we go from there. Two hours later, I leave. She wanted to give me a prescription for an antidepressant but I refused.

"No drugs." I'm firm about this.

"Fine. It'll be harder without them. Your need to fight is worrisome."

"I can control it."

"Reese, Skylar has chosen her path. You have to decide if you want her in your life with the decisions she's made. You can't control her. You can only control yourself. And this *is* what it's all about, isn't it? You want her to change her lifestyle. You want her to quit enabling her mother. And while you're correct in what you say, those are *her* choices and hers alone. What you have to decide is if you want her in your life as is. That's what love is all about anyway. It's accepting someone just as they are without changing them. Taking them with all of their flaws. Think about this: if she accepts you, she's not exactly getting the perfect guy, now is she?"

"No, she's not. She's getting a fucked-up piece of shit."

"I wouldn't go that far. What I would say is that she's getting a human being that has issues too. One that she won't be able to control either."

"But when we were together, I felt balanced."

"And you knew about her choices. So what changed?"

My brain goes back to that day at Luna Park. The day she told me all about her life growing up. And how I wanted to protect her. How I ached inside for what she'd been through. And I tell Dr. Martinelli.

"Reese, you realized you're in love with her. And that's when you recognized you didn't want to share her anymore. Is that right?"

"Yeah, I guess."

"No, no guessing. What is it?"

"Yes, I love her."

"Then tell her."

"I don't know if I can. Because I don't think I'm good enough for her."

Dr. Martinelli stares at me for a second. "So really it's about *your* self-worth then."

"I don't know."

"Yes you do, Reese. Tell me."

I'm on my feet faster than I can even think.

Dr. Martinelli's calm voice stops me. "Two things, Reese. We have to get to the bottom of this, and we will, painful as it may be. It will help you in the long run. Will you hate me? Probably. But in the end, you'll thank me. The other—if you need me, call. Any time, day or night, I'm available. Here's my number." Her hand is extended and between two fingers is a card. It's blank, with the exception of ten digits. "I mean it, Reese. Call if you need to talk. And I'll see you in a week."

I don't ever want to come back here again. The first stop I make is the restroom, where I puke my guts out. She's disturbed something deep inside of me that I don't even care to begin the process of digging through. How the hell am I going to get through this? This was a very bad idea.

Twenty-Three

Skylar

TODAY IS MY BIRTHDAY BUT I WISH I HADN'T REMEMBERED. Mom is waiting for me when I get home. After the attack, I went home for a couple of nights, but then decided to crash at Jimmy's, and then Cara's. So now I'm back at home and she's drunk, a bottle of vodka in her hand.

"Where the hell have you been? I've been waiting for you for two days. I'm out. All out." No, *Happy Birthday, Skylar*, for me.

Her hands shake and she rocks back and forth. As I look around I notice how dirty the place is. I was gone for two nights and she was able to trash it this fast.

"Where's your stash? You had plenty when I left here the night before last."

"Don't you question me, girl. I'm your mother."

The cabinet where she keeps her drugs is empty. Nothing. She had enough meth and crack in there to last her another week, at least. She must've given it to someone.

"Mom, what happened to your supply?"

"None of your damn business, girl."

This is it. She just added that final straw. You know, it's not the last straw that breaks that poor camel's back. It's the load he's been lugging around for years and then finally some dumb jerk adds one more tiny straw, and doesn't think it'll matter. But it does. Boy does it ever. That poor creature's spine snaps and he's dead. Bam. Just like that. Well, this girl's spine isn't going to break. Instead, I stiffen the darn thing and walk up to my mom, snatch that vodka bottle out of her hand and throw it across the room. Then I grab her shirt by the collar and haul her ass off the threadbare chair her butt is planted on.

"You listen to me, Mom, and listen good. I'm done. Through. This is it. I almost got raped a few nights ago dancing, in order to earn money to support your lousy drug habit. And then I got stabbed because I fought back. See?" I yank my shirt up, exposing my bandaged ribs. "But this is the end of the line. I'm not doing it anymore. You understand what I'm telling you? I quit! I'm finished with you and your drugged up life. If you won't go to rehab and get help, then fine. Find a way to get your own stupid drugs. I'm not funding your addiction any longer." I release her shirt and she falls back into the chair, creating a slight breeze. Jeez she stinks.

"You can't mean that."

"Oh, but I do," I snarl. "I'm so over your crap, it's not even funny. Sleeping with men, doing things that make me want to vomit. For this? I'm beyond finished. You want 'em. You get 'em yourself."

"But Skylar, you know how much I need my medicine. Please, baby, help your Mama." Her whiney voice grates on my very last nerve and it takes all my strength not to take a swing at her.

"Stop saying that. It's not medicine. My 'Mama' needs rehab for her addiction. Not me buying her drugs. Get real, Mom. You're sick, and you need to face it. And you smell like a skunk.

When was your last shower?" I march into my room and start to clean it up. Then I look at my bed. Now I am furious.

Through clenched teeth I say, "Get out of here. How *dare* you bring men into *my room*." Then I yell, "*Get out of this house!*" My voice reverberates off the wall and my throat hurts from screaming so loud. She whimpers behind me, but I'm past reason. My hands latch onto her shirt once again, and I push her out of the apartment. A vein throbs in my temple because I'm so angry. Then I lock the door behind her. She starts to pound and pound.

"Let me in, you whore. Let me in!"

I ignore her. She bangs all afternoon. My hands are gloved up as I rip all the sheets off the bed. Then I bleach everything in the bathroom and the rest of the house. Any surface that can possibly be contaminated, I put bleach to it.

The laundry room is two levels down, but I've no choice if I want clean sheets to sleep on and clean towels for a shower. Bundling everything up in the laundry bag, I head out. She's lying in the hall as I leave.

"Let me back in," she begs.

"No." I march on past her and stay down there until my chore is complete. Then I return home and she's still there.

"I need a fix, baby. Pleeeeeease. I'll be good. I promise."

"Then go to rehab. Cuz you're not coming back here. Narcotics Anonymous isn't far from here. They'll help you. Go on. Scram."

"Why you little bitch." She tries to get up, but I'm back inside before she can manage it.

Then I break down and call Reese.

"Skylar?"

Through my tears, I explain that I've kicked her out and she's in the hallway on the floor. Withdrawing, most likely.

"What do you want me to do?"

"I don't know. I don't even know what to do with her."

"Want me to come over?"

"Would you?"

"On my way."

Thirty minutes later, he knocks and I open up.

"This isn't good. She can't walk."

"Does she need to go to the hospital?" I ask.

"That would be my best suggestion."

"Okay."

He hails a cab and we take her to the hospital. On the way he asks what she takes. I tell him about the meth, coke and crack. Also the vodka.

"The alcohol withdrawal is the most dangerous. Let the medical staff handle the withdrawal. Then she'll need to decide what she wants to do. And Skylar, you did the right thing."

My mom smells so bad, I have to pinch my nose. The odor permeates the cab. "God, she stinks something awful."

"Yeah. I've smelled worse though."

"Thank you, Reese."

He smiles.

I glance down and notice that I'm wearing my fuzzy bunny slippers. I didn't even think to put on shoes. Reese follows my line of sight and laughs.

"Nice."

My failed attempt at a laugh prompts him. "It's going to be okay."

"She's not allowed back in my house. She let her nasty men sleep in my bed. She had sex in there with them." I feel the bile rising up again. My hand covers my mouth as I force it back down.

My mom starts moaning. Her greasy gray hair hangs in strings around her face. She's skin and bones and her skin is sallow.

Reese's hand is on mine, his thumb moving back and forth. Turning my hand over, I lace my fingers with his and hold on tightly. He responds. The cab pulls up to the emergency room entrance and we get out, Reese carrying my smelly mother.

He's just risen up dozens of levels in my mind. What kind of guy does this? Most would run like their butts are on fire and not look back. I pay the cab driver and follow Reese inside. He knows the drill because he explains to the lady at the window what's going on in detailed terms. Someone wheels out a gurney and then takes my mom back. Now we sit and wait.

"Can I get you some water?"

"No, thanks."

"Skylar, you did the right thing by forcing her out. Look at me." My head slants up to his and his brilliant cobalt eyes grab mine. "Believe me, please. I know you don't feel like it right now. But you did."

"My anger took over, Reese. I shoved her out the door. Literally. She yelled and screamed but I wouldn't let her back in. Then I took all the nasty bedding and towels to the laundry room …" I shudder. His arms wrap around me and hold me against his warmth. My hands hug his waist and I bury my face in his chest. God, I love the way he smells. "What if she dies?"

"I doubt she will. But if she does, she chose to live this way. You have to remember that people make choices for all different reasons. She decided on this path when she knew better. Remember that, babe."

"I miss you, Reese. Every day."

His arms tighten their hold. My disappointment mounts when he doesn't say anything.

"What happens next?" I ask.

He walks me through the steps, how they'll keep her until she's done with detox and then they'll most likely recommend a rehab facility.

"Is that what you did."

"Yeah. I went somewhere out of state, but there are places associated with the hospital. And then she'll need to go to NA."

"What if she refuses?"

"That's a very real possibility. And that's what you'll have to face. Are you strong enough to say no to her? Can you keep her from moving back in if she doesn't agree to all of it? This is where tough love comes in."

"Right now I hate her."

"That'll pass."

The doctor calls my name. Reese joins me. He pretty much repeats what Reese told me. I leave him my cell phone number and tell him to call me when she's ready to be released. I don't want to talk to her until then.

"One other thing, Ms. O'Donnell. Your mother has liver disease. It's from the alcohol abuse. She doesn't need to drink anymore."

"No surprise there, doctor."

Reese and I leave. We walk in silence. I feel bad about these thoughts, but I don't want her to come home. Ever.

"You'll change."

"How did you know ...?"

"Just did. And don't feel guilty. You have every reason to hate her."

Stopping, I turn and throw myself in his arms. "You're the biggest reason. If not for her, I'd be with you right now." Then I pull away and run all the way home.

Busying myself, I put the sheets back on the bed, but I know I'll never sleep on it again. They're balled up in my hands as I stare at them. The couch will be my bed until I can get a new one. Matter of fact, it's time to dump this whole apartment. Hunting for a new one becomes my day's obsession. I pour over online ads and make several appointments for the next day. These are all for 1 bedroom units. Mom is on her own. I'm leaving her with no place to live so she has no choice.

Later that afternoon J.D. calls and I tell him I quit. He's not surprised, but he's genuinely sad. And in a way, so am I. J.D. rescued me from Mikey all those years ago. He spied Mikey slapping me around one night and sent one of his bodyguards in and took me away forever. Mikey never came after me or bothered me again. J.D. offered me a job at *Exotique-A*, contingent upon my ability to dance. Then he put me to work in a safe environment, where drugs weren't involved and all my customers were decent guys. Yeah, they have some weird fetishes, but they've never laid an unwanted hand on me or did anything I didn't agree to. J.D. saw that I was well cared for and he also made sure I earned top dollar for my services. He allowed me to call the shots, too, as far as what I was willing to do. So I've had it pretty good with him.

"You ever change your mind, baby doll, you come see Big Daddy. He'll help you out. You hear?"

"I hear and thanks Big Daddy. I'm gonna miss you." And it was the truth.

"You too, doll baby, you too."

Now I have to get a real job. This is what scares me the most. My education is absent. I never graduated from high school. Back to the computer. I check into what it takes to get a GED. Apparently I have to fill out some forms online, so I begin that lengthy process.

At about six in the evening, my stomach hollers out. Hell, I haven't eaten all day long. After checking all the cabinets and the refrigerator, I head out for a bite to eat.

There's a pizza joint a few blocks away that makes awesome pizza. I walk inside and Reese is seated in a booth, chatting with a very attractive dark haired woman. His brow is furrowed, like he's upset about something. My legs are frozen. He looks up and our eyes lock. My breath jams in my lungs. My face tingles, maybe because I need oxygen. I don't know. I do know I need to get the hell out of here. But my idiotic legs won't respond to my mental commands. *Go legs! Move. Now!*

Oh, God, no! He's getting up and walking toward me. And finally, praise Jesus, whatever vice grip was attached to my legs, releases and I turn and dart out the door.

"Wait! Skylar!"

Run, legs run! Go, faster! All I know is that I have to get away from him. Anything, I can handle anything: tossing my mom out on the street while she's in withdrawal; almost getting raped; getting stabbed; quitting my job, my only source of income. But I can't deal with seeing Reese chatting it up with another woman. A beautiful woman at that. Now I understand why he didn't respond when I told him I missed him. Oh God, I've made such an utter fool of myself.

Run, I keep telling my brain. And I do. I don't know how long or how far. But when I stop, it's dark. And I'm alone on some deserted street. In a section of town I'm unfamiliar with. *Crap!* What have I done? My head darts around, hunting for a street sign. I spot one in the distance and head for it. Oh my God. I've run all the way to the end of Manhattan. I need to get back so I start jogging, and my side aches tremendously. When I'm close to home, I breeze through a grocery store and grab some items to eat. I don't even make it out the door before I tear into the bag of chocolate covered peanuts. The candies have me so engrossed, I don't even notice the large figure hunkered on my steps. He stands when I get there.

"Skylar."

Gasp! Those candies are choking me now.

"Well shit." He spins me, and puts his arm below my sternum.

Heimlich. He knows I'm choking.

Once, twice, and a gooey peanut flies out of my mouth. I cough some and then I turn and punch him in the arm. Hard. Right before I start to cry. What the heck is wrong with me? I don't want to cry. I want to act like I'm fine and strong and that I don't care that he's seeing someone else. But my stupid darn tear ducts won't listen.

He grabs my hand and tugs me up the steps. When we get to my door he holds a hand out for my keys and I hand them to him without a word. I am such a weak pussy butt. I have no strength when it comes to Reese, and I hate myself right now.

We walk inside. He takes my groceries and puts them away. Then motions for me to sit. And like a stupid puppy dog, I obey.

The only thing missing is a leash. I wonder if George would lend me his leash and harness?

He makes a glass of ice water and hands it to me.

"Drink."

Why isn't my tongue hanging out with my tail wagging and me panting? Of course, I drink the glass of water.

"Wanna tell me what happened back there?"

"No."

"Skylar." There's a warning edge to his voice.

"You have to ask?" My snarky side emerges.

One side of his mouth curls up. "Uh, yeah. You see, I'm sitting in my favorite pizza place, having a meltdown with *my shrink,* and in you walk. And then you turn around and haul ass. Hell, Skylar, I couldn't even keep up with you. You ever run track? You friends with Usain Bolt or something?'

His shrink? He was eating pizza with *his shrink?*

"Your shrink? As in psychiatrist?"

"Yep. Dr. Martinelli. She works a lot with substance abusers. In fact, I was gonna recommend her for your mom. But no, you take off like someone lit a firecracker up your ass. So you gonna tell me what that's all about?" He's smirking now.

God, I'm such a loser.

"Uh, yeah, I thought I left the oven on."

"So, you what? Decided to go somewhere else first? Cuz I've been here for an hour."

I drop my head in embarrassment.

"Skylar, were you jealous?"

"Yes. No. I don't know. Hurt. Oh darn. I saw you there with her and it just hurt me. So I ran."

That beautiful mouth of his breaks into a big grin. My stomach tightens and a current zips down to my core. My breath rushes out and I lick my suddenly dry lips.

"Now you know how I feel."

"I quit. My jobs. I called J.D. and told him. And I'm hunting for a new job. But I have to get my GED." This is so embarrassing. My head drops down again and my face burns like fire.

His fingers are beneath my chin and they lift it, forcing me to meet his eyes.

"Why the long face?"

"I'm a drop out."

"So? I'm a drug addict."

"So? I'm a stripper?"

We laugh. Then his mouth catches mine in a kiss that melts the clothing right off of me. Or so it seems. Somehow I'm naked and he's feasting on my granite-like nipples.

"God, you taste so good. Sweet and salty."

"Reese, I need to shower. I ran and got all sweaty."

"Love sweaty."

"No. I'm not clean."

"I like you dirty. Besides, I want to do the dirty to you." He stands and removes his shirt, then pants. His muscles stand out, powerfully. He's so much more sculpted now than before. Huge.

His cock is fully erect and my mouth waters at the sight of it. I wrap my hand around it, and its heat makes my desire spike. He sits on the edge of the sofa and says, "Face away from me and ride it. I know you're already wet, aren't you, babe? Work your slickness around my head, and then sit on me." He commands, I obey. I inch down on him and it seems like forever since I've felt this kind of ecstasy. His cock stretches me until I don't think I can take anymore and then he starts thrusting. I'm just about to topple over that ledge, when he stops and lifts me off of him.

"What are you doing?" I whine.

"Prolonging your pleasure." He grins.

"I don't care about that. I just wanna come."

"Oh, you will, Skylar. You will. Turn around and face me."

He puts my legs around his waist. Then he starts that motion again. His cock moves so deep I want to scream. He touches me in places that I love . Nerve endings spring to life and shoot their pleasure currents into me.

"Kiss me." I do and I'm lost in the combined sensations of his tongue against my tongue and his cock sliding in and out of me. While we kiss, he takes my legs and puts them over his shoulders and now he's even deeper, he's at the pleasure-pain threshold and I'm getting ready to tumble into another orgasm.

He rolls my nipples and I moan. Then he squeezes them until they hurt. Soon they become numb from his pinches.

"Now ride me hard, baby."

I ride him hard and fast and in the middle of my joy ride, he releases my nipples and I scream as I come.

"Ohmigod, ohmigod, ohmigod!" Then he takes his finger and flicks my nub. Over and over. And I slip into that wonderful land of climax-ville. His hands grip my ass cheeks, spreading them as he rocks his hips fast and hard into my slick sex. He groans as he comes, and I feel his warmth spurt into me. His lips caress my neck and move to my mouth, where he hungrily kisses me, fucking my mouth and taking everything in that kiss he possibly can.

Then he stops and murmurs against me, "I've missed the hell out of you too, Skylar."

Best birthday present ever.

Twenty-Four

Reese

THIS ISN'T SUPPOSED TO BE HAPPENING ... I WANT SKYLAR
with every living and breathing molecule in my body. But I'm so
fucked up right now; I don't think the timing is right. Dr.
Martinelli has convinced me I have some issues that need to be
dealt with before I can function in a healthy relationship. But
what about her? Her background is every bit as screwed up
as mine.

Dr. Martinelli eyes drill me as she waits. "Reese, tell me.
You've been vacillating on this too long."

Sometimes I want to strangle the woman. But she's good. She
sees through all my bullshit ... all my smoke and mirrors.

"Yeah, okay. I was little. Maybe five or six. It didn't mean
much then. I overheard my mom and dad. They were arguing,
about my mom and her ballet. She was good. The principal
dancer at one time. My aunt claims there was no one like her ...
ever. The most stunning lines ... curves and leaps ... and she

183

could hold a position forever. That's very difficult, you know. Your muscles are exhausted and frazzled to the extreme from everything they've been through and the final movement is no movement at all. It's still … a freezing of the body in a position in which the human body was never meant to be." Lost in images of myself doing the same, my mind drifts.

"Reese, you still with me?" She snaps her finger in front of my face. "Keep going." Her soft voice brings me back.

Rubbing my face, I say, "Sorry. Anyway, my parents were arguing and my mom said something like, 'It's all his fault. I can't do it anymore. My body's different. My hips don't move the same.' And my dad was arguing back, disagreeing with her. And they went on and on. Doors slammed and I could hear my mom crying. I asked my dad why they were yelling and he shouted at me to go and play with my toys. It scared me so I ran to my room. I wasn't used to hearing them yell at each other. I hid in the closet and stayed there for a long time until he came and found me. He pretended everything was fine, but he took me that night and to stay with my aunt for a while. When I came home, my dad said that my mom wouldn't be dancing any more. The older I got, the more it made sense. Then one day, I came right out and asked my mom. She denied it, so I went to the person I could always count on. Aunt Emmy. She told me that my mom was angry, not because she got pregnant with me and that her body changed, but because she never intended on loving me so much. I didn't believe her. My mom's true love was ballet and she never intended to get pregnant. I killed her career. I ruined her plans. She pretty much let me know that too. If it hadn't been for Aunt Emmy, I would never have been allowed to dance. She snuck me out of the house and took me to lessons. She persuaded my mom to enroll me in the different dance academies. And then when it came down to it, she was the one who bargained with them to allow me to go to London to train with the Royal Ballet School. After that when I wanted to diversify my training into contemporary, Aunt Emmy was the one who made them understand the importance of moving to the Joffrey Ballet School. When I started auditioning, my mom told me I didn't have what it took to make it to the lead. That I would never become the principal dancer. She never believed in me. And I knew it. It was my Aunt Emmy I would dance for. Not my mom or my dad. My dad was better, but he would've rather I'd been aiming for goals as a New York Ranger. So now you know."

"That's it?"

"Yeah. Me. The unwanted kid."

"That's all you got for me? No molesting by some toothless uncle? No fondling by some sweet old aunt or nanny?"

"No, damn it. My mom didn't want me. She got pregnant and I ruined her career."

"I'm throwing you under the bus on that one, Reese. She might have whined and maybe felt sorry for herself because none of her contemporaries had to go home and be energetic after a long day of practice or whatever for a child the way she did. Think about it. You lived that life. You know how draining it was. Now think how hard it would be to take care of a child on top of it. But you want to know the truth? Your aunt was dead on right. If your mom wanted to dance, she would've let the damn nanny raise you and danced her heart out. But the truth of it is, she loved you more than she loved dancing and it bowled her over. She never expected it. So, my dear, the unwanted became the wanted. And the loved. She probably didn't want you to go to London because— how old were you when you went?"

"Twelve."

"Well jeez. I would never let a kid of mine go away to school, overseas no less, at the age of twelve. Are you kidding me? That would destroy me. And perhaps she wanted to dissuade you from that life because she knew what kind of a toll it takes on a human being. And she realized how much of life you'd miss growing up. All the teen stuff. Prom, girlfriends, school events, that sort of thing."

She's debunked my theory and throws it back in my face in a matter of minutes.

"Get over yourself already and move on."

"Aren't you being a little harsh?"

"Life's harsh, Reese. You of all people should know that."

Boy do I ever.

"While you mull that one over, let me run through this whole thing again. Mom gets pregnant and has Reese. Quits ballet. Dad wants a hockey player. Gets a ballet dancer instead. Reese thinks he's not loved. Oh, wait. Were your parents ever cruel to you?"

"Of course not."

"Just verifying you weren't abused."

"Stop being an ass."

"Only if you stop feeling sorry for yourself. Here's the deal. You're one hell of a package. So you dropped down the rabbit hole and spent some time in Wonderland. However, you figured out that it wasn't so wonderful after all. You got your head together ... well, partly ... and straightened up. You're back in school and you have one heck of a goal, my friend. Give up that vigilante crap and you're good to go. Quit worrying about how unworthy you are for Skylar and do something about your relationship with her. Help *her*. You have the ability to do that."

"But she's got issues."

Dr. Martinelli shrugs. "Issues shmissues. I have issues, you have issues, the world has issues. Who doesn't?"

"Hers are terrible."

"She seems like she's handling everything just fine. You're the one who has issues with *her* issues."

"But, she's ..."

"Reese, you can't fix her. She's not a plastic toy with a cracked doohickey. You're not in here to discuss Skylar's issues. You're here to talk about yourself. Now what else for today?"

My shrink shut me down.

"Thank you." I stand to leave.

"Reese, how are your compulsions?"

"Much better."

"No urges?"

"No, ma'am."

She inspects me. "Are you having sex?"

This is unexpected.

"Well?"

"Yes."

"With Skylar?"

"Of course. Who else would I be having sex with?"

She narrows her eyes. "Reese, I'm not blind. I'm sure you could have your pick of any number of women."

"Not interested."

"Be careful with Skylar. You're in love with her."

My ass plops back in the chair. My throat feels like a clamp is crushing it.

"Right you are, as always, Doc."

"She doesn't know, does she?"

"I imagine she suspects it, but I haven't told her."

"You're both fragile right now. You know where to reach me if you need me."

My mind is munching on everything she just fed me. All this time I've been groveling around, feeling sorry for myself because of my mom. How did she figure everything out in a few minutes? And Aunt Emmy—she was right all along. Which reminds me, I need to call her. She's left me two messages and I haven't called her. Later ... right now my brain needs to process everything from this session.

SKYLAR LEFT ME A TEXT AND WHEN I CHECK IT, IT'S ABOUT her mom. Something's happened. As soon as she answers the phone, her voice tells me what I need to know.

"I'm on the way." I hop in the first cab I can and meet her in the ICU waiting room.

"What happened?" I ask.

"Her heart. It went into some weird rhythm or something and they don't know if she's going to make it." Her body sinks into mine as she shudders with the force of her tears. "Oh, Reese, this is my fault. I shouldn't have left her in the hallway so long."

"Shhh, babe. This is not your fault. Her heart was probably weakened from all the years of drug and alcohol abuse. You can't use like she did and expect not to have some kind of consequences on your body. Look at her liver. This was her choice."

Skylar looks so sad I want to erase all of her hurt. This dirty mess her mother's made, and now her life is hanging by a thread, angers me. For everything she's put her daughter through, this is the icing on the cake. There is a row of chairs close by so I walk to them, bringing Skylar with me. When we get there I sit and have her sit too.

"How long have you been here?"

"I don't know. A few hours, maybe."

Tucking her into my side, I put her head on my shoulder. "Everything's going to be fine."

We sit together, just like that. Not much later, the doctor comes out and calls her name.

"Ms. O'Donnell?" She flies to her feet and I follow her.

"I'm sorry. We did everything possible. We simply couldn't get your mother's heart to maintain a normal rhythm. She had several seizures, which is typical in cases such as hers, but her heart must've been too weakened by all the drug abuse. Her heart couldn't withstand everything she'd put her body through and the liver damage only made things worse. Would you like to see her?"

"No, I want to remember her as she was before this. When she wasn't an addict."

"I understand. We'll have some paperwork for you and then

we'll need to know what you want to do with her," the doctor says.

"Do with her?"

"Her ..."

"Skylar, a funeral service, babe." Skylar's eyes register pain. Then it settles in and she squeezes them shut as tears dribble past. She buries her face in my shirt.

"Doctor, we'll figure it out."

"Thank you. And I'm terribly sorry for your loss."

"Thanks."

Once the floodgate closes, but while she's still wrapped in my arms, I ask, "Do you have a funeral preference?"

Her head shakes back and forth. "No funeral. Mom had no friends. I don't know of anyone that would come. I want her cremated and I'll put her ashes somewhere. I don't even know of a place that was important to her. The only things she cared about were drugs and vodka. Maybe I could find a poppy field somewhere. Or maybe a liquor store."

Her humor makes me smile and she chuckles for a moment.

"Skylar, would you like to talk with Dr. Martinelli? I know you feel you're to blame, but you're not. Maybe talking to a professional would help you see things more clearly."

"Maybe, but I sure I can't afford her."

"She'll work with you. Let me call her for you after we get this cremation thing settled."

"Thank you, Reese."

Soon, a nurse meets us and expresses her condolences. Then she hands Skylar some papers to sign and we make arrangements with a mortuary.

We leave the hospital and during our walk home, I call my shrink and explain the situation. She says she'll gladly talk with Skylar. I hand my phone over to her and they set up an appointment. Well, isn't this nice? One big happy family at Dr. Martinelli's. Maybe we can all go together for a group session, I chuckle to myself.

Twenty-Five

Skylar

ALTHOUGH IT'S BEEN AGES SINCE MOM WENT TO CENTRAL Park, it was the only place that came to mind when I rummaged through my memories of happier times. Reese and I carry her ashes here on a sunny afternoon and sprinkle them on the edge of the Jacqueline Kennedy Onassis Reservoir. She used to enjoy watching the ducks swim here, so we agree this would be an appropriate spot for her final resting place. Weirdly enough, I feel no sense of sadness, only relief that she's no longer fighting the demons that controlled her.

My appointment with Dr. Martinelli is tomorrow. There are so many things I want to discuss with her. I wonder how she's going to peel the layers of my onion. I almost feel sorry for the poor woman. My lips vibrate with the bubble of laughter that sneaks past.

"Did I just hear you laugh?"

"Yep." Then it gushes out of me.

"What is so funny?"

When I can talk intelligibly, I explain. "Dr. Martinelli is going to think I'm a freak. Oh my gosh. First, the ugly divorce. Then the wicked stepmom. Then the drugged out mom. Then the hooker life. Then the stripping. Holy crap, Reese. She's gonna flip when she hears my mountain of a story. And after I tell her about some of my clients ... ugh!" My hand flies to my mouth as I suck in my breath because I never ever wanted to go there with him.

He shakes his head. "Skylar. I'm not stupid. It's not like I don't have an imagination or can't think about things you did."

"But they never ... I mean ..."

"I know. You told me once. They were never allowed to kiss you or to have intercourse with you."

"When did I tell you that?"

"I don't remember," he hedges.

"No. I never told you. No one knows that. Except J.D. and the clients. No one knows my lists of rules. How did you find that out?"

He shrugs. "I just did."

We've been walking this entire time, but I stop and cross my arms. How the hell did he figure that out? I'm not letting this drop.

"Reese!" He's ahead of me and turns around to look. When he sees that I've stopped, he takes three long steps and stands in front of me.

"Yeah."

It's not a question ... more like a demand. This has to be handled now.

"I demand an answer."

He runs his lower lip between his teeth and damn if he doesn't look hot ... hotter than sin.

"See, here's the thing, Sky." He's never once called me Sky. "I don't do well with demands. Or orders. Yeah, we don't get along too well."

Then damn if he doesn't turn around and start walking again. His tight jeans hug his ass and his shirt clings to the sinews of his back. The man sure is sexy. My core tightens and I squeeze my legs together. He stops, turns and says, "You coming?"

I want to say, *just about.* I scurry to catch up.

His arm extends and he throws it around my shoulders. "You're not going to tell me, are you?"

"Not much to tell. Now let's go home because I suddenly have this urge that needs to be tended to."

Yeah, you're not the only one.

Tilting my head up, I find his eyes are on me. It should be against the law for someone to look this delicious.

My appointment with Dr. Martinelli is the batshit nuttiest thing I've ever done. She listens to the saga of my life and sits there going from tearing up to doing her best not to laugh. Of course, my ridiculous, descriptions of some of my clients are so bizarre, she has trouble believing me initially.

When I get to the point where I describe my sessions with George the howler, that does her in. "Oh, God. I'm sorry, Skylar. But this is ... is this real?" Her hand cups her mouth in a poor attempt to quiet the loud noises erupting from it. No doubt she thinks I'm delusional.

"I tried to warn you, didn't I? And yes, it's real."

"You did. But honest to God, this ought to be a movie!"

"And you haven't even heard about Lester. Lester liked to wear beehive wigs and dress up like a woman. Once I went there and he was all decked out in granny panties and a polka dotted bikini top. He had me chase him around the room yelling, 'Surf's up!' The worst part of all was Lester was the hairiest dude you've ever seen! My eyes!"

"How did you not laugh?"

"I did! I'd cover it up with a coughing fit. It was awful."

"Skylar, in all seriousness, your sense of humor has carried you miles."

"Yeah, well, it didn't help much in dealing with my parental units."

Dr. Martinelli is quiet for a few moments. Then she asks me, "Tell me about your childhood."

Here it goes. Holding nothing back, I give it my all. The worst part is the guilt I feel about my mom.

"Your mom was an adult, before you were even born. She made the decisions that ultimately destroyed her career, her marriage, and unfortunately, you got in the way of it all. I'm sorry you had to live through that, but you can't carry guilt over a decision that wasn't yours."

"But I refused to help her in the end."

"Honestly, the only thing that you could have done differently was refuse to help her sooner. But she was your mother, and that's a very tricky situation to be in. Other than that, you didn't do a single thing wrong. You were trying to be a good daughter. Let me ask you something. And it's a yes or no answer. Is being responsible for your own actions important?"

"Well, yes?"

"Another question. Are you responsible for your own actions or is someone else?"

"I am."

"Think about what you just said. And apply that to your mother."

"Point made."

"Saying all of this is so easy, but shedding the guilt isn't. There are ways to do that. But I want to ask you something else. Do you think your mother was happy?"

"How could she be?"

"I don't think she could. It's going to be very difficult to forget the way she was and the things she did. And normally I would say to remember the good times, but there don't seem to be any. Drugs ruled her life for so long that happiness couldn't have been a part of it. Have you thought about moving into a different place?"

I tell her of my plans and that I've found somewhere else to live.

"That's an excellent step toward progress. Again, I'm not saying this will vanish in a week, but you're certainly on the right track. Now I need to ask you another question. What about your father?"

"What about him?"

"Have you communicated with him at all?"

"No. When he moved me back in with my mom, that was it. No calls, letters, nothing. It was as though he disappeared. His wife hated me. She lied about me to him. Made up things. So I don't have anything to say to him."

"Okay. We'll leave it at that. For now. But this is something I want to discuss more later."

"There's nothing to say. He didn't want me in his life. End of story."

"True, but you must feel some resentment towards him."

"Resentment? It's more like hate, disgust. He forced me to go back with my mom, knowing what she was. And he didn't believe me when his wife made up all of those lies about me and never bothered to ask my version of the story. I was a little kid and so lost in life. He threw me away like I was nothing more than a piece of trash. Little did he know that's exactly what I turned out to be," I scoff. "He walked out of my life without so much as a good-bye, adios, or see ya. He's never even sent me a birthday card. I don't really want to talk about him anymore." Bringing all of this up burns like acid in my gut. It's terrible to know that neither of your parents ever cared a thing about you.

"Here." Dr. Martinelli hands me a box of tissues and I look at her like — *what the hell are these for?* I don't even realize I'm crying until the tears plunk on my hands. Big fat drops and I stare at them in fascination, wondering where they came from.

"It's okay to cry."

"I'm not crying over it. I'm ... shoot I don't know what I'm doing. Why'd you have to bring that jerk up?"

"Part of the healing process."

"Doesn't feel much like healing to me." This tiny room has gotten smaller all of a sudden. The walls are closing in on me and I need some air. My hand is on the knob, attempting to open the door, when her voice stops me.

"Take a slow, deep breath. Running won't help, Skylar. Those memories, those feelings will always be there. You can try to bury them, but they're still there, lurking below the surface. You'll have to confront them sooner or later. Why not sooner? Why not learn how to cope with them?"

The truth of it is I don't want to confront them. My dad plunged a knife into me and annihilated any feelings I had for him when he never came back for me. He knew what my mom was doing. He knew she was messed up on drugs and doing all sorts of bad things. Yet, he left me with her, knowing he was putting me in danger. That's how little he cared for me. Not to mention all the terrible things his wife did to me and he never once intervened or put a stop to it.

"I don't want to confront them. Basically, I think of him as dead. Dr. Martinelli, are you close to your parents?"

"We're not here to discuss me, Skylar."

"Well, if your parents never did anything like this to you, it's not possible for you to understand."

"Let's look at it another way. If you don't confront this, it'll always be there screwing with your head. I don't know about you, but if I were you, I wouldn't want that. I would want to be free of that."

"Then how am I supposed to confront it?"

"There are several ways. You can call him. Or write him."

Holy ever loving hell. There is no way I would call him. Ever.

"I will never speak to him again." My head moves back and forth so fast I'm giving myself whiplash.

"Skylar, please sit down. You don't have to call him. That was only a suggestion. What I was also going to suggest was to write him a letter and spill your guts. But," she holds up her hand as I get ready to speak, "don't send it. Write down exactly how you felt when he walked out of your life. How it made you feel when he sided with his wife and never gave you the opportunity to tell your side of the story. How you've felt over the years. Write every last word on paper, even if it's twenty pages long. Then stick it in an envelope and put it away. You don't ever have to do anything with it, but it can be cleansing. It can rid you of all these things you've shoved so deep inside of you, thinking they're tightly locked away. But they're not. They're always there. Ready to burst out and hurt you. If you tackle them head on, there's less chance they can harm you. Does that make sense?"

My brain digests what she's said. "Dr. Martinelli, my dad wounded me and those scars won't ever go away."

"Maybe not. But if you confront them, you can deal with them. Look at you right now. You almost hyperventilated a few minutes ago. If you learn to deal with him, he will eventually become another unpleasant thought. Will what he did always hurt? You bet it will! What he did was wrong. Terribly wrong. But you can choose to let it destroy you or choose to go forward and be strong. If you continue with our sessions, your homework is to begin writing this letter, even if it's one paragraph at a time. I think your father is the root of your issues, not your mother. Yes, you feel guilty but you're smart enough to know that you tried to help her and she wasn't going to get cleaned up for anyone, not even you. Your feelings regarding your father are what you need to work on."

As painful as it will be, I know she's right, damn it.

"Oh, and another thing. You can be pissed off at me as much

as you want. I don't care. Just start writing the letter. How about next Tuesday, same time, for your next session?"

"Sure." Not even bothering to say good-bye, I practically run out of there. This session was so disturbing, every muscle, every tendon in my body is in knots. There's only one thing that will get rid of them and it's dancing.

My running shoes tear up the sidewalk between the good doctor's office and my apartment, where I grab my bag with my dancing gear. I'm back out the door, running to the subway.

An hour later, I'm into my routine, dancing to hip hop and moving to the music like my life depends on it. I throw myself into it, not bothering to stop until I'm drenched in sweat and my muscles are weakened from exertion. Walking over to my music, I shut it off and drop to the floor. Only then I notice the petite figure standing by the wall, and it's only because she starts clapping.

"If you danced like that during an audition, there's not anything on this earth that would prevent you from getting the part."

My head whips around and Marianna stands there, with a huge grin on her face.

"Yeah, well, my mind was a little occupied."

"My darling Skylar, you were brilliant. Admittedly, hip hop is not my area of expertise, but I recognize raw talent when I see it. And dear, you are blessed with it. But that's not why I stopped by. I'm having a small party the Saturday after next and I'd love for you to come. It would be a nice opportunity for you to network. And I know things have been difficult for you lately. Please say you'll be there."

She makes it impossible for me to refuse. "Of course I'll be there, Marianna. I wouldn't miss it for the world."

Marianna smiles and claps her hands. "Wonderful dear. I'll see you Saturday after next then. At four. And keep up that dancing."

"Oh, Marianna, what should I wear?" I ask as she's leaving.

"Casual, dear, but not jeans."

"Okay, see you next week. And thank you."

Honestly, I dread it, but I would never say no to her. Not after everything she's done for me.

Rising to my feet, I pack up my things and head on home. After I shower, I'll start that letter I dread writing so much. It'll probably begin—*Dear Dad. Got to hell. No, scratch that. Dear Dad. Fuck you.*

Twenty-Six

Reese

TWO DAYS HAVE PASSED WITHOUT A WORD FROM SKYLAR. I'VE left her several text messages and now I'm beginning to worry. It's time to pay her a visit. When I knock on her door, I can hear her moving about but she doesn't answer.

"Skylar, I know you're in there. Please let me in."

She finally opens the door and she looks like she hasn't slept in days.

"What happened?"

She waves me in and begins telling me about her visit with Dr. Martinelli. She been writing a letter to her dad and desperately trying to find a job.

"This letter is killing me. I really hate that man. And if I don't find a job soon, I don't know what I'll do."

"Okay, one thing at a time. The letter. Did she tell you to write the whole thing at once?"

"No. Just a paragraph or two."

Leave it to Skylar, trying to take on too much at once.

"Then my friend, you know the one who helped me get that audition? She invited me to a party at her house and I don't really want to go it, but I couldn't say no. She's been so kind to me. It's the week after next and I'm already worried about it."

"How 'bout we do this one step at a time. First, the letter. Write a couple of paragraphs at a time, like Martinelli suggested. You're taking on too much at once. As for the party. Go. It's not for another two weeks so calm down about it. Besides, if your friend got you one audition, she may know others that can help you. You never know. Someone may be at that party that can help you connect with the right people."

"I didn't think of that."

"If you like your friend and think so highly of her, then her friends should be pretty cool too."

"True."

"Now for the job part, I have a friend that's been looking for an admin. Do you have any skills like that?"

"No. That's why I can't find anything. The only thing I qualify for are waitress jobs. And I'm trying to get my GED but the paperwork to begin the process is taking so long."

She is in a bind.

"Let me check with Case. Maybe he can train you. You know how to use a computer, right?"

"Only the basics. My computer is ancient. It's pretty hopeless."

"One thing I learned in rehab is you have to take it one step at a time and sometimes even down to a minute at a time. It can be an ass buster, but that's how it works, babe."

"Thanks. For this. It makes me think I'm overloading myself."

"I think you're dead on. Want to get out of here for a little bit? I'm starved."

She laughs. "You're always starved."

"I'm a growing boy." Her eyes move to my crotch and widen.

"I'll say." She waggles her brows.

"So, dinner then."

"Yeah, sure."

Later that night I give Case a call to see if he's still looking to hire someone. He is, but he's a little concerned about Skylar's lack of skills.

"Can you at least talk to her? She's super bright and trying to get her GED. I know she could learn anything. If it doesn't work, no worries."

"Send her over on Wednesday. I'll interview her."

"Oh, and Case, act like you don't know a thing about her past."

"No problem."

"Thanks."

When I pass this information on to Skylar, I can tell she's nervous. She wants to know if she should tell him about her past and I recommend she does.

"Look, babe, Case is awesome. He's my sponsor at NA. He's been in a messy place himself. He's not judgey at all. If you come clean with him, he'll respect you for it."

"Okay."

WEDNESDAY ROLLS AROUND AND I GIVE SKYLAR HER PEP TALK before going to meet Case. She promises to call afterward. I'm up to my neck in coursework. The semester is bearing down on me with Thanksgiving around the corner. And then finals will be here. It's all work this week and no play for Reese because I have to make straight this semester. Law school is very important to me and their requirement is an excellent GPA.

Skylar calls and Case is going to give her a chance. She finally heard about getting her GED and will begin night courses in January. Some are online and she can get it in a year. Or maybe less, depending on how fast she completes the required work. She starts working for Case next Monday and he's going to train her.

Thursday I meet with Dr. Martinelli and my session goes fairly well. She notices I'm much calmer than I've been. My aggression has eased, although just last night I pounded the crap out of some dude when I caught him beating up on this girl. I figured it was his girlfriend. Told her she needed to stay away from him, though I doubt she will. Also told her to go to an abuse shelter for help. She looked at me like I was nuts. After I called 911, I left. The girl had two black eyes and a busted up nose but the guy was left in much worse shape.

My parting words to him were, "How does it feel to have someone bigger than you kick the shit out of you, asshole?"

Dr. Martinelli wasn't happy. "Reese, why didn't you just call 911 and wait for them to arrive?"

"Because you know as well as I do that he would've gotten off and she would've gone back to him and ended up worse off the next time. She probably will anyway, but at least this time, he knows what it feels like and maybe, just maybe, he'll stop and think about it. And you know I'm right."

She huffs out a long breath and shakes her head. "You're so hard-headed. You can't be the police, judge and jury. And not to mention, one day you're gonna get hurt."

"Nah, I'm too big and fast for them. Plus I have something they don't."

"Oh? What's that?"

"The element of surprise."

"Well. Mr. Smart Ass, what if they have the element of a weapon? Ever stop to think about that? What if they slip a knife into you and puncture your aorta? You'd bleed out in a matter of minutes. Stop this nonsense. You've cheated death once. You really need to step back from this. If not for you, do it for Skylar."

That statement brings my thoughts to a screeching halt. Not because she's right, but because it makes no sense. It's because of

Skylar that I do this at all. She's the one that put me on this path to rightness … that put me onto this goal of mine. It began the night of her rape and that's what triggered it all. I can't *stop* for her because I *started* it for her.

"Reese," Dr. Martinelli interrupts my thoughts, "what's going through that mind of yours? I can see your wheels spinning."

Shaking my head, I say, "You have it all wrong, Doc. Stopping for her, that is. She's the bottom of why I'm doing it." And I explain.

"Whoa, whoa, whoa. Let's back up and analyze this. Back to the beginning. You interrupted Skylar getting raped. Correct?"

"Yeah."

"But then this vigilante behavior of yours continued, even after you stopped seeing her. Why?"

"Because I wanted to stop people from getting hurt. But it's not like I hide in the shadows, lurking there, or go out looking for these attacks to take place. I interfere when I happen to run across them."

"But why?"

"Because I don't want anyone to go through what I did. If someone had interfered with my attack, I'd still be dancing today."

"So where does Skylar play into that thought process?"

"She doesn't."

"And there it is. Reese, think about what you just said. You started it because of *you*, not her. So why don't you *stop for her*? Because if she knew you were doing this, don't you think it would scare the hell out of her. That she would worry about you?"

"Well yeah. That's why she doesn't know."

"Then *stop*."

"But …"

"I'm not saying stop helping people. When you see something, call 911 and wait until the cops arrive. You can still help. Just don't involve yourself."

When I leave her office, it's with a troubled conscience. Is it me being selfish going forward with this, or am I helping people? The thought of one of those thugs having a weapon and using it on me never occurred to me. Well, that's not exactly true. It occurred to me, but I've always thought I'd be invincible and could outsmart them. But she's right. One day, I may not be able to do that, and then what?

By the time I get to the library, I'm in a shitty mood. It derails my studying, so I head to the gym to work out my frustrations. A couple of hours and a shit ton of sweat later, I'm back at the library with my head on straight, ready for a long night of work ahead of me.

Friday rolls by and I'm whipped. I'm up until three in the morning studying and it kills me. Classes all day and then more studying. Skylar calls and we talk, but when I start dozing during our conversation, she says good night and I'm out.

Twenty-Seven

Skylar

I'M ABOUT TO FINISH PACKING UP MOM'S THINGS TO EITHER toss out or donate to charity. Since I'll be moving next week, I'm making a pretty good dent in organizing so the move should go smoothly. Mom didn't own much, so this whole weeding out process should be done in a matter of hours.

Her closet and drawers are empty and I decide to take a break. Reese is studying today and will drop by when he's done later tonight. My goal is to have everything of mine that I won't need, packed up as well. It's after five and I've worked throughout the day, not stopping for anything. I'm just finishing up my ham sandwich when there's a knock on my door.

My building has no security, but I have multiple locks on the door with several chains. Reese must've finished early, but I'm always cautious when opening the door. Leaving the chains intact, I crack it open, just enough so I can see who's there.

"Yes?" and when I see who it is, my heart rate speeds up so fast I think my chest may explode.

"Hi, Skylar. May I come in?"

There are so many things I want to say … and many of them are written in that damn letter, but right now, not a single one will come to mind. I don't want to let him in. I don't even want to speak to him.

"Please, Skylar. Can I please come in and talk to you. I heard about your mother."

How in the hell did he hear that? I start pacing the tiny room because, frankly, I'm in a quandary. Should I let him in and listen to his lies? I'm positive that's why he's here. To tell me lies about why he never came for me.

"What do you want?" Bitterness edges every word.

"I want to talk. Please."

Okay, I'll let him speak. I want to hear what kind of excuse he has for me. I unlock the door and open it wide for him to pass through.

He walks in and looks around.

"Looks like you're moving."

"Pretty observant of you. I decided that a change of scenery was in order. You know, one that didn't include any memories of crack pipes, syringes, needles, male customers, that type of thing. Get the picture I'm painting here, *Daddy*?"

He cringes. Then squeezes his eyes shut.

"Skylar, I can't begin …"

"No you can't. Ever. There's not a thing you can say to me that will make things easier. But maybe you should've thought of that ten, no, eleven years ago. When your sweet little wife was making up all those lies about me. Did it ever occur to you, one time, that she was lying?"

He flinches, indicating the level of his discomfort. Good. Maybe he'll suffer just a tiny bit. I begin to wonder why he's even here. He can't even look me in the eye.

"Well?"

"Er, well, I don't …"

"It's a simple yes or no question, Dad."

"Yes."

I shake my head. He knew she was lying and said nothing. His answer … the truth of what he tells me, sickens me. "You sent me back here knowing what it would be like? You didn't even care enough about your own daughter to check up on me? To see what was going on? What Mom was making me do? And you acted like you believed all those lies your wife told you. What kind of man are you?"

He still can't face me. He speaks so quietly, I have to strain to hear him. "Not a very good one, I'm afraid."

Then a thought occurs to me. The letter I wrote. It's done and sitting on my nightstand. Now's my big chance, my opportunity to give it to him. He's going to know exactly how I feel after today.

"I would have to agree with you on that. Let me give you something, *Daddy*. You see, I'm going to a psychiatrist now and she's the one who recommended I write this. I never intended for you to have it, but since you're here, well, you may as well read it." I head to my bedroom to retrieve the letter I was in such turmoil over. When I return, I hand it over to him.

"I want you to have something, Skylar. I wasn't a father to you. Maybe the first few years of your life, but when your mom and I split, well, I have no excuses. Anyway, here."

He hands me a piece of paper and I look at it and it's a check for fifty thousand dollars. I laugh. Uncontrollably. And I can't stop.

"Read the letter. Then you'll know why I'm laughing."

He opens the envelope and takes out the many sheets of paper and begins to read. My eyes zero in on his face because I want to see his reaction. I want to gauge how sincere he is. It takes him quite a while to get through it because he breaks down and cries several times. At times it's so bad he has to pull a handkerchief out of his pocket to wipe not only his eyes, but his entire face. No doubt, my letter has shaken him up.

I'm silent, refusing to speak. When he's composed himself, he finally has the balls to look me in the eyes.

"Your mother was a smart woman. Sailed through pharmacy school like she was eating a piece of candy. She landed the first job she applied for at the hospital and climbed the ranks quickly. She worked long hours and so did I. Then she started coming home, acting strange. At first I thought she was having an affair. I never dreamed she was using drugs. The idea never occurred to me. Then one day, I found her supply. It shocked me. I couldn't believe what it was at first. It was a plastic case and inside there were small syringes and vials of morphine and other things I'd never heard of. There were pills too. So I confronted her and that's when the fighting began. I was convinced she would quit. She swore she would. But she didn't. Then she got caught stealing and you know the rest of that story. I was a mess. I really loved her, Skylar. I know it's hard for you to believe now, but I was crazy in love with her. Only she changed ... became a different woman. She was so pretty, so smart. I ... well, I don't need to go into all of this. Suffice it to say, by the time she went to prison, that sweet, smart, happy girl I married didn't exist anymore. I lied to myself and made myself believe that she would change for you. Of course, she didn't.

"I'm not telling you this for you to forgive me or anything like that. What I did to you ... the way I left you and never checked on you was ... unconscionable. I'm sorry for that, and if I were you, I'd hate my guts too. But that day that young man came to my house and showed me your picture ... the one of you eating cotton candy for the first time, the pretense of the world I had built around me couldn't be maintained anymore. It all crashed around me. I had no idea things had gotten as bad as they had. That Mary would stoop to the levels she did. And when he told me ..."

My head spins with his words. *Showed me your picture ... the one of you eating cotton candy for the first time.*

"Wait! Who showed you a picture of me?"

"I don't know his name. He came to my house and let me have it—verbally. Then he shoved this in my face and left."

My dad pulls out a folded up picture of me. It was one of the photos that Reese took of me the day we went to Luna Park. What the heck is going on here?

"What did this man look like?"

"Young, big, dark blond hair."

Oh. My. God. I stagger backwards to the couch. What has he done?

"Are you okay, Skylar?"

I can't answer that right now. Instead, I look for my phone and when my eyes land on it, I make a dash for it. My hand shakes as I tap in his number.

"Hey babe. You finishing up?" he asks cheerfully.

Damn his sexy as hell voice. My resolve to be pissed wants to shatter, but I buck up and say, "How soon can you come over?"

"What's up?"

He knows something's wrong.

"Just come here as soon as you can."

"Skylar, are you all right?"

"Yes. No. Just get over here, Reese."

"On my way, babe." His voice is firm, all sexiness is gone. Well, not really but he's much more *aware.*

I'm up on my feet, pacing. My father watches me, unsure of what to do. A thought hits me.

"Where do you live?" I ask my dad.

"In LA."

I scrunch up my face and shake my head. "You live in LA now? He came to your house in LA?"

"Yes. He did."

"What the hell," I mumble to myself.

"What?"

"Nothing."

The muscles in my neck feel hard as a rock so I dig my fingers in them, trying to relax them. It's been months since I've smoked weed or even had a drink, but I sure could use one of the above right now. Or maybe I should call Dr. Martinelli. I feel like I'm hanging off a cliff by a frayed rope and only one tiny thread is left intact.

The loud knock on my door startles me and I jump.

I take the few steps to open the door and let Reese in. When he walks in, he knows immediately why he's there.

"Mr. O'Donnell."

My dad nods.

"Reese, what the hell is going on? And when did you go to LA?"

My dad looks lost. Completely. Reese looks between us and asks, "Are you okay? Physically?"

"Yes."

"May I speak to you privately?" Reese asks.

"Ye…"

"Skylar," my dad interrupts, "look, I came here to apologize and to give you that check. I think I need to leave so you and this young man can talk. He obviously cares enough about you to fly across the country and tell me what needed to be told. I know I don't deserve your forgiveness and I'm not asking for it. But if you ever want to talk, here's my number." He pushes a square of paper in my hand and lets himself out.

I can't decide if I want to laugh or cry over this situation.

"What did he tell you?" Reese asks.

"That you let him have it—verbally and then shoved a picture of me in his face."

"Well, he got that right."

"How did you find him? And what made you do that?"

Whenever Reese gets uncomfortable with something, he looks away and scrapes his lower lip between his teeth. Then he moves his neck from side to side, as if he's relieving the built up tension there. He's so easy to read.

"Sit." When he tells me this, I know I'm not going to like his explanation.

I take a seat on the couch. He pulls up a chair and sits across from me.

"When you first started coming to my place, I got hooked on you. No pun intended. I couldn't stop thinking about you. I still can't. But then you'd disappear for a few days. So I asked Case to investigate you."

"You did what?"

"I hired Case. To do a little detective work on you. That's how I found out you worked at *Exotique-A* and also that you were a ... a ..."

"A prostitute?" I say it for him.

"Well, yes. That night when you came home, the night you sprained your ankle and I said those terrible things to you, was right after I got all the information back from Case."

"Oh God. You hired someone to dig into my background. To ... Reese, how could you?"

"You kept disappearing on me, Skylar. I wanted to find you. That was the only way I knew how. Case's report came back and it was there in your background about your mom and dad. That day we went to Luna Park and you told me about your stepmom and how your dad left you, something snapped in me. I came home and had all those pictures of you ... how beautiful you looked and how happy you were. I captured you eating your first taste of cotton candy, and your first bite of a funnel cake. Things like that. I stared at those pictures for hours, wondering how could any father ... any man, not listen to what his daughter had to say? Not even give her a chance? And that's when I knew I had to tell him what I thought of him. How he'd abandoned you to an incompetent mother who cared nothing for you. So I had Case find out where he lived and we both flew out there, went to his house, I gave him a piece of my mind and we flew straight home. Never in a million years did I imagine he would come to New York."

At this point, I'm not sure what to think. Should I be angry with him for snooping into my affairs? Or should I be pleased that he's the only one who ever cared enough to stand up for me?

"Are you angry?" he asks.

"I don't know. At first I was. But when you explain it like this, I've never had anyone to champion my cause before. You must've made an impact on my dad for him to come here and tell me he was sorry. He gave me fifty thousand dollars, but I don't want it."

Reese puts both hands on my legs and says, "Take the damn money, Sky. Put it in the bank. Don't you dare tell him you don't want it. After everything you've been through, it's the very least he can do."

After I think about it for a second, I say, "But it's like he's paying me off."

"No, it's not. It's money he should've been paying for child support all those years. Does he feel guilty? Hell yeah. And he should. But he owes you. And a hell of a lot more than that, too. The man has a big house and two Mercedes. He can afford it. Take the fucking money. Even if you never see him again."

"Maybe."

"Please take it." He begs me. Maybe he's right. He makes sense, but I sure wish my dad had come through years ago.

"Please don't be mad at me, Sky. I didn't do it to be nosy. I did it to find you." He moves from the chair to sit beside me on the couch.

"Stop, Reese. I know what you're doing and I need space right now." He backs right off.

"Do you want me to leave?"

"I think that'd be best." I can't trust myself to look at him so I keep my focus on my hands, which are clasped in my lap.

"Sky, please reconsider."

"I can't yet, Reese."

"Okay. You know where to reach me. I'll be waiting for you."

I don't trust myself to speak at all because if I do, I'll tell him not to leave. But I have to sort this out in my head. I need to talk to Dr. Martinelli. My feelings for Reese are so tangled up with the sex, I can't separate the two. And I need to in order to do what's right for me. Even though he didn't do anything out of malice, the fact that he went so far as to hire a detective to find out about me, speaks volumes on how controlling he is. I've figured that out by his demands in the bedroom. But this is another thing altogether. And I'm not going to leap into something that has potentially dangerous consequences if I can help it.

My phone sits on an end table so I pick it up and scroll through my contacts until I find the number I seek. Then I hit the call button.

"Martinelli here."

"Hi. Dr. Martinelli, this is Skylar O'Donnell."

"Skylar. Everything okay?"

"I need to talk."

"Go."

"Now?"

"Isn't that why you called?"

"Well, yeah, but I was thinking that I could make an appointment."

"Skylar, you have one for Tuesday. Remember?"

"Yes, but I need one sooner."

"Go ahead and tell me what's going on."

"It's Reese," I begin. I piece the giant puzzle together for her so it doesn't sound like some crazy soap opera. In the end, I do a terrible job of it and she laughs.

"Skylar, don't ever try your hand at journalism."

"No, ma'am. Wouldn't think of it."

"That's a crazy train of a story, but why are you so concerned?"

"His stalkery!"

"Stalkery? Is that even a word?"

"Yeah, because I just made it up."

"Is there anything else?"

"What do you mean?"

"Other concerns, Skylar?"

"Um, no. I guess not. But it was so intrusive of him. Who does crap like that?"

"Me," she answers.

"You?"

"You bet. In this day and age, I wouldn't think twice about running a background check on someone I dated. And let's go back a bit. Did Reese not give you a key to his place, before he even knew much about you?"

"Well, yeah."

I can hear Dr. Martinelli's fingers thrumming on a table or desk. "So he trusted you enough to give you a key to his home and he didn't even really know you."

"But don't you think hiring a detective is controlling?"

"How so?"

"Because he's digging into my past."

"Maybe because you were so mysterious."

"Okay, I'll give him that. But what about flying all the way to LA and telling my dad off."

"All right, I know this is unprofessional and I probably shouldn't say this, but open your eyes. He was defending you against someone who should've taken care of you and never gave a darn about you. I actually think that's rather noble. That's the unprofessional part."

"Dr. Martinelli, will you be my friend and just hang out with me sometime?"

She laughs. "Yeah, let's grab a glass of wine one afternoon."

"I need one right now."

"Where are you?"

"Home. I've been packing up this mess of an apartment."

"How about a beer instead?" she asks.

"Are you serious?"

"Completely."

She suggests we meet at the pizza place I saw her that night with Reese. Thirty minutes later, I'm out the door.

Dr. Martinelli sits across from me and we're sharing a pizza and drinking some beers. We laugh at how inept I am in this relationship.

"Look, if it makes you feel any better, I'm the worst. I've had such losers, it's not even funny. My track record on boyfriends borders on ludicrous. I've even considered those speed dating lunches, just so I won't be trapped in a miserable situation for endless hours."

"I think I'm in love with him."

"You think or you are?"

"I don't know. I've never been in love before."

"Never?" Gabby asks. "Not even puppy love?"

"Think about who you're sitting across from before you ask that question."

She squints at me. "I'm talking like junior high. Thirteen, fourteen years old."

"Nope. I didn't have any friends. Everyone knew about my mom. No one would let their kids hang out with me. Fun times, right?"

"So, Skylar, what you're really saying here is that Reese is not just your first love. He's your first relationship?"

"You got it, Doc."

"Well, no wonder you're freaking out. Listen up. He's a good guy. I can't reveal anything else. But I can say this. Reese Christianson is a good ... no, he's a *great* guy. Understand me?"

My eyes widen, my ears perk up and I lean in closer. "Really?"

"Yes. Really. Now, go with your gut instinct on him. And this controlling thing you're worried about? Don't be."

"But when we have sex, he's very controlling."

"Do you like it?"

"Yeah!" Just the thought practically makes me drool, but I don't tell her that.

"Then what's the biggie? As long as you're both satisfied. You are satisfied, aren't you?"

Satisfied. No, it's way beyond satisfied. It's exquisite.

Gabby snorts. "Don't bother answering that. From the expression on your face, I'd say you two are a perfect match."

I hold my bottle in the air and wait for her to do the same. Then I clink mine against hers. Definitely the perfect match as far as bedroom mates are concerned.

"So, can I ask you something?" she asks.

"Shoot."

"What was it like? Being a working girl?"

"At first, awful." She knows about how horrible is was with Mikey from our sessions. But then I explain how my clients with J.D. were high society and she wants to know how I felt about them.

"Meh, they were nice guys and good to me, I guess. And before Reese, I never gave it much thought. But after Reese, I couldn't stand it. I didn't want them to touch me. It made my skin crawl even worse."

"You're in love. It wouldn't have changed if you didn't have such deep feelings for him."

"You need to meet Cara. She's my best friend. Heck, she's my only friend. But she and I worked together for years and she's completely different. She can be in love with someone and still go to work and it not bother her. She loves the highs of being able to control men. That's what it's all about for her."

"I would love to dig into her psyche." She practically rubs her hands together, which makes me chuckle.

"Hey, I'll get her out with us one night. She's the most gorgeous thing you've ever seen. And you'd love her. And Jimmy too. He was my bodyguard at *Exotique-A* and my other bestie. Oh, the stories we could tell. I'm still trying to figure out how to get Reese comfortable with my relationship with Jimmy."

"I can see how Reese wouldn't like that at all. He's protective of you. I mean his trip to LA showed just how much. So what are you going to do about him?"

I close my eyes for a moment. "I'm sure I'll give in and we'll be together by tomorrow night."

She looks at her empty bottle and then at me and says, "Well, I think this is it for me, kiddo."

"Yeah, same here. I have to finish packing tomorrow. The big move is next week. And I start my new job on Monday."

"Oh, right. Case. You'll love working for him. He's awesome."

"Yeah, I hope he can put up with my incompetence."

"Okay, now your friend is putting on her shrink hat and telling you that you're not incompetent. You just need to be trained and there's a huge difference."

"Thanks, Doc."

"Hey, I'll see you on Tuesday for your appointment."

"Right. Till then."

I turn and head towards my apartment, thinking about Gabby, Reese, and everything in between. Maybe I am paranoid. Or perhaps it's just insecurity or inexperience. I'm afraid of being hurt, abandoned, controlled. After all of that, there's not much left to be afraid of. But now when I think about it, it was pretty amazing of Reese to fly all the way to the west coast, just to tell my dad what a POS he is. I bet he scared the crap out of him too. I wonder if the evil stepmom witnessed any of it. I sure hope so. It would give me great pleasure to know she had seen someone like Reese give my dad a tongue lashing. I'm still grinning over that when I get home, and so I do what I figured I'd end up doing. I pick up my phone and hit his number, hoping to have a long conversation with him before I fall asleep.

Twenty-Eight

Reese

THE LOOK ON HER FACE ... IN HER EYES, TELLS ME WHAT I need to know. She doesn't want me here. So I get out. I walk. And walk. And walk some more. And then I go home. It's times like these I wish I still drank. Or did other things. But that's not an option. Once I'm home, I know this is not going to work, so I change and head to the gym.

The treadmill is my starting point. After eight grueling miles, my next stop is the free weights room, where I pump enough iron until every muscle is at failure. Then I break for about twenty minutes. My brain is still jacked up so I hit the bag for my last stop. By the time my session with that is over, I'm wasted ... completely given out. I pack my shit up and head home, where I stand under a hot shower to let the water soothe my aching muscles.

By this time, I'm ready to collapse. But my stomach tells me how pissed off at me it is. Heading to the refrigerator, I make a huge sandwich to satisfy my starving body. When I'm almost finished eating, the phone vibrates. I almost don't answer it, but something makes me check the caller ID, and I'm surprised to see who it is.

"Skylar."

"Hey."

I hear a smile in that word.

"Hey back. What're you doing?"

She lets out a tiny laugh. "I was just getting ready to ask you the same thing."

"I'm stuffing my face."

"Anything good?"

"Just a sandwich I made."

"Want some company?"

"You never have to ask me that. Door's always open for you."

"I'm on my way."

"Hey, Sky. Take a cab."

"Reese, it's only a few blocks."

"Please. For me."

"You got it."

We end the call and I sit and stare at my phone. Why did she change her mind? Why isn't she pissed off at me anymore? Or is she? She didn't sound like she was. I stuff the rest of my sandwich down my throat and go brush my teeth. By the time I'm done, she's walking in the door.

Every time I see her, it's like the very first. Her face always looks so fresh to me … as bright as the sun. Her wavy blond hair begs my fingers to wrap themselves in it and her luscious pink mouth is ripe for my kisses. But I hold back and do nothing except eye her as she walks up to me.

"Your hair's wet. Did you just shower?" Her hand slides through my hair, but I trap it and kiss her palm before releasing it.

"Yeah. I hung out at the gym tonight."

"Did you beat yourself up?"

"Yep. I'm pretty fucking whipped, actually."

"Reese, I ..."

I stop her. "You know what? All I'd love to do right now is crawl into bed with you curled up next to me. Would you mind that too much? My eyes feel like they have lead weights in them."

She doesn't say a word, but grabs my hand and leads me into the bedroom. Off comes my shirt and she orders me in the bed.

"Not the pants?"

"Sure, if you'd like."

I peel them off and slide under the sheets. She locks the place up and hits the bathroom. I hear her brushing her teeth, but I don't even feel her come to bed. I'm asleep before she gets in.

Her luscious mouth is on my cock and it's still dark in the room. Her wet tongue is like hot cream coating me. She cups my balls and squeezes as she sucks and strokes me with that sweet mouth of hers.

"Sky, get up here. I want your body wrapped around mine."

She slides up and covers me with kisses as she moves. My hands reach for her hips and I flip her on her back. I check to see if she's ready for me and she is, as usual.

"Roll on your side, babe."

When she does, I lift her leg and wrap it around my waist. Then I rub my dick around her opening, and slide it up and down her slit until she sighs. Normally at this point, I would plunge it in hard and fast, but for some reason I want it slow. I inch in, and watch her face. Her tongue peeks out and wets her lower lip and that's all I can take. My arms pull her close to me so I can taste her mouth, feel that tongue on mine. We kiss. Sensuously. Slowly. Just like we fuck this time. I take her breath in mine and we watch each other. It moves me so deeply it's nearly impossible to process. The whole picture of Skylar, as she lies next to me, is quite extraordinary. Her breasts scream for my mouth, her abs beg for my touch, her hands reach for me but her eyes pull my heart to a place it's never been before. My hips rock into her and she receives each thrust with perfect rhythm, like we were made for each other. It occurs to me that this is the first time I've ever made love to anyone when it wasn't hard and dirty. This is soft. Perfect. Beyond beautiful.

"Reese."

The way she softly says my name pulls me back. Then her hand cups my face and she tilts her head back. I can feel her tightening around my cock and then her spasms take over. My body quickens on its own, my thrusts increasing in intensity and I climax right after her, calling out her name. Afterwards, I'm absolutely speechless. Because this was the most moving experience of my life. Not because it was the greatest fuck. But because it was the most tender, the most intimate moment I've ever shared with anyone. And I know I never want this woman to leave. I am so in love with her.

She stares at me and I crush my mouth on hers, kissing her as if my life were ending. My hands pull her on top of me as my arms hold her tightly against my heart. With profound clarity, I realize that it doesn't matter she was a prostitute and slept with a lot of men and she danced naked for dozens more. She's pure to me and that's all I care about. She makes me feel like I've finally found my oasis after wandering the desert for years. I'm the man who's finally been treated to the gift of water and she's the only one who's been able to quench my thirst.

"Are you okay?" Her voice even has the ability to soothe me.

"Oh, much better than okay. You're perfect, you know." I smooth her hair back.

She lets out one of her laughs. She has no confidence in herself. That's fine. I'm going to change that. One day, she'll see herself as I do. The most beautiful girl in the world and the only girl that stole my heart.

"You are, Sky. You can't see what I do. But you will one day. So, I take it you're not angry with me?"

"No. I met Dr. Martinelli for some beers and pizza."

"Dr. Martinelli." I stiffen. What. The. Fuck.

"Don't get all uptight on me. It's all good. She's opened my eyes."

"Oh, and how exactly did she do that?" This ought to be good. "And while we're on this subject, when did you two become such great chums?"

She laughs. "Tonight. I called her. Here's the deal, Reese." She kisses my nose and my body relaxes. How does she do that? "I thought you were being stalkery."

"Stalkery? Is that a word, Sky?"

Laughter rumbles in her chest. "That's exactly what the doc said."

"Well, it's nice to know she and I think alike."

"You wouldn't believe how much."

"Why don't you tell me?" Though I try to refrain, I can't keep the irritation from invading my voice.

"You're jealous." She pokes a finger into my ribs.

"No. Jealous isn't quite the emotion I'm feeling. But please go on."

"Well, I was worried because you're so controlling."

This comes as a shock to me. Totally. "You think I'm controlling?"

"Well, yes. I do."

"Why?"

"Reese." She's actually admonishing me. "Seriously? You went to LA and scolded my dad. You try to tell me what to do. Like take a cab or whatever."

"Whoa, whoa, whoa. You think that's controlling?"

"Uh huh."

"Sky, I only do that because I worry about you. The taking a cab part was because I envision that night when we first met. Where that guy was … I can't even go there because it disturbs me so much. And then when you got stabbed." I pull her close to me and wrap her in my arms. "This is about your safety, babe. The part with your dad was about letting him know what a dickhead he was to you. And that he should've cared enough about you to check on you." I pull away from her so I can look at her face. "All this is because I care. I don't want you to get hurt. Now does it make sense why I do those things? It's not safe for you to walk around alone at night."

"You're the only one who's ever cared about me, Reese. And yes, I understand. But because you're the only one, to me it feels controlling. But after I spoke with Dr. Martinelli, she helped me look at it in a different way. And the part about you checking into my background? I can understand why you did that too. I'm not saying I'm particularly fond of it, but I get it."

"Is that all she said? Did she say anything about me?"

"She did. She said that you were… how did she put it? Oh yeah, she said, 'Reese Christianson is a great guy.' And that's it. And I didn't want her to say anything else, not that she would."

"She said that?"

"Yes. But I knew that already. I mean, how many guys would want to have a relationship with a hooker. Or a private dancer. Do you want to discuss my past? In all of this, you've never asked me about it. And I don't want it to come back someday and bite us both in the ass."

I stop and think for a minute. There're a couple of things I want to know. "No one ever had you, did they?"

"Yes. They did. Before J.D. When I still worked for Mikey, he forced me to do things, Reese. He raped me too. I was only sixteen and, it was pretty bad. J.D. found me and took me away from him. That's when my life changed for the better. J.D. allowed me to make my own rules. That's when I stopped letting them have me like that. After Mikey, no one ever had me again. J.D. sent me to the doctor he uses for all his girls and had me checked out. Once my health was cleared, I decided I would never risk it again. So that's when I said no more intercourse. Ever. And no bare back blowjobs. I'm sorry if this upsets you." Her hand cups my face.

My hand reaches for hers and I cover it with mine. "It upsets me that you were hurt so much." I turn my face into her hand and kiss her palm. "Were your clients ever mean to you?"

"Oh no! Not after I left Mikey. J.D. had the best clients and mine were really great. And they paid well too. Some of them were weird as heck. Do you want to hear?"

Since I already know some of it, a part of me wants to hear it from her, but another part of me wants it locked away forever. So I say, "I think I'll let you keep that to yourself."

Pulling her under me, I frame her face with my hands and kiss her, softly at first. Then I take her lower lip in my mouth and suck on it until she moans. I repeat the same with her upper lip and then she pulls my tongue in her mouth and sucks on it, literally blows it like she does my dick, until my cock is hard as a piece of wood.

"I need you again. Tell me you want me too. This time hard and fast."

"Yeah, Reese. I want you too. Hard and fast."

Rolling to my side, I get up and pull her onto her knees so I can move behind her. In no time, my cock finds its home and we're both seeking our own orgasms. Leaning back, I pull her onto me and she rides me until we both come.

"I love when we do it like this."

"So do I," I laugh, "and I'm glad you love it too." Moving her so she's on her back with her legs spread, I gaze at the picture before me. "You're just too much to resist." Yeah, this has been the perfect interruption to a great night's sleep.

Twenty-Nine

Skylar

MONDAY MORNING I WALK INTO JORDAN PRIVATE Investigative Services, or JPIS. I'm prepared to learn everything I can. Case meets me at the front of the office and introduces me to the receptionist, Patsy. Then he walks me to the back, where we go into a small room that has a desk, a computer and two chairs waiting.

"So, let's get started. Just so you know, the kitchen is down the hall there. Do you need any coffee? We're all addicts here," Case says. "Coffee that is." He smiles and I grin back.

"Yeah, that'd be great."

"Come on, I'll show you."

We walk to the kitchen and he shows me where everything is and we fill our cups. When we get situated back in the small room, he wastes no time in getting started. Case is to the point and all about business. One thing about him though is he's an excellent teacher and pays attention to the smallest detail. He's helpful with my lack of knowledge in this more up to date computer system. But I'm a quick learner, thank God. The morning flies but I enjoy everything he teaches me. This business is fascinating and Case is involved with law enforcement too. They work together and he hires a lot of cops when they need to make extra money.

"So what do you think so far?" he asks as we break for lunch.

"It's great. Love the computer stuff. I'm amazed at how much you can do."

"My connections with NYPD have helped. Did Reese tell you my background?"

"No, sir."

He laughs. "Uh, you can dispense with 'the sir.'" Then he goes on to tell me about the shooting and his consequent involvement with drugs.

"I never would've guessed."

"I was a mess. That how I ended up at NA. Which led me to start this business."

"Wow. That's an amazing accomplishment. You should be proud of this."

"I am, which is why I'm a perfectionist here."

"Case, if I don't do something to your expectations, I hope you'll let me know. I want to be the best at what you hired me to do. So please tell me."

"Oh, don't worry about that. Did you bring your lunch?"

Holding up a brown paper sack, I say, "Yep."

"That's what most of us do here. It gets pretty pricey eating out every day."

"I'm sure. Well I think I'll get back to it and work during lunch."

"You don't have to do that, you know."

"Yeah, but I want to get a jump on things. And I'm moving this week too so I'll need to take off an hour early on Wednesday, if that's okay."

"No problem. I'll catch up with you this afternoon. If you need anything, just holler."

My first day at an official job ends and I leave the office with a sense of pride I've never known before. But there's so much to do at home, I hurry on my way so I can get things done. Over the years, I did my best to keep the apartment organized, but Mom stashed crap everywhere as I'm now finding. In her drugged up mind, she had trash stuffed in the back of cabinets and closets that I never imagined was there. There's no telling how many garbage bags I fill and take to the trash chute, but by bedtime, I have it all cleaned out.

After I shower, I fall into bed and call Reese. Our conversation is brief and soon sleep takes over. The alarm wakes me at seven.

By the time Wednesday afternoon arrives, Case lets me leave at four. The movers are outside waiting on me when I arrive home. Reese offered to help, but I refused. He's so busy with classes now I didn't want to bog him down even more. Everything is packed in boxes and ready to be loaded in the truck anyway. Several hours later, I say a final good-bye to my old apartment and a happy hello to my new. A new start ... a new beginning with newer happy memories.

The next day I arrive at work and everyone is grinning at me. Since I'm so new to this office stuff, I think it's because I'm the new kid on the block. After my round of "Good Mornings," I make it to my little space so I can get my work done. Case sticks his head in and asks me to join him in the kitchen. Not thinking a thing about it, I follow him down the short hall and when we get there, all ten members of JPIS are there, plus one extra—Reese. They hold up a big plate of tiered donuts and Reese hands me a giant bouquet of flowers.

I'm confused because it's such a surprise. And I'm not sure what all the fuss is about.

"What's going on?"

"Happy new apartment and new job!" Reese says. Then he

kisses me. I really wish he hadn't done that. We haven't been together in two days and as soon as his lips touch mine, my need for him blossoms. When he tries to release me, my hands curl into his shirt and I hold onto to him tightly. Letting go is not something I want to do.

Case clears his throat and a few of the people laugh. Reese finally eases himself out of my grip and moves his mouth to my ear, "Um, babe, you just gave me the biggest stiffie, but this isn't exactly the appropriate place."

Whoa! What the heck am I doing? I drop my hands and grin. "Oops." Then I turn to everyone and say sheepishly, "Thank you guys. Donuts are my favorite."

Case laughs. "Seems to me Reese is."

I vibrate with laughter. Then everyone joins in. We all eat some donuts and I say, "Well, I need to get back to work. I have this new boss that can be real tough at times. And I don't want to get fired."

Reese says, "Yeah, I have to get to class too." He leans in close and whispers, "I'll catch you later, babe."

My body heats from his touch, his words, and the idea of what awaits me at the end of the day. I hope this day flies. And it does.

By the time I get home, my heart pounds in anticipation. Reese texts me and says he'll be over around seven with dinner. This is my fairy tale. And I'm the princess.

A shower calls and I make sure I'm smooth and clean for tonight. Then I slip into something comfy. Yoga pants and a cami will do. Reese has never said anything about the way I dress, but I get the feeling from the way his eyes darken that he prefers me in casual clothes. My hair still hangs in damp tangles when the buzzer goes off. It's exciting to know I now have security in my building. I giggle as I say, "Yes?"

"Hey, it's me."

"Um, can you please identify yourself, sir?"

"Yes, I can. I'm the man that will tie you up and spank your ass until it's rosy and pink if you don't buzz me in right this second."

I bust out laughing as I punch the buzzer and then I stand in the doorway, waiting for him. When he steps up the final stair, I want to devour him. My eyes are glued to his ass as he walks inside my apartment and I close the door behind us.

"Do we have to eat right now?"

He spins on his heel and scans me from head to toe. Without uttering a word, he walks into my kitchen and sets the packages down. I hear him open and close the refrigerator door and the crinkling of paper bags. Then he walks back to me and in a husky tone says, "Get rid of those clothes, Sky." His eyes are half open and lust filled and a million butterflies in my body flutter.

My pants slide off first, followed by my cami. I'm wearing no bra or panties so he stares at my nude body, causing chills to speed up and down my spine.

"Touch yourself and show me how wet you are." I do as he asks and walk to him, sliding my fingers into his mouth.

"Tell me, Sky."

"I need you, Reese."

"How?"

"Any way you want."

"Not good enough."

"I want your tongue on me."

"More specific."

"On my pussy."

"Get on the table."

My table is small, only enough for two chairs. But I don't question him. I sit on it and wait for my next order. He pulls up a chair and sits in front of me.

"Spread your legs as wide as you can."

Now this I can do. I'm flexible so I can do a split if he wants.

"Oh, look at how hot you are here." He takes his fingers and slides them up and down my slit, circling around, but never touching my clit. He teases me, and it drives me crazy. He dives in to lick me and mimics the same movement with his tongue, never touching my clit. I moan his name. He licks everywhere but the places I need him to. And I'm dying.

"Reese, please," I beg.

He doesn't answer, but keeps up his torture. Then he stops and slaps me, right there. And I come with a scream. As soon as I start coming, his tongue works me over like he's playing a delicate instrument. He knows exactly which spots to lick, suck, and press on and I'm so out of it, I don't even realize he's stopped until I feel him enter me. When I look at him, he's standing and my ankles are on his shoulders. He pulls me closer and begins to move at a faster pace. I don't know how, but he hits me exactly right every time he thrusts and I'm going to climax again.

"Ahhhh. Reese."

"You good?"

"Yessss."

"That's it babe. Let me feel you. Let it go. I love it when you come for me."

I orgasm, sending ripples of pleasure over us both. Watching him is the sexiest thing ever. I sit up, pulling him closer, running my hands up his torso, and playing with his nipples. He surprises me when his hands grip my ass cheeks and he picks me up. We're still joined but he carries me to the bed and we fall down, me on top, and kiss.

Reese breaks away and traces my nipples with the tips of his fingers. "A fucking carnival babe, every time."

ON FRIDAY, I'M AT WORK AND CASE IS TEACHING ME HOW TO file. He has things set up as active and inactive. We go over everything and then he hands me a banker's box of inactive files and tells me to go file the contents. It's done alphabetically and paper files are kept for five years and then moved to a data storage bank. I'm going through them when my hands land on one: Skylar Mara O'Donnell.

It shocks me so much my breath disappears for a second. And then I remember. Reese hired Case to find me. That's when I thought he was being stalkery. Should I open this and check the contents? Or leave it be and go on? Do I even want to know? The file is in my hands and my eyes are locked on it. This will eat me alive if I don't look inside. So I open it.

Everything I never wanted anyone to know about me is in here ... from the day I was born until the day Case turned the information over to Reese. He was thorough; I'll give him that. It even details my mom's arrest, subsequent trial and prison sentence. Then the years I lived with my dad and evil stepmom all the way until my mom sold me to Mikey. This is where the details are sketchy. They don't have that information. It's "suspected" that I went to work as a prostitute at the age of sixteen, but nothing's definitive. He knew everything. The job at *Exotique-A*, my life as a hooker, who my damn clients were, what my mom's addiction was, the whole shebang. Nothing was sacred. He even knew my stipulations with my clients. This is so much more than what I thought. Yeah, maybe he told me about this, but he didn't go into all the details with me. He acted like he only knew a few of them. Even the other night when the subject came up, he didn't let on. I feel so exposed. And Case knew everything too. What am I supposed to do?

My butt hits the chair because I'm stunned. One part of my brain is saying, 'Yeah, he told you all this.' But the other side says, 'But did he really? And is this okay?'

"Everything okay in here?"

Case's voice startles the crap out of me and I nearly fall off the chair. My face heats and I feel like I got caught with my hand in the cookie jar.

"Er, yeah, well ..." I can't help but stammer.

"What's wrong?"

Lying was never one of my strong suits. I hold up the file and say, "I found this. I know it wasn't my business to look inside, but I did and, well ..."

"You're upset."

"Yeah," my voice cracks. Oh God, don't let me cry. I have to keep it together.

Case takes a seat near me. "He was taken with you and didn't know anything. I wasn't totally comfortable with it, but it's really hard to say no to Reese sometimes."

"But, he told me about this, only he wasn't as forthcoming as he should've been. Everything's in here."

Case grabs my hand. "Listen, Skylar, don't for a second think I judged you for this. I judge no one, at any time. If you even knew some of the things I did, you'd understand."

"But, *Reese* knew. And he ..." I blow out my breath.

"Do you need to go home?"

"Wh-what? No, I'm at work. It was just a setback. I can work. I'll deal with this and Reese later."

"You sure?"

"Yes. I'm fine, Case."

"Don't be too harsh on him, Sky. He's a good guy underneath his faults."

"Case, would you mind if I have this?" He hesitates and I relieve him of his decision. "Never mind. I don't want to put you in the middle of this mess. You did nothing wrong. Forget I asked."

"It's just that this is confidential and ... you really should never have seen it."

Now I've put him in a bad spot too. "Do you want me to keep quiet about this?"

He shakes his head. "No. You found it by doing your job. It was an accident really. And you need to get this off your chest."

"Thanks."

"You bet.

I finish up the day, knowing Reese is expecting me at his place right after work. With a heavy heart, my feet carry me there, while my mind tries to figure out what to say.

Thirty

Reese

When she lets herself in, I grab and hug her, but immediately sense something's wrong.

"What happened? Bad day at work?"

"You might say that. Case put me on file duty today. While I was putting things up, I ran across something. A file on me."

Damn it!

"Sky, I'm sorry."

"But Reese, you told me you had me investigated and I could understand that. Only this was so detailed. You knew *everything*. I mean every last tiny bit about me. And so did Case. I felt so *exposed*. And other people in that office probably know all about me too." I pinch my lips together in an effort to stop them from trembling.

"When I asked Case to find everything he could about you, he was thorough."

Now even my stupid voice quivers. "The other night you

asked if my clients ever had me or hurt me. Why bring that up when you already knew the answers? Why did you act like you didn't? Were you testing me?"

He closes his eyes and rubs them. "I don't know. No, that's not true. I wanted to hear it from your own lips. I wanted to hear that they never had you. Reports are one thing. But your word is another."

"But it's so belittling to talk about. I want to be completely honest with you, but you already knew it all."

"I didn't look at it that way, Sky. I would never belittle you. That wasn't my intent. Not at all. I ... I have feelings for you. I care for you. But ..."

"But what?"

I'm stuck. But what exactly? I love her, yes. I'm in love with her, yes. So what's stopping me from saying those words to her? Is it her former job? Is it the old life she led? Is it the possibility my parents will disapprove of her? Or is it *my* past? What is it?

My hands tear through my hair and no words will come out of my mouth. I look at her pained eyes and know that once more, I've hurt the person I love the most. What's wrong with me that I keep doing this to her?

"Sky, I ... I don't know what to say."

"Obviously. But I do. This doesn't sit well with me at all. My whole life has been dictated to me. But I won't let you do it too. This has to end. I can't be with you under these circumstances right now. My head isn't right with this. I need to talk to Dr. Martinelli ..."

"What the hell does she have to do with this?" My anger busts through now. I don't want her telling our shrink all of our secrets. Is this a logical reaction? Probably not. But I can't lose her again.

"She helps me sort things out. You get me all messed up in my head."

"No, Sky. Things aren't messed up. We're together and that's how it's meant to be."

"But you can't even tell me your true feelings, Reese."

"Well, can you tell me yours?" I throw her statement right back at her.

Her mouth works around a little, like she's testing what she wants to say. But I don't want to give her a chance. "See? You can't either. Can't you just be happy for us to be together for a while? We've come a long way. Can't we just see how things develop between us?"

"Yeah, I thought that's what we were doing. Until I found out you'd been dishonest with me."

"Well, pot meet kettle. You wouldn't even tell me a damn thing about yourself at first. You'd leave my bed before I woke up. And here you are, wondering why I had you investigated? I gave you a key to my home, for Christ's sake!"

She stands there before me, her smoky gray eyes clouded with tears and her mouth opened in shock. My belly twists up in knots as I stare at her. What the hell have I done? She backs away and makes a run for the door.

"Wait! Sky don't go!" I call out to an empty room. She's gone. And I can't blame her. I was all but screaming at her. What was I thinking? I know how she hates yelling. That's what her parents did to each other. The words I spoke may have been the truth, but I could've handled it in a much better manner.

An hour later, after calling and texting her repetitively and not getting a response, I hit Case's number.

"Wassup?"

"Case, I need your help."

"Skylar told you about the file, didn't she?"

"Yeah and I didn't handle things well. I yelled and she ran out of here and won't answer her phone. Will you try calling her? I'm worried about her and I want to know if she's okay."

"Sure thing. I'll call you right back."

The jackhammer in my chest doesn't let up one bit and when the phone rings, it picks up even more speed.

"Case?"

"Hey man, she's okay. She needs some alone time and she needs to talk to Martinelli. Let it settle for a couple of days. She cares about you. A lot. She'll come around."

"I don't know. I think I fucked it up."

"Well, fix it up then. You know how."

"Thanks for getting in touch with her."

"You know it. See ya."

After I stare at the blank wall for about thirty minutes, I know it's time to make another call. I grab my phone and search the contents for the number I need. Then I tap it in.

"Martinelli here. Speak."

"Bow wow."

"Who is this?"

"Reese Christianson. I need you, Doc."

"Well, it's nice to be needed. Funny, I'm in need a lot tonight."

"I figured you would be. I fucked up."

"You think?"

"I know."

"Talk."

She gets the lengthy version of my story and I omit nothing. When I'm done, she says, "Well, Reese, you did make a good point. I do think you had a solid reason to investigate her. But you also didn't handle it very well tonight, by your own admission. So, what would you have done differently?"

"I'm not sure."

"Then we need to hang up and you need to reassess things."

How can she say that to me? "What do you mean?" I ask.

"I don't know how I can be any more clear."

"Okay, I shouldn't have yelled at her for one."

"Go on," she urges.

"I could've been more honest with her about the investigation."

She lets out a breath. "Reese, quit beating around the bush."

"I could've told her I'm in love with her."

"Hallelujah! The man finally makes sense. And what else?"

"What do you mean?"

"Reese, does Skylar know about your past?"

I freeze. Solidly. Like an ice sculpture.

"Hello? Reese are you still there?"

My throat is stuffed with cotton and I can't swallow. "Yes," I croak.

"Deep breaths. Nice and easy now."

After a few panic-filled moments, I gain control and say, "How the hell am I going to tell her when I can't even stand to think about it?"

"And that, my friend, is what you're going to have to figure out."

SATURDAY MORNING SUNSHINE WAKES ME UP AND I HIT JOE and Mo's on the way to the gym. Then it's back to the library to study. I'm supposed to meet Aunt Emmy later today. I'm excited to see her but a little leery about telling her what's going on in my life. Part of me wants to tell her about Skylar, but the other part doesn't. Maybe it's best I don't mention her today, since I haven't heard a word from her since last night. I hit the shower, get changed and then I'm on the subway heading up to her place, right on time, since she hates anyone being late.

When I walk through her front door, I'm surprised to see the room filled with people. She never said anything about other people being here.

"Reese!" she exclaims. "My goodness, look at you! I almost wouldn't have recognized you. What are you feeding yourself these days? Fertilizer? You're huge!"

She always makes me laugh. "Thanks, Aunt Emmy." I wrap my arms around her and give her a huge hug, lifting her up and swinging her around in a circle. "I've missed you. You look gorgeous, as usual."

"Oh, hush, now. I'm old as the hills and you know it."

"You are not and you're as beautiful as ever."

"And you're as handsome as the devil. You're wearing your hair longer and I like it. It's sexy."

"Aunt Emmy! You're not supposed to say things like that to your nephew."

"Who says?"

She's stumped me there. "I don't know." We both laugh.

"So, a party, huh?"

Her eyes twinkle as she says, "Yes, dear. I knew if I told you about it, you'd make up some cockamamie excuse and wouldn't come. So you can be angry with me, but I got you here so now you're stuck. I want you to meet some of my friends. Are you hungry? I have way too much food."

She holds my hand and drags me through the room, and I nod at a good many people I already know. This isn't the most comfortable thing for me. I haven't seen many them since my dancing career ended, but it had to happen sooner or later, so I smile and pretend I'm happy to be here. We get to her dining room, where all the food is spread out on her table, and she walks me around and fills a plate for me. As we move through the room, she says, "Reese, there's someone in particular I'd like you to meet." Then in a louder voice, she calls out, "Skylar, come over here and meet my nephew, Reese." My heart skips the next hundred beats and stops all together. Then I see her turn, look straight at me, and notice how her face registers surprise as her mouth gapes open.

"Reese? What are you doing here?" Skylar asks.

My voice has just taken a hike, I believe to Alaska, or maybe even the Arctic region, because it's paralyzed … my vocal chords are useless. Nothing will come out of my mouth. Aunt Emmy keeps pulling me closer to her and I'm positive my legs move by some unforeseen force, because it's not by my command.

"Skylar, Reese is my nephew."

"Your nephew?" she asks.

"Why, yes. Do you two know each other?"

I have to get out of here. Now. Skylar knows nothing about my past and I never intended for her to learn about it like this. How in the hell did I not put two and two together? A friend who was helping her ... the studio ... the auditions ... this party even? I'm so damn stupid!

"Yeah, Skylar and I know each other Aunt Emmy. But I'm suddenly not feeling very well. I'm so sorry, but I'm going to have to leave. Please forgive me." And I'm out of there. Like my ass is loaded with a damn surface to air missile. And I don't bother looking back at their faces. Aunt Emmy will know, but I can only imagine the hurt that will be written all over Skylar's and that's something I can't take right now.

Thirty-One

Skylar

WHEN REESE DASHES OUT OF MARIANNA'S HOUSE, I'M LEFT standing there not knowing what to do. But when I move to follow him, Marianna's hand grips my arm and she says, "Let him go, Skylar."

"But something's wrong."

"I know. How long have you known him?" she asks.

"About a year now. And why does he call you Emmy? He's talked about his Aunt Emmy before."

Marianna laughs. "When he was a little tyke, he could never say Marianna. So I told him one day to call me M. And it turned into Emmy."

That makes sense. "He adores you."

"Follow me. I want to show you something."

She leads me upstairs into a den where the walls are covered in pictures. Some are of a young Marianna in her ballet costumes, and others are of another beautiful ballerina and then there are dozens of pictures of a young man. When I look closer, I recognize him as Reese.

"What's going on here?" Seeing a young Reese as a ballet dancer bewilders me.

"Here."

She hands me a scrapbook of sorts. I open it and begin reading. It chronicles the career of a young boy, then an adolescent at the Royal Ballet Academy, named Reese Christianson, stage name Reston Blakely. I'm stunned. Reese is *the* Reston Blakely. The famous ballet dancer who was beaten and left for dead almost three years ago. I recall hearing about him on the news. The scars on his leg and body—the ones he would never talk about—now all make sense. That day he helped me with my sprained ankle. No wonder he knew so much about it.

As I continue to read, I want to run to Reese and hold him. Comfort him, like he comforted me when I left my mom locked outside of the apartment. He attended the Royal Ballet in London to study and was pronounced, "The dancer of the decade." Then he left London to return to New York to study contemporary ballet at the Joffrey Ballet. It was there he was picked up by the Metropolitan Ballet Company and became their youngest principal dancer. He was a phenom, destined for greatness … until that one devastating night. Oh my God. The tragedy of it all makes me tragically sad for him. Everything tumbles into place … the drugs … why he became an addict.

I look up to see Marianna standing there. "You're in love with him, aren't you?"

"Yes, I am." It's something I've known for a long time. "I never knew any of this. I asked him about his scars once, but he wouldn't answer, so I never asked again."

"He won't ever talk about this. But with you, maybe he will. We almost lost him, you know. Not only to the assault, but in the aftermath, too. Something happened though, and we got our Reese back, but a better version of him, I think. Go to him, Skylar. But be patient. He's never been an easy boy. His whole life has been difficult. His mother, my niece, was selfish. She didn't want to be pregnant. It was a huge surprise. And then she didn't want to love Reese, because she wanted her career. You know, she was a principal too? And the best. A beautiful dancer. But when she returned to dancing, after he was born, she couldn't bear to be away from him. She tried her best to hate him for it, but she couldn't. She loved with him with everything she had. But when he showed such great promise as a dancer himself, she did everything in her power to keep him away from it. I pulled all kinds of shenanigans to get him to dance lessons. And boy did we have fun together. Juliette, Reese's mother, would be so angry. Her father is my brother and we would come up with all kinds of schemes. Then when Reese wanted to go to London to study... bah, it was a mess. I suppose I can't blame her. Can you imagine sending your twelve-year-old son off to school abroad? She was furious with me. Oh, I didn't think she'd ever speak to me again. But she did. And she ended up being so proud of him. He was a beautiful dancer. I wish you could've seen him." She snaps her fingers and says, "Wait!"

She moves to a shelf, pulls out some DVD's and puts one into the player. Then she turns on the TV and there he is, dancing. I sit there, mesmerized, as he leaps and turns, his graceful beauty astounding me. The DVD is a recording of his final performance in *Shatter*, the last time he ever danced. I wasn't aware a human body could move like that, displaying such strength in motion, fluidity, and grace all at the same time. His elegance and lines are so dramatic and the height of his leaps are so grand as he extends himself, I find that I can't breathe as I watch. When the dance is over and Marianna removes the DVD, my face is soaked from my tears.

"No wonder he was destroyed," I mumble through my tears.

"Go to him, Skylar."

"What shall I say?"

"Whatever is in your heart. The truth."

"Do you think he'll want to see me?" I ask.

"Probably not. But the things you want the most in life are what you fight the hardest for. Fight for him. Show him that you care and that it doesn't matter to you. And it doesn't, because you fell in love with Reese, not Reston."

My head bobs up and down. Marianna's right. I care about Reston because it hurt him so badly, but Reese is the one I love.

"Yes. You're right. I never knew Reston. Only Reese."

"And Skylar, we need to work on your next audition."

During my train ride home, all I can think about is Reston Blakely and his dancing. As I start to climb the steps to my place, I change my mind and go to Reese's. I ring the buzzer and he answers.

"It's me. Can I come up?"

He doesn't answer. I wait a little bit and I'm getting ready to lay on the buzzer again when it sounds and I push the door open. Taking the steps two at a time, I make it to his door, to see him standing there with it half open.

"Skylar, I ..."

I cut him off. Holding out my hand, palm facing him, I begin, "I know this is ass backwards, but I'm going to say it anyway. I'm in love with you, Reese Christianson. I don't care about Reston Blakely. Well, that's not exactly true. I do care about the fact that he was so deeply hurt and that he can't dance anymore, because I've never seen anything so utterly beautiful and stunning in my entire life. Other than one thing. You. Right here, standing before me as Reese Christianson. I fell in love with Reese, not Reston. And despite everything that's happened, even your stalkery, I'll love Reese forever. I know I'm the other side of the tracks girl, the one you'll never want to take home to meet Mom and Dad. I get that. I mean, who really wants their parents to meet their girlfriend who's a former prostitute and exotic dancer? I'm willing to live with that. Just ..." and this is where I stop because, damn it, I'm trying my hardest not to be a big pussy butt, but those stupid tears are making it very difficult right now. "I just wanted you to know that, well, that I love you Reese."

I pivot and haul butt because I just made the biggest fool out of myself. Riding the subway home from Marianna's, I'd built myself up in my mind. But in reality, I *am* that girl from the other side of the tracks. And honestly, what *can* I give Reese? A good blow job? A good piece of ass? Yeah, I'm down for that, but what else? Because that's all his parents will think of me when they find out the truth. They'll see me as a paid whore and nothing more. If my kid came home with someone like me, that's exactly what I'd think. The roaring in my ears drowns out all the city noises and I want to scream. When I get home, I close the door and lean against it, eventually sliding to the floor. Getting involved with Reese was a mistake, but staying involved with him was epically wrong. It's destroying me now and putting myself back together will not be easy.

My apartment has darkened with the night sky and I'm still sitting against my door. What's the point of getting up? I can't call Cara because it's Saturday and this is her big night. She's really my only friend, other than Jimmy, and he's working too. Mom clinched the friend deal for me.

When Sunday morning breaks, I put on my running clothes and head out the door. My body is achy from spending the night curled on the floor and I need to let off some steam. I run all the way down to the tip of Manhattan, around Battery Park and back up again. When I finish, I stop by Joe and Mo's to grab a latte and a muffin. As I'm leaving, in walks Reese. We both stop and stare at each other and then I nod and walk past him.

"Skylar, wait."

My breath picks up again, like I'm still running. I'm scared to death to turn around. This guy does bad things to my body and I turn into a minion around him.

"Yeah?"

"Can we talk?"

No!

"Okay." *Traitor! Lame butt!*

"Give me a minute." He walks to the counter and orders, then joins me. "Come back to my place?"

"Sure." *Double-decker lame butt minion!*

"Looks like you've been running."

"Great observational skills there."

"Yeah, I'm known for them."

"Uh huh." I can't think of anything at all to say. So I only sip on my coffee. We get to his apartment and he ushers me inside. "May I please have a glass of water?"

He looks at me and laughs.

"What?"

"So formal?"

"Oh," I shrug as he hands me the water. I guzzle it. "More?"

He hands me another one and I guzzle it too.

"Thirsty much?"

"Yeah, running usually does that."

"Yeah, I suppose it does."

"May I sit?"

"Damn, Skylar, do you really have to act so formal? Yes, sit!"

"Jeez, you don't have to get all mad about it." I drop to his sofa. This is awkward.

"Well, you're acting like you've never been here before. Shit, you lived here for how long?"

My cheeks heat and I scrunch my eyes shut. "Right. Maybe this was a bad idea," I say as I rise.

"No, sit, please. We need to talk."

"It's okay, Reese. I know I made a gigantic fool out of myself yesterday, so I'll save you the trouble of saying it. It's not you, it's me. Isn't that what you're supposed to say? I'm not really sure because I've never been in a relationship before." I rub my eyes. "I never imagined this would be so uncomfortably weird."

"Skylar, would you just be quiet for a minute?"

I look at him and his brow is furrowed.

"Can I eat my muffin?"

"Yes!" he snaps.

My shoulders droop, because he's in such a bad mood. I'm really not comfortable. But I am starving after that run, so I dig in and munch away. He watches me. And watches me ... until I squirm. Finally, I ask, "Would you like a bite?"

"Oh yeah. But not of that muffin. I'd prefer to have a taste of the one between your legs."

The bite of muffin I just took shoots out of my mouth as I cough in surprise. After I recover from and clean up my mishap, I look up to see him smirking at me.

"Finish your muffin. Because I want my muffin too."

My throat is so dry, I can't swallow. "I'm done," I say as I set the muffin remains on the coffee table. *Triple-decker traitor pussy butt minion!*

"Take your clothes off and get in the shower."

"Didn't you have something you wanted to tell me first?"

"It can wait."

"Can I brush my teeth first?"

"Since when did you start asking?"

Scurrying into the bathroom, I grab Reese's toothbrush and scrub my teeth. My clothes are torn off and I hop in the shower.

"What's your hurry?"

"Eeeek! You scared me!"

"You didn't think I was going to let you wash all the sweat off of you by yourself, did you?"

Yeah, I did. But I can't talk. The only thing that comes out of my mouth is a squeak, when he rubs body wash all over me. His hands stop to tweak my pearled nipples, which, if they could talk would moan themselves. My girls are clapping and high fiving each other while my muffin is getting more impatient by the second. His hands roam all over my body, sudsing me up and caressing my skin. But when they finally make it between my legs, I purr out my pleasure. He soaps me up so well that I protest when he stops.

"I'm only rinsing you off, Skylar."

"I don't want to be rinsed."

"What do you want?"

"I want to be fucked. Now."

"You have a wicked muffin."

His mouth crashes into mine and all I can think of is what's coming next. He takes my leg, pulls it around his waist, and thrusts into me. I moan against his lips.

"Suck my tongue."

I pretend I'm giving his tongue a blow job. My tongue swirls and sucks his and then I move to his lips, first the upper and then the lower.

His fingers sink into my ass cheeks but then I feel a soapy finger slide into my back door.

"Ahhh."

"Tell me to stop if you don't like this."

"Don't stop. It's good."

"We're gonna do this hard and fast now, babe. I want you to come fast for me. Hold on tight."

He backs me against the cold tile and starts to pound into me so hard that I can barely take a breath. As he thrusts, he moves up and down, so slightly, but it's enough for him to drive me over the edge.

"Oh, oh, yeah, right there Reese."

"Let it go for me, babe."

Between his finger and the motion he's got going, there's absolutely no hope for me … at all. I call out his name as I come. Then he grinds his hips against mine as he finds his own release. The water pours over us as we hold onto each other.

Then he says, "Always a carnival, Skylar."

"One that came with a muffin, too."

He laughs. "And a more perfect muffin never existed."

Thirty-Two

Reese

IT'S TIME. TIME FOR ME TO TELL HER EVERYTHING, BECAUSE I haven't been fair in holding back. As I gaze into her beautiful eyes, and know that she's bared everything for me, it's wrong to not do the same. Reaching for the shampoo, I squeeze some into my hands and then transfer it to her hair. She loves for me to wash her hair. So I take my time, massaging her scalp. Then I rinse and condition it with the conditioner she keeps here.

"Mmmm."

"You like that?"

She hums her delight.

"Step aside so I can do mine." I only take a minute or so, then I turn off the water. Reaching for a towel, I wrap her in it. When she's nice and snug, I grab one for myself and dry off.

She's wrapping her hair in a towel when I surprise her by picking her up.

"Wh-what are you doing?"

"Putting you to bed."

"But my hair. It's soaking wet and tangled."

"I know. I'm going to comb it."

After she's covered in the sheet, I and start combing through her tousled waves. It takes a while, because her hair is so thick.

"So about that talk," I begin as I set the comb down.

"Yes?"

"Yesterday rocked the Earth off its axis. Didn't know how to handle things. See, the thing is when I got hurt, well that's how it started with all the drugs. It began with the morphine in the hospital. Then I was released on Lortabs. But I found it zoned me out. Made me not think about how my career had been ripped away. So I decided to try other things. Stronger stuff. And I fell into a cave ... that rabbit hole if you will. Skylar, I didn't care if I lived or died. There were many nights I wished I *had* died. That those guys did kill me because they robbed me of everything I had ever dreamed of ... the only thing I knew how to do. I spent my entire life working toward that goal and never thought about an alternate plan."

She takes her finger and begins to trace all my scars, starting with the ones on my chest. Eventually, she gets to my leg. They're long and deep from all of the surgeries. But her hand splays out and travels along the length of it, following all the indentations. My throat tightens with her gentle touch and my hand rubs my forehead in an effort to keep my tears at bay.

"Remember that day you asked me about these? I just clammed up. I get so uptight when I even think about it. But then you never brought it up again."

"Your reaction told me you had no desire to discuss it. Reese, these are the visible scars, but I don't think they're the ones that hurt you the most. The ones inside, you know, the invisible ones are those that cause the most pain. Your Aunt Emmy told me everything. She even played me the DVD of your final performance. You were amazingly beautiful."

"Sky." Her words bring the memories of that night back to

me. How the exhilaration of the dance felt and my hand moves to my busted up leg.

"I'm so sorry you lost what you loved the most, but what I said last night is the way I feel. Look how far you've come. You come. You run, lift weights. You're in school. You've overcome your addiction and are in recovery. Those are amazing accomplishments."

My hand wraps around her neck and I say, "Stop! Wait a minute." Her words fly through my head again and my eyes don't leave hers. "Ballet *was* the most important thing to me back then, but it's not anymore. *You* are. Please tell me I haven't lost you."

"I'm here, aren't I? And I don't love Reston. I love Reese. The man with the scars. Nothing else matters because I didn't know you then. And from what your Aunt Emmy tells me, you're a much better person now than you were before anyhow."

"She said that?"

"Yes, but ..."

"But what?"

"You're from a good family. You have parents who care ... really care about you. Your aunt loves you too. You don't need to be with someone like me."

Her lips quiver. And I'm the fool.

"Skylar, yes, my parents care. I'm lucky. But that doesn't have a thing to do with you. I love you. I need to be with you because I'm in love with you. I never told you about who I was in the past because it's so painful for me to talk about, but maybe it's time I change all that, starting with you. See, I have connections in the dance world. And I can help you. No, I'm not versed in your style, but my name can open doors for you. I want to do that for you. It won't get you the part, but it *will* get you the audition."

"What will your parents think? About you being with someone like me?"

"First off, they'll think you're a young lady who works for a private investigator. They love Case so they'll approve of that. Second, they'll adore you for the beautiful person that you are. Just ask Aunt Emmy about it. And third, my mom will be all over you when she finds out you're a dancer."

She balls up her hands and it tells me she's not buying it.

"They'll find out. Eventually. This is a small world. We'll have to tell them."

"Maybe. Someday. But Skylar, if I don't care, why should they?"

"You know why. I can't begin to understand the world you came from. It's like an alien planet to me. Before I turned sixteen, there were days I'd go without eating. So when you talk about having a nanny and things like that, I can't relate."

Jesus. Going without food, and here I sit, living off my trust fund.

"Okay, you're right. And I can't understand your world either. But that doesn't mean we can't make it work. The only way we can find out is to try. Take it a day at a time. And if you say you love me, and I *know* I love you, then what's the harm in giving our love a chance? Everything in life's a risk, Skylar. Let me be your risk." I pull her into my arms and kiss her, showing her my love. Usually I kiss her with a roughness, an edge, but not this time. This time, it's soft and gentle as my hands glide into her wet tresses and I pull her body into mine. When her arms reach around me, I know she's giving me her answer. But I want it in words too.

"Tell me you're mine. And that you'll let me be your risk."

"Yes. I'm yours Reese. Even though I'm not sure it's the right thing."

"It *is* the right thing. My heart knows it. And you'll see in time. We may not have started out like most relationships do, but I guarantee, there isn't a couple out there that can out do us in the bedroom. And about the other night, I'm so sorry about the terrible way I handled things. Dr. Martinelli had to listen to me on the phone and I have a lot to learn, but I swear I'll get better at this. I know I have a long way to go, but one thing I can say for sure. I've never been afraid of hard work. And I'm willing to work my ass off for you."

"Reese, don't work too hard because I love your ass just the way it is now."

She makes it impossible for me to keep my hands off her, but when I try to pull the sheet down, she stops me.

"Before you do any of that, I want to know what every one of your tattoos mean."

"Every one?"

"Every single one."

"Slide over." She moves and I slip into the bed next to her.

And so I begin with my leg. "These were to cover up the scars. I started out in anger so the first ones were symbols of death. All in black ink. I didn't want any color anywhere, because my life was so dark at the time. After a while, I stopped with my leg and got into script. That's what's all over my torso. I didn't really care about covering up the scars. I was so angry though, I wanted to scream all the time. And I did, a lot, when I wasn't on drugs. Thank God I did most of this in Asian or Greek because my body is covered in death, hell and all sorts of stuff now. But the way it is, no one really knows what it says."

"Tell me."

I point to the largest one that runs down my left side. "This one says, 'Life is death.' I'm glad I made it small. I love ink, don't get me wrong. But this one is so morbid to me now that I'm in a better place."

"What about this one?"

"I had this done when I started to see the light again. After I met Case. *'I tried hating life but I couldn't. I tried dying but I didn't. From this day forward, I'll accept what I did wrong and strive to do what's right.'*"

"That's so profound."

"It means a lot because when I was using, I hurt a lot of people. Some of them I was close to, such as my parents, but others I didn't even know that well. I hated myself every day for what I was doing, but didn't know how to stop. Now, I try to take responsibility for my actions."

"I think you're amazing to be where you are after what you've been through."

"Sky, I was a fucking bastard, so you shouldn't say that."

Her lips touch my cheek and then she points to a series of tic marks. "What about these?"

I grin. "Those are my sobriety days. I started getting one a day and when I reached thirty, I went to one a week, then one a month. I'm super proud of them. And now, I've switched to actual numbers. That's what the '1' means."

Her fingers dance across them and then move to the script on the right side of my torso. "And this?"

"Read it."

She gives me one of her smart ass looks. And then reads, *"Every day is a blessing. Count it as one. Life is a challenge. Live it as one. Cheat death, not yourself. Think of others, not yourself. Care enough to learn to love."*

When she finishes, she looks up at me and her eyes glisten. "Did you write that?"

"Yeah."

"It's beautiful." She leans in and touches her lips to the inked words and I'm lost. My hands lift her onto my lap and we kiss. Then I lay her on her back and get up. A few seconds later I tell her to close her eyes. I have a surprise for her ... one that's going to drive her to the brink of sexual madness.

Thirty-Three

Skylar

MY EYES ARE CLOSED AND I WAIT IN ANTICIPATION. I CAN hear his footsteps as they come nearer. He wraps something silky around my head, covering my eyes, and I'm plunged into darkness. Then his hands grab mine, pulls them above my head, and he wraps something soft around my wrists. When he releases me I try to move, but can only go so far. He's anchored me to the bed. Next, he moves to an ankle. He bends my knee and spreads me wide open. I feel cool air graze my core as he wraps it in something rough. Again, when he releases me, I can't move. He repeats this to my other one and now I'm stretched out and bound on the bed. My excitement mounts as my chest moves up and down with each rapid breath I inhale.

"Skylar, what a sexy sight you are." There's nothing now but silence except for the sound of my panting.

Soon, though, he returns and puts his mouth next to my ear. "I'm going to fuck you silly, Sky."

His hand trails down my neck, and over to my breast. When he reaches my nipple, he bites it gently at first and then harder. I moan. Then he moves to the other nipple and does the same. Back and forth he alternates, effectively torturing me. I try to move, but can't. I'm strung so tightly to the bed that any movement is impossible. Soon I feel his hot, delicious tongue travel down my stomach, until he reaches the apex of my thighs. I beg him to lick me, but my words make no impact on him. Instead, he moves to my inner thighs and sucks me, hard. His teeth sink into me and I cry out, sure I'm going to come. Then his mouth moves to my calves, teasing each one alternately, and finally the arches of my feet. My senses reel with his touch but my nerve endings are on fire with need.

"Reese. Please."

He doesn't acknowledge my pleas, but forces my hips up with some pillows. Then he leaves me again. When he returns, he's back to biting my nipples. But then he pushes something icy cold inside of me and I nearly scream. What is it? I don't have time to think because an intense orgasm slams into me. "Oh God," I moan. I came and he never even touched me.

"Skylar, you weren't supposed to come. Now I'm going to have to paddle your ass."

"Yes. Please." Anything. I need him to do anything. I'm so excited by all of this play that even my orgasm didn't relieve me.

"But not yet."

Disappointment fills me. But not for long. Because his hot tongue drills into me and I cry out. It circles my clit and in no time I'm orgasming again.

"Oh, Skylar," he says, "You're a very naughty girl. Now that's two orgasms you weren't supposed to have. Two punishments you're going to have to receive from me."

"Please," I beg.

He pushes my legs up, which in turn lifts my ass off the bed and he slaps me. Hard. It shocks me since I wasn't expecting it. He smacks me again. And again. I count up to seven and stop.

Because I'm gasping. Not with pain, but excitement. My God, this is turning me on beyond my limits. My butt is on fire and my sex is aching with need. When he finally stops spanking me, he flicks my clit rapidly and I come. Hard. I don't even notice he's untied me until I find myself on my knees and feel him slamming into me.

"Ahhhh."

The intensity of the way he fills me is indescribable. My body is so ready for him, but every nerve ending of mine feels each stroke, each tiny motion, and I'm so full as he stretches me beyond what I think I can take. But then his tip kisses me against those places that push me over and everything tightens, then contracts. And I multiple on him.

"Let it go baby. Damn, Sky, I love to feel you do this to my cock." Then he growls deep in his throat, and I have this pressing need to hold him. But I feel him spurting into me, as I draw every last drop from him. His warmth deep inside me is a balm and when he's finished, I look over my shoulder at him. He's pure, raw sex as he stares back.

"Kiss me, Reese."

He moves so fast, I can barely track because I'm so lethargic right now. I'm caged against his body and he pulls me on top of him as he lies down. Then I kiss him tenderly, passionately, and with all the love I feel.

"Reese, I …" I'm terribly emotional all of a sudden and I choke up.

He cups my face and the action is so sweet I melt. "I love you, Sky." He rubs his cheek against mine. "You've stolen every inch of my body and mind, including my heart and soul. And babe, that was the best carnival I've ever been to. I hope you liked it too."

I start thinking, and it's strange how life throws curves at you. Like the night he prevented the rape from happening.

"What? Your face is all scrunched up again."

"If that guy hadn't tried to rape me, you and I never would've met. I was just thinking how strange life is."

"Oh babe, and if I hadn't been beaten like I was, I wouldn't have been in school, walking home at two in the morning either. So it works both ways. Life is weird."

My hands move all over him, because I love to touch him. His skin is perfect beneath my hands. I don't care about his scars. They make him all the more real and all the more mine. I never knew the other Reese and from what he's told me, there's a good chance I wouldn't have liked him. He probably wouldn't have given me the time of day anyway.

"Hey. We need to go see Marianna today. We both kind of left in a hurry yesterday."

He flashes me a smile and he's so handsome I can't stop myself from pulling his mouth to mine. We kiss briefly and then decide to get up and pay his aunt a visit. There are all kinds of things we need to do.

"I want you to meet my parents too. And you need to start focusing on your dancing. There are some people I want to introduce you too. Oh and do you want to call our shrink and see if she wants to meet for dinner tonight? And I'd really like to meet your friends, Jimmy and Cara."

My arm flies out and I hold out my hand. "Whoa. Calm down buddy. One thing at a time. And don't you have some studying to do?"

He casts me a sheepish look. Then laughs. "Guess I got carried away."

"You think?" I shoulder nudge him. Damn he's huge. I feel his muscles. "You're like a beast. You know?"

"Frustrations. I take them out in the gym."

"Me?" He gives me another sheepish look. "Don't be shy about it."

"Then yeah. It was you. At times, I felt like pulling my hair out."

"Same here."

We gaze at each other, then laugh. I hold up my fist and he bumps it. Then his face turns serious. "I want to be yours, Skylar. All yours. Every day and every night."

"And I want to be yours too, Reese. I love you. But remember, I've never had this before. This is new to me, so be patient."

He wraps me in his arms and hoists me up, so our faces are even. "As long as you're patient with me, we'll be fine."

MARIANNA IS GLOWING WHEN WE GET TO HER PLACE. SHE tells us how she wanted to arrange for us to meet, but didn't want to meddle.

"Knowing Reese, I knew he'd be so angry with me."

"Marianna, what do you think Reese's parents are going to say?"

"Aunt Emmy, Skylar's worried about ..."

Marianna only knows about my life as a stripper so I decide to tell her everything about me. I interrupt Reese and explain every last gory detail.

"I think Mr. and Mrs. Christianson need to know the truth about me. It'll come out one day and I'd rather they hear it from me than find out the hard way."

"You're right, dear. And if they don't like it, to hell with them."

"Marianna!"

Reese laughs. "Sky, this is typical Aunt Emmy. She calls it like she sees it."

"Yes!" Marianna says as she claps her hands. "Now, when are we going to get this girl dancing?"

"But," I protest.

"Skylar, darling, if they don't like you at first, it won't last. They got over the fact that Reese was a drug addict. They'll get over the fact that you were a lady of the evening. And look at you. You're gorgeous. Juliette will be all over you because you dance. Now let's move on to setting some auditions up for you. Reese, I want you to use that Blakely name of yours to get things moving."

Jeez, she relentless. Then a thought rolls into my head.

"Hey, where did your stage name come from, Reese?"

I look at him and he looks at Marianna. So I glance at her to see her smirking. What's with that?

"I'll let Aunt Emmy explain."

She laughs. "Blakely is my maiden name, as well as Juliette's. And Reston is my last name. I thought you knew that, Skylar."

When I sit and think about it, I realize I never knew Marianna's last name. "Oh gosh, I never knew your last name." Then I grin because I realize what an honor Reese paid Marianna by using her name in reverse for his stage name.

We leave Marianna's late in the afternoon and the November sky is gray with clouds. It's chilly and looks like rain may be headed our way. When we exit the subway station, Reese has decided to walk with me to my place so I can grab some clothes. I'm going to stay with him tonight. My apartment is closer to his now than it was before, so when I'm finished, we head over to his. As we walk, we're chatting and we hear a scream. I tense up and Reese looks around, then spies a couple getting attacked.

"Reese!"

"Call 911," he shouts as he takes off toward them.

"Reese, stop!" I grab my phone and call the emergency number. They answer and I report the incident. The operator instructs me to stay on the line and I do, but I run toward the screaming and shouting. The operator tells me the police are on the way and to stay back, but I yell at Reese to get back. All I can see are his fists flying and two guys going at him.

"Reese! Get back!"

I hear sirens in the distance and then a shot rings out. My head snaps toward the melee and the three men are still struggling. The couple is huddled on the ground and I can't tell if one or both of them are injured. I want to move closer, but I'm afraid.

"Reese, please," I scream. I don't care about those thugs. I don't want him to get hurt. Then another shot rings out and something burns like fire in my chest. The sirens are real loud now, but I still can't see them. Reese and only one of the thugs are standing. The burning in my chest turns into a fierce pain and I try to call out to Reese, but I can't seem to breathe. I open my coat and see the red stain spreading across my shirt. It's completely surreal as I gape at it. All my strength is instantly sucked out of me, and I drop to my knees. Air, I need air, but my chest won't expand. The warm sticky blood is all over my hands now and my ears buzz as my vision becomes foggy. Though I'm still on my knees, I know it won't be for long. I'm afraid if I go all the way to the ground, no one will notice and I'll die. So I fight. I fight to stay upright.

Everything moves in slow motion. Reese turns to look for me. He sees me on my knees, then sprints toward me, but when he speaks, but I can't hear anything.

Thirty-Four

Reese

SKYLAR. COVERED IN BLOOD. WORST CASE SCENARIO possible. I pick her up as the police arrive.

"She took a bullet to the chest."

"Ambulance is on the way."

It arrives and I carry her to it before it even stops. They load her up and try to tell me I can't go. To hell with that. I climb in the passenger side, punch the dashboard and say, "Let's go."

The doctors take her immediately to surgery. They can't tell me a fucking thing other than she's critical. My brain is on short circuit. I call Case and he arrives. Numbness rules. Case calls my parents. Then Dr. Martinelli. We're all in the surgery waiting room, waiting for the surgical team to come and report. Sitting isn't an option. This is my fault.

Turning to Dr. Martinelli, I say, "You predicted this. I should've listened."

Case says, "Oh, man. Stop. She wasn't even in the mix. You were helping. It was a stray bullet."

Dr. Martinelli jumps in and says, "Reese, look at me."

I do. Her face is intent.

"This was an accident. Clear?"

"She tried to get me to walk away."

Doc grabs my arm. "Doesn't matter. It was still an accident. The gun went off and she got shot. You can't blame yourself."

"Then who else can I blame? I'm the one who stopped. If I'd have kept on walking we would be sitting at home right now, eating dinner or doing something other than this."

"It. Doesn't. Matter. This was unintentional. You cannot blame yourself."

"Doc, the only way I won't blame myself is if she doesn't die."

Six hours pass and finally the surgeon walks out. Thank God Dr. Martinelli is there for all the doc-speak. She's touch and go for the next twenty-four hours, but if she pulls through, each day she makes it, her survival rate increases, barring she doesn't develop an infection from the ventilator she's on to help her breathe. *Fuck!*

"I need to see her."

The surgeon looks at me and says, "Sorry. You can't see her until she's out of recovery and moved into the unit."

"Unit?"

"She'll be in ICU after this."

"So when can I see her?"

"I'd say in a few hours. Go home and get some rest. Come back in the morning."

"Are you serious? Go home and get some rest? When my girl's life is at stake? What kind of crazy are you?"

"Reese, calm down," Dr. Martinelli says.

"No, I will not calm down. That's the most ludicrous thing I've ever heard." I look her square in the eyes and ask, "Tell me if you think it isn't. Would you go home if the love of your life just got out of surgery? A surgery that was touch and go? Would you go home and get some rest and come back in the morning? What the fuck, Doc?"

"No, you're right. I wouldn't."

She turns to the surgeon and says, "Doctor, I'm throwing down the doctor and the psych hat here. That wasn't a very comforting thing to say to a family member of a patient. I'm the patient's psychiatrist. When can we see her?"

The surgeon looked at Doc, and then me. "Let me see what I can do. And sorry about that. It was a long surgery."

My eyes bore into his, but I keep my mouth shut.

A couple of hours pass before we're allowed in. They allow Gabby (which Doc has asked us to call her) and me into the unit to see Sky. She looks like I did, I suppose, after my incident. So damn frail, with tubes and wires poking out of her, and machines everywhere. But I couldn't care less. She's the most beautiful thing to me and I pick up her hand, kiss it, and break down crying.

"Jesus, babe, I'm so sorry this happened. If you can hear me just know I'm here waiting for you. I'll always be for you. You're mine, for now and forever, Sky." I stay there, holding her hand until they make me leave.

But I don't leave the hospital. At all. Gabby takes me into the doctor's lounge so I can bathe and Case brings me clean clothes. My parents bring me food and I tell them everything about Skylar ... everything single detail. My mom cries when I explain about her parents and the terrible life she had growing up. And then she says, "Skylar is going to be just fine, son. She was sent to you. To help you. I just know it. I can feel it in here." And she pounds her chest.

On the fourth day, Skylar wakes up. She panics because of the breathing tube. I talk her through it, knowing exactly how she feels. My whispered words in her ear calm her immensely and she hangs onto my hand tightly, giving me hope.

"You're going to be fine, babe. Everything's going to be okay."

That same afternoon, they take her off the ventilator. Her throat is killing her.

"Don't try to speak. I know you're dying for water, ice, anything to put out the burn. But it'll get better in a day or so. I promise. And as thirsty as you feel, your IV is giving you all the fluids your body needs. It's mainly discomfort you're dealing with." I brush her tangled hair off her face. "Are you in any pain?"

She shakes her head.

"Good. Good. I don't want you to hurt at all, if possible. I'm so sorry babe. This is my fault. If I hadn't stopped ... "

She squeezes my hand. When I look at her, she shakes her head. Then pulls me a little. I bend down and she puts her arm around my neck and croaks, "Love you."

Then I shudder with the force of my sobs.

"Don't cry. All's good," she whispers.

It takes me a while to compose myself, but I tell her how my mom has been here with me most of the time and how I told her everything. About how much I love my girl, no matter what her background is. During my little speech, my voice breaks and a relief so great swells my chest that for a moment it suffocates me. This feeling has me all but pulling her into my arms, and if she didn't have so many damn tubes and wires attached to her, that's exactly what I'd do. When I'm able, I also tell her how my mom doesn't give a damn about any of the things Sky was so worried about and is only excited to meet the girl who stole my heart.

She gives me a weak smile and her eyes drift shut.

Skylar is transferred into a regular room and when my mom comes to visit, Sky is initially shy. But my mom wraps her arms around her, thanks her for loving me so much and soon, the two of them act like they've known each other forever. Sky is healing up nicely and the doctor says she should be able to leave in a few days.

I still haven't left the hospital and don't until the day she's released. When she's discharged, she has too many flowers to carry home (mostly from me) so we give them to the nurses. She doesn't go home because I won't let her. She moves in with me so I can take care of and spoil her.

Her first night home, I cook her lasagna, and make a salad. She doesn't stop saying, "Mmmm," the entire time she eats, which has me grinning like a fool.

When she's finished, I clean up. As I stare at her sitting on the sofa, I can't believe how lucky we are.

"I feel so guilty."

"Reese," she groans. "You just ruined it."

"Ruined what?"

"How great everything was going. You have to let it go. It wasn't your fault. You were only trying to help," she says.

"That's what Gabby said."

"She should know. She's the expert, so stop thinking about this damn guilt of yours. I don't blame you so you shouldn't blame yourself. You ought to be thinking about something else."

"Yeah. Like what?" I grin.

She laughs, and asks, "Well, are you up for a dirty night? Because I'm long overdue."

"Sky, you can't do that. You just got released from the hospital."

"True, but I asked the doctor and he said no vigorous activity. We can do things that aren't vigorous, can't we?"

I chuckled. "I believe I can think up a thing or two."

"Then what are you waiting for?" she asked.

"How dirty you wanna get?"

"Maybe just a tiny bit smudged."

Thirty Five

Skylar
One Year Later

"*Now remember, chin up. Look every auditor in the eye. Smile when appropriate. Romance them. Hell, eye fuck 'em if you have to, babe. Keep your carriage upright and don't ever drop it. Never relax. And just let it fly!*"

"*I'll never remember all of this,*" I groaned.

Reese kisses my nose, slaps me on the ass and says, "*You'll do great.*"

I heard my name. "*Skylar O'Donnell.*"

"*I'm so nervous.*"

"*Good. I'd be worried if you weren't. Now go get 'em. And remember, I love you.*" Whack.

My butt stung after that one and I thought about what he did to me last night, damn him.

I took my position. The music started and I began to dance. As soon as my feet pick up the beat, something took over and I lost myself. All the instruction Reese gave me flew out the window so I had to rein myself back in and remember what he said. Crap, my carriage! I pulled myself up to my full height and carried on, spinning across the floor. My legs separated into a full split in the air. Everyone looked amazed at the height I achieved in my jumps. Even Reese said I was spectacular, but sometimes I think he had lover's blindness. When my song ended, it felt like it had just begun. My final movements landed me right in front of the three auditors and I looked every one of them in the eye, as Reese told me to, and ended with a bow. Then I walked off the stage into his arms.

"You were brilliant, Sky. Absolutely perfection. Not one error."

"You're just saying that."

He pulled away from me and says, "No, I'm not. You know me better than that by now. I am a harsh critic when it comes to dance. If you don't get this part, they're blind fools."

Eight days later the call came and not only did I get the part, I was second to the lead female.

I STAND IN POSITION, WAITING FOR THE CURTAIN TO RISE ON opening night. It's been a thrilling year, but I won't say it's been an easy one. My body has been pushed more than I ever thought possible and Reese ... let me just say he's the bossiest thing when it comes to dancing. We've had our share of arguments over this, but I've always had to concede because he's the master when it comes to dancing and performing. I smile when I think about what happens after our disagreements too. Makeup sex is the best. And I have to admit to starting an altercation or two, just to experience this magical phenomenon.

The music begins and I'm off. Everyone's nerves are on edge because this production has been buzzed about for months now. *Edge* is exactly like it's title ... edgy. It's an ultra-modern musical showcasing homeless life on the streets of New York. The critics are already weighing in on this one. They're split on their opinions and they haven't even seen the thing. So we've decided to throw down the towel and dance our butts off.

When the orchestra plays its final note and we take our last steps, the audience brings down the house. Everyone one of us is dripping in sweat, our tattered costumes soaked. The stage lights shine so bright in my eyes, I'm disappointed because I want to see Reese's face, but it's not possible. I begged him to stay back-stage, but he said he wanted to watch me from the audience's perspective.

After several ovations, we finally drag ourselves off stage and there he is, waiting for me, with a huge bouquet of white roses and a smile that could rival the stage lights.

My excitement is at an all-time high as I run into his arms and he swings me into the air.

"You were outstanding, Sky. That was the best show I've ever seen. It made me want to dance again."

My breath catches when he says those words. "Oh, Reese."

"No, babe, it's a good thing. It made me feel right. You know?"

I can't say that I do, because I'd like so badly to give back what was stolen from him. So I do the only thing I know and I lean in and kiss him, intending for it to be just a short peck on the lips. I should've known better. None of our kisses are ever just short pecks on the lips.

"Hey, break it up O'Donnell," I hear one of the cast members say.

Reese runs his thumbs lightly beneath my eyes, swiping up some of the moisture created from my sweat. "You're a mess, babe."

"Right? I'm drenched."

He shoots me a look that promises all kinds of things and I become drenched down there as well.

"I meant from sweat. But now ..."

"Now what?" he smirks.

"I'm in bad need of a shower."

He smirks again. "Oh, the possibilities."

"I'm also in need of some ice."

"Are you intentionally trying to give me hints?"

"Reese!" I scold him.

He laughs. "Mom, Dad and Aunt Emmy are waiting. We need to meet them."

"You didn't bring them back?"

"Yeah, but they wanted us to have our moment alone."

"Aw, they're so sweet to us," I say.

He takes my hand and leads me to them where they all want to hug me. I won't let them, because between my running pounds of makeup and smelly sweat, I know I'm a nasty mess. They say they don't care, but I do.

After they leave, I head to my dressing area, while Reese waits behind. Since I don't have the lead role, I have to share so it's quite crowded. Hurrying, I rub the goopy gunk off my face and strip off my clothing, leaving it for the crew to be cleaned. We have several costumes that we alternate wearing, so we don't have to wear the smelly ones the next day. I quickly clean up with the wipes I keep—a trick I learned from my stripper days. As soon as I'm changed, I run back to where Reese is waiting.

He throws his heavy arm over my shoulders and hugs me next to his hard body. It never fails to amaze me how his touch affects me.

"You hungry?" he asks.

"Starved," I say, licking my lips.

"That could very easily be misinterpreted."

Smiling, I say, "Hmm, you catch on quickly."

"I have been told I'm fast."

"You also told me you were dirty."

"Oh, babe, the dirtiest."

"Well, guess what?"

"What?"

Standing up on my toes, I whisper into his ear, "I love dirty. In fact, I'm in the mood for something real dirty right about now."

He faces me and says, "Is that right? And how dirty are you thinking?"

"Filthy dirty."

"I guess that means we're in for a dirty night then."

My arm slips around his waist and I say, "I was hoping that's what you'd say."

"Hey, one thing first. Can I just say that I'm so happy our dirty nights are no longer secret nights?"

I fist bump him, grinning. "I'll second that."

THE END

Thank you for reading Secret Nights. I hope you enjoyed it. This book inspired a series called the **Hart Brothers Series**, where Gabby is the star of the first two books, **Freeing Her** and **Freeing Him**. **Freeing Her** is currently FREE.

FREEING HER

This is the beginning of a story ... the story of two people who were meant to be together. Why? Because unknown to them, they shared terrifying pasts and the cruel circumstances of their births doomed both of them to a life of hell.

Two strangers ... one night ... one accidental meeting that changed their lives forever.

Gabriella Martinelli, Manhattan psychiatrist had only one goal in life—to help abuse victims avoid the horrors she'd experienced herself. She worked late, volunteered, and donated her services to anyone who needed them. Life was good ... until her nightmare resurfaced. **He** found her, and began stalking her, and she knew he wouldn't stop until he destroyed every ragged piece of her.

Kolson Hart, Manhattan's most eligible bachelor, was ruled by his dark past. He liked control, from the boardroom to the bedroom and didn't care to be involved with someone whose life was just as screwed up as his. But one look at Gabriella short-circuited everything. Want ... desire ... need ... will sometimes drive a man to do things he swore he never would.

He freed her from a life of fear ... when he couldn't even save himself.

FREEING HIM

Kolson Hart and Gabriella Martinelli... destined to be together, fated to be torn apart.

After avoiding his father for years, Kolson knew asking his father, Langston Hart, for a favor would be like selling his soul to the devil. Only the devil wants more ... more than Kolson is willing to pay. But some promises can't be broken, not without losing what's most important. For Kolson, that's Gabriella Martinelli.

Left with two choices—pay up or risk everything—Kolson's only way out is to do something drastic, something so monumental not even Langston will be able to interfere. The question is: Will it be enough to guarantee Gabriella's safety from his father?

Kolson freed Gabriella from her past, and now he's risking everything for her again. Will she be able to save him from the demon that hunts him? Or is fate too strong for them to fight?

As the suds rinse, I stare at and memorize everything about her. A deep clenching pain rips through my gut, and then I know it's not true what they say about your heart breaking. It doesn't even come close. Your heart doesn't break. A gash splits your gut wide open and then it expands straight on up to your sternum until your heart explodes out of your chest.

Follow Me

If you would like to hear more about what's going on in my
world, please subscribe to my mailing list on my website at
http://bit.ly/AMNLWP
You can also join my private group — Hargrove's Hangout — on
Facebook if you're up to some crazy shenanigans!
Please stalk me. I'll love you forever if you do. Seriously.

www.amhargrove.com
Twitter @amhargrove1
www.facebook.com/amhargroveauthor

https://www.facebook.com/anne.m.hargrove

www.goodreads.com/amhargrove1
Instagram: amhargroveauthor
Pinterest: amhargrove1
annie@amhargrove.com

For Other Books by A.M. Hargrove visit www.amhargrove.com

The West Sisters Novels:
One Indecent Night (Spring 2019)
One Shameless Night (TBD)
One Blissful Night (TBD)

The West Brothers Novels:
From Ashes to Flames
From Ice to Flames
From Smoke to Flames

Stand Alones
Secret Nights
For The Love of English
For The Love of My Sexy Geek (The Vault)
I'll Be Waiting (The Vault)

The Men of Crestview:
A Special Obsession
Chasing Vivi
Craving Midnight

Cruel & Beautiful:
Cruel and Beautiful
A Mess of a Man
One Wrong Choice

A Beautiful Sin

The Wilde Players Dirty Romance Series:
Sidelined
Fastball
Hooked

Worth Every Risk

Secret Nights

The Edge Series:
Edge of Disaster
Shattered Edge
Kissing Fire

The Tragic Duet:
Tragically Flawed, Tragic 1
Tragic Desires, Tragic 2

The Hart Brothers Series:
Freeing Her, Book 1
Freeing Him, Book 2
Kestrel, Book 3
The Fall and Rise of Kade Hart, Book 4

Sabin, A Seven Novel

The Guardians of Vesturon Series

Acknowledgements

As always, my readers come first. Without you, I wouldn't be doing my dream job, nor would I have the inspiration to keep writing every day. So I extend my deepest gratitude to all of you for continuing to take a chance on my books.

It always takes a team, and without my team, a book wouldn't be possible. I'd like to thank my book wifey, Terri E. Laine. She puts up with all kinds of grumbling, helps me with blurbs, plots, writers block, and everything bad about life in general. You are my sister from a different mister and I love you to the farthest star and back.

Thank you Amy Jennings, travel companion, book lover, chat buddy, and bestie. I can't think of a better person to hang with and laugh with. One word — raclette. Enough said.

Nasha, I'd be lost without you and I am praying I get to meet you this year, my beautiful friend.

Diane, you have been the most amazing friend and assistant I could ask for. All the things you do, that I don't even think of. You are full of awesome — I don't know what I'd do without you, my lovely friend and team leader. I thank you hard!!! By the way, I love when you swear in French!

Thank you Maria at Steamy Designs for turning out such a hot cover and also for our whacky conversations! I don't think I've ever laughed so hard.

Harloe— you are indispensable —enough said.

If I've forgotten anyone, it's because my brain is on empty this week and I apologize.

About The Author

One day, on her way home from work as a sales manager, USA Today bestselling author, A. M. Hargrove, realized her life was on fast forward and if she didn't do something soon, it would be too late to write that work of fiction she had been dreaming of her whole life. So she made a quick decision to quit her job and reinvented herself as a Naughty and Nice Romance Author.

Annie fancies herself all of the following: Reader, Writer, Dark Chocolate Lover, Ice Cream Worshipper, Coffee Drinker (swears the coffee, chocolate, and ice cream should be added as part of the USDA food groups), Lover of Grey Goose (and an extra dirty martini), #WalterThePuppy Lover, and if you're ever around her for more than five minutes, you'll find out she's a non-stop talker. Other than loving writing about romance, she loves hanging out with her family and binge watching TV with her husband. You can find out more about her books www.amhargrove.com.

To keep up to date with my new releases subscribe to my newsletter here: http://bit.ly/AMNLWP

Made in the USA
Las Vegas, NV
10 August 2021

27934947R00169